Saving
MISS LILLIAN

ANNE LOVETT

WORDS OF PASSION • ATLANTA

SAVING MISS LILLIAN

Copyright © 2017 by Anne Lovett.

Published by Words of Passion, Atlanta, GA 30097.

Editorial: Nanette Littlestone
Cover: Brandi Doane McCann
Interior Design: Peter Hildebrandt

ISBN: 978-0-9960709-7-3

Library of Congress Control Number: 2017946011

DEDICATION

For my parents and grandparents, who first took me to the islands.

CHAPTER ONE

The hospital halls were dancing with light, or so it seemed to Sunny Iles. She practically waltzed down to her next patient, garnering strange looks along the way from passing doctors and visitors. *Tonight, tonight*—she hummed to herself, picturing Natalie Wood spinning down an alley in Brooklyn, as she'd seen in that old movie *West Side Story*. Then she stopped in front of Room 413 and came down to earth with a thud. *Stirling, Lillian*. She never knew what to expect from this sharp-tongued lady with the spiky white hair. Lady, definitely, not woman.

Lady or not, the patient had sworn like a sailor when they first brought her in. A high-class sailor, like Prince Harry or somebody, though she didn't know if Prince Harry swore. Or was even a sailor. It was odd how many of the staff here seemed to know Lillian Stirling, as though she'd been a patient often, or was on a reality TV show.

She pasted on her confident nurse's smile, walked in, and froze at the sight. "About time you got here," the elderly woman grumbled, half out of bed, hanging on to a chair. "I've got to pee."

"Whoa, Nellie!" Sunny rushed to her side and grabbed her elbow. "I came as soon as I could."

"You barely beat the puddle, sassy pants." A smile crept over the older woman's face. "And don't call me *Nellie*. Miss Lillian will do just fine."

Relief washed over Sunny that she'd arrived in time and brought the portable potty.

After she'd settled Miss Lillian back in bed and taken her vital signs, Sunny plumped the bed pillows and straightened the plant on the window sill. Her champagne mood began to bubble again. "What a gorgeous spring day it is outside, Miss Lillian," she said. "The roses are starting to bloom."

Miss Lillian wrinkled her nose. "I'd rather see my own roses." She sat up further and shook out her covers. "I thought they weren't going to keep me here. When do I get out?"

Sunny gathered her equipment and placed it on the cart. "The doctor says you'll go home tomorrow. You had a pretty bad fall, and since you hit your head on the stairs, we need to watch you for concussion."

"My head's okay," Miss Lillian said, "despite what you-know-who says."

Sunny was puzzled. "You mean Dr. Brown?"

"Not the doctor, silly girl. That woman who's trying to kill me."

"Not one of us nurses, surely." Sunny said it lightly. Was Miss Lillian making a joke?

Miss Lillian cocked her head and lowered her voice. "I mean my son's wife. Have you met her?"

"I haven't had the pleasure," Sunny said cautiously. Maybe Miss Lillian did have a head injury that could cause paranoia. Her son had come in with her, she understood, but she hadn't met him, *or* his wife.

"It won't be a pleasure to meet *her*," Lillian said darkly. "She keeps telling Alex that I have dementia. If only my husband were still alive, there wouldn't be this nonsense."

"Dementia?" Sunny's eyebrows rose. "Have you been diagnosed?"

"Of course not!" Lillian spat. "Nothing's wrong with me! And she's trying to shuffle me off into one of those *homes*, just because I've had this fall. It wasn't an accident, I tell you."

"Now, now, Miss Lillian," Sunny said. "Do you have someone to look after you when you leave here?"

"Of course!" Miss Lillian waved one arm for emphasis. "I have a perfectly good butler who can cook and drive me around, and I have a crew come in to do the heavy cleaning. *And* I have a yard man. He says to call him Gopher, but his name is Rodrigo."

Well, she's obviously well off, Sunny reasoned, trying not to giggle. Gopher indeed. She shouldn't have a problem hiring someone.

"Your staff is all male, right? You'll need a woman caregiver to help with baths and such. With that ankle having a compound fracture, it needs to be kept immobile. I can give you a list of agencies for you or your son to call."

"Agencies? Pah!" Miss Lillian focused her laser gaze at Sunny. "I like *you*, my dear. You're the best nurse I've seen, and I've seen plenty. I want *you* to come work for me. You're not a little young snip. You have experience. And I don't see any wedding ring. You're perfect."

"*Me?*" Sunny stopped in her bustling tracks, her face warming. She hated to be reminded she was thirty-eight and currently single. "Now, Miss Lillian, you don't need a skilled nurse. A caregiver would do just fine."

"The cost doesn't matter. I'll pay well."

Sunny heard voices in the hall, the wail of a siren in the distance, all the familiar hospital sounds. She liked the hospital. No matter what Miss Lillian claimed, she'd heard many wealthy people were miserly, and paid the help as little as they could get away with. Still, right now the main attraction of the hospital was Dr. Troy Bentley.

She smiled at the lady with the spiky white hair. "Miss Lillian, your offer is tempting, but I like my job here, and this caregiving job would only be for a few weeks, until you're healed."

Miss Lillian snorted. "Ha! What's so great about this place? Arrange for some time off. I'm serious."

Sunny wasn't about to say yes, but she didn't want to disappoint her patient, which wasn't good for healing. "Let me think about it" was a good thing to say.

She glanced at her watch. Her shift was up, and she needed to get home, wash her hair, and give herself a manicure before Troy picked her up. "See you tomorrow, Miss Lillian," she said. "Unless you leave first."

Miss Lillian nodded. "If we miss each other, you call me and tell me your decision. Write this number down."

Sunny dutifully pulled a phone from her pocket and began to tap the keys as Miss Lillian gave the number. She wished the old lady would be quick.

Miss Lillian's bright blue eyes regarded her shrewdly. "You're in an awful hurry, young lady. I'll bet you have a date tonight. Are you going to that ball?"

Sunny's mouth dropped open. "How did you know?" Had Troy Bentley blabbed to the whole staff?

Miss Lillian sank back in her pillow. "Just a lucky guess. My son and his wife are going. They go to all these fund-raising galas, because she's the social buzz bomb who wants to be Queen Bee. Her best friend is the chairwoman of this thing."

"I've never been to a ball before," Sunny confessed.

Miss Lillian nodded slowly and gave Sunny a mysterious smile. "I see. In fact, I see stars in your eyes, my girl. I wonder who it can be. Some doctor?"

Sunny's warm cheeks gave her away, and she poured Miss Lillian a cup of water for distraction.

"So it's like that, is it?" Miss Lillian said, taking the cup. "You look out for yourself tonight."

"I will, thanks," Sunny promised, as she headed out the door. She felt a little gray cloud gathering overhead, and didn't know quite why.

In the huge parking deck that smelled of concrete and oil, she noticed a tall and rangy man, good-looking in a Han Solo sort of way, gazing at the confusing overhead signs. His sun-streaked brown hair needed a haircut and he wore a faded plaid shirt and rumpled chinos. Something in him tugged at her, something elemental. She just *had* to speak to him.

"Can I help you?"

He glanced at her in surprise, then smiled. "Yeah, thanks. What's the shortest way out of this maze? I'm going to see my mother-in-law, fourth floor of the hospital."

Well. So he was married, and *she* had a boyfriend, a blond one with smooth good looks and a winning smile. Still, she regretted passing this hunky ship in the night. He looked as though he had . . . *soul*. She told him her favorite shortcut, he thanked her, and she hurried along toward the stairs. She was still thinking about him when she literally ran into Troy Bentley exiting the stairwell. They bumped, and he caught her. "Oooff!" She just stared at him, blinking wildly.

"Hey, hey, beautiful!" he crowed. "No harm done!" She felt her cheeks warming, guilty that she'd been thinking about somebody else. He swooped her into his arms and gave her a long, smacking kiss. Surprised and delighted, she melted like peach ice cream in July.

"Somebody might see us," she murmured through her fog of enchantment.

He shrugged. "So what?"

She smiled stupidly. "It seems, well, unprofessional."

There was that grin again, and he chuckled. "I just couldn't wait until tonight. Say, you look frazzled."

She decided to rally. "Miss Lillian will do that to you."

"Miss Lillian? You mean Lillian Stirling?"

Sunny blinked again. "You *know* her?"

"Half Atlanta knows her, sweetie. I'll be by at eight. Adios, cherie." He rushed off toward the hospital building.

"But, Troy . . ." He was out of earshot, but he would have some "*splainin*" to do tonight, about Miss Lillian.

She was still mulling over why everybody seemed to know Miss Lillian except *her* when she unlocked the door of the townhouse she shared with her fifteen-year-old daughter, Avery. Avery would be so impressed that her mom was going to a ball! It was a charity thing for—what? She wasn't sure. There were so many breakdowns of the human machine, and they all needed funding. "Dancing for Disease," Troy had called it.

How had she arrived at the age of thirty-eight without ever going to a ball? At a country club! She'd been dating Troy for seven and a half months and he'd never taken her to a country club, although she suspected he belonged to one. Maybe this meant he was getting serious.

She hummed "Someday My Prince Will Come" and studied the dress hanging on the back of her closet door. Well, it hadn't been transformed by a fairy godmother, but it was the best that Le Carrousel, her favorite consignment shop, had offered.

A retro white fifties model with a full chiffon tea-length skirt and a tight bodice, the gown was gauzy and glittery and went so well with her blonde hair. Well, she had blonded the locks a little more than was natural. Her natural color tended to look the shade of somebody's mother's support hose.

Her daughter Avery didn't like the dress, of course, said she looked silly in it, like she was about to dance *Swan Lake*, and the nude heels didn't help. Nor did Avery like Doctor Troy Bentley. Sunny was glad Avery was at a sleepover with her school friend Mariela tonight.

Sunny hoped that Troy would come back home with her after the dance and they could make love in her bed, instead of his, and she could roll over and go to sleep afterwards. Usually, at his place, she had to get up and come home for Avery, or he would bring her home.

She called Avery's cell phone just to make sure she was at Mariela's house, and had the girl hand the phone to Mariela's mother, Maria. "Those boys aren't coming over tonight, are they?" she asked. Maria knew she meant the football players the girls liked.

"Of course not," Maria said. "You worry too much about that child, Sunny. She's just like the rest of them, you know. Those girls are going to have a great time, and Manny and I'll be home."

Sunny grinned and stripped off her garments—first the shoes, and then the pants, and then the top, and then the patterned support socks she wore on duty, and then her bra and candy pink striped undies. She flung the latter two across the room and drew a white strapless bra and some lacy white bikinis out of her top drawer.

Sexy innocence.

She was putting the finishing touches on her makeup when she heard a ping from her phone. She found the device among the lipstick and eyeshadow, foundation and hair pins that cluttered the makeshift dressing table with the poofy flowered chintz skirt. There was a text message. From Troy, of course. She caught her breath. Please please *please* not bad news, she prayed.

It wasn't.

TROY: *Cant wait to see u sweet lips.*

But he had just *seen* her. This was exciting. She texted back,

ME: *Me too.*

TROY: *Luv that red hair. All of it.*

Red hair? Face burning, she clicked off the phone. She shivered all over. She felt sick. Avery had *told* her Troy was a good-time guy, but he was so much fun. Avery had *told* her she was building castles in the air—but he had sent her a vase of roses tonight!

They were yellow roses. Avery had scoffed. "Yellow's for friendship, Mom."

Friendship wasn't what she wanted.

When he arrived to pick her up only ten minutes late, she faked her cool, collected appearance. Inside she was like jelly in an earthquake. She'd tucked every stray curl into an updo she'd copied out of *People* magazine, and she hoped that she looked like Cate Blanchett at a Hollywood awards ceremony. She waited impatiently for a compliment, but he didn't give one, only a kiss. She thanked him for the roses. He smiled distractedly.

She told herself that he had patients on his mind and brooded all the way to the club. He didn't help by chattering on about some hospital gossip she'd already heard, about somebody's divorce and leaving town. Her spirits lifted when he escorted her into the club's foyer, where the high ceilings, the tasteful neutral décor, thick damask draperies, and glittering chandeliers combined to give her a feeling that anything might happen tonight.

Then he led her into the spacious ballroom where a five-piece dance band was playing hits of the 80s. Away from the dance floor, tables covered with white cloths held flickering candles in hurricane lanterns. Sunny surveyed the crowd, and her heart sank to see that most of the other women were wearing slinky dresses that clung to their well-toned shapes or Grecian-urn types of gowns that showed a lot of leg. Avery had been trying to tell her that. Well, hell! With her curvy figure, she didn't look good in slinky. And she cared about people, not about fashion.

Now one of the slinky women was approaching them. Over a toned, freckled tan, she wore a silky turquoise gown that plunged into a V-neck just this side of indecent exposure. With it the woman wore a cocktail ring as big as a nugget of Hershey's chocolate and gold sandals with red soles.

And her hair was *red*.

"Hel-*lo*, Troy!" The slinky woman leaned over and kissed Troy on the cheek. And then she nodded to Sunny, still addressing Troy. "This must be your little friend."

"Sunny Iles," Sunny said, extending her hand. So she, Sunny, was Troy's little friend? They had been talking about her?

"I'm Sydney Fairbanks," smiled the woman, giving Sunny a limp fish to grasp.

Sydney. The light bulb came on. "Sydney" would be right after "Sunny" on the phone's contact list. Troy had hit the wrong name to send his message. She gladly let go of the fish hand.

Sydney shrugged and inclined her head. "The bar's over there, dear hearts. Go have a drink. The food's almost ready." She smiled patronizingly at Sunny and walked over to greet some new arrivals.

"She's the chairman. Does so much for charity," Troy remarked. Sunny gazed at the retreating turquoise dress, and dread crept into her soul, destroying the last remnants of her beautiful castle in the air. Through the pile of dream-rubble she saw clearly that Troy was sleeping with Sydney.

She raised her chin and told herself it was just a fling, really, but inside she was tied in knots. Troy, back to his usual buoyant self, danced with her, and he also danced with Sydney. A *lot*. Too often, Sunny found herself at a table sipping champagne and being chatted up by various husbands or boyfriends who had lengthy tales of wives or girlfriends who had changed for the worse.

When a doctor she knew slightly, Roger Humbolt, approached her and asked her for a turn on the floor, she sighed and rose from her chair. Better than sitting. He was fiftyish, tall, and impeccably dressed, with a long face punctuated by a mustache and topped by a head of well-groomed gray hair. "I love your dress," he said. "It makes you look like a ballerina."

Startled, she stumbled and almost fell, but he executed a smooth move that disguised her faux pas. She was so grateful she forgot about being self-conscious and followed his expert lead. She found that she was smiling.

"Having fun?" he asked.

"This dance with you is fun," she said truthfully.

"But you're not enjoying yourself as a whole," he said. "Troy's leaving you alone too much, dear girl."

A sob caught in Sunny's throat. If Roger Humbolt had noticed that Troy was ignoring her tonight, maybe others had noticed too. She scanned the crowd and saw that Troy was over by the bar, laughing with Sydney. She gulped back tears, and dove in her bag for a tissue.

"I guessed it, didn't I?" said Roger Humbolt.

She nodded and blotted away a tear. "I think it's over."

Roger glanced over at the bar. "He's being a cad. Why don't you just walk out and let me take you home right now?"

Sunny blinked. "I thought you were married."

The older man shrugged. "We're getting a divorce," he said. "I brought my sister tonight, who's visiting from Cleveland. She won't miss me for a few minutes. Do you live far?"

Sunny wanted to leave, but she wasn't sure of Dr. Humbolt's intentions, and she didn't want to get mixed up with anybody else right now. "Thanks, but I can manage." Maybe it was all a mistake. Maybe Troy wasn't planning anything. Maybe he was just networking. Maybe he'd make up his negligence later.

The music ended, and Roger walked her back to the table. "Can I get you a drink?"

She thought another glass of champagne would be just the thing. He was smiling as he returned with two bubbling flutes and took the chair next to her. "To a happier future," he said. He clinked glasses, drank down his champagne, and ordered a dry martini from a passing waiter.

Then he draped an arm over the back of her chair and leaned closer. "I'd like to ask you something," he said.

She had drunk several glasses of bubbly already and was feeling a little light-headed. She hoped he wasn't going to ask her out. "Okay," she said, and glanced over at the bar, where Troy's arm circled Sydney's waist.

"I've heard you're a good nurse," the doctor said. "Got a great way with patients."

Well, *this* was a weird prelude to asking somebody out. Sunny took another gulp of her champagne. "People have been talking about me?" Not Troy, she hoped. Blabbermouth.

Roger smiled like a kindly uncle. "I've been asking around. I'm moving to Pinehaven, North Carolina, to start a practice there, and I'll need a good office nurse."

Her gaze tracked back to Troy and Sydney. She wondered whether he would even notice if Roger took her home. She suspected that the yellow roses had been a message that Avery had decoded for her. Just then Troy noticed her talking to Roger, patted Sydney on the arm, and headed her way. Was he jealous? He didn't look jealous. The lout, he was grinning!

So, Roger Humbolt was making Troy's cruel intention easier? She thought of having to see Troy at the hospital later if this was good-bye. She thought of having to work with him.

She turned to Roger Humbolt. "When would you need somebody?" she asked.

CHAPTER TWO

"You should have gone to the back," the man in the black suit told her.

"Oh, come on," Sunny said, her face warming. "This isn't 1912." She was standing at the front door of a mansion on a hill, facing a mahogany-skinned butler who spoke like the butlers she'd seen on *Downton Abbey*.

A lavender mobility scooter whined into place beside the butler, and the woman with short spiky hair peered at her with bright blue eyes. "Ah, you're here. Never mind all that, Harris. Come on in, dear."

Lillian Stirling had been delighted when Sunny called and told her she could work for a few weeks, until she started her new job in North Carolina. Miss Lillian had asked her to come in for an interview first, because, she said, her son had insisted on it.

Miss Lillian now appeared very much the grande dame, wearing a luscious coral cashmere cardigan draped over her shoulders, a lighter coral silk blouse, and a pair of beige wide-leg pants. Her ankle was thrust in front of her, immobilized in a fiberglass cast.

"Now," Miss Lillian said, "welcome to Stonehaven." She tilted her head. "I've been wondering. Is Sunny your real name?"

Sunny winced to hear the familiar question. "No, ma'am. My mom named me Susannah Nadine, but with a last name like Iles, well, Sunny just came naturally to a lot of people."

The older woman looked Sunny up and down. "I like it. Come this way." She pressed a button and scooted off. Sunny padded after her, casting a glance at well-worn books stacked floor to ceiling—there was even a ladder—and comfortable green leather club chairs. And then she saw the silver-framed photograph on a side table. Just the thing to further sink her day!

A bride stood tall and beautiful, hair blowing in the breeze, and the groom—! *That* man looked like the hunky man she'd met in the parking lot! So he was married to Miss Lillian's daughter? Then *why* wasn't the daughter here looking after her mother? Sunny had looked after her own mother enough. She shuddered at the memory of those days and hurried on through the French doors into a tiled sunroom so bright she blinked at the pink and cream décor.

"Help me off this machine," Miss Lillian was saying, but she was pushing with her cane, already half onto a cream-painted wicker settee before Sunny could reach her. Sunny drew in a breath. That settee, those flowered cushions—oh, it was like the set Troy Bentley had on his back deck, except these cushions were rose and cream, and Troy's were maybe coral and blue, or was it yellow? She ought to remember, they'd made love on them more than once.

"What on earth is the matter with you, my dear?"

She felt the color rise to her cheeks. "Nothing."

"Are you sure you don't need a doctor?"

"Miss Lillian, that's the *last* thing I need."

Miss Lillian tilted her head expectantly. "Oh? Something happen at the dance?"

Sunny didn't know what to say. Was the woman psychic? Fortunately Harris arrived with a tray loaded with mint-sprigged iced tea in crystal glasses, a plate of cheese straws, and sugar-coated pecans in a silver bowl. Sunny licked her dry lips while Harris arranged the tray.

After Harris left, Miss Lillian offered her a glass and a dainty linen napkin. Sunny accepted with thanks and took a long sip of the heavenly sweet brew. She glanced around for a paper napkin before she dabbed her mouth with the embroidered linen, and was horrified to see she'd left a lipstick smudge.

Miss Lillian didn't seem to notice or care. "Now, Sunny. I told you I wanted you to work for me, and I still do. I just want to ask you a few questions."

"Sure. Fire away." Sunny had nothing to hide. Except her beginnings. And *that* had nothing to do with her qualifications. Miss Lillian cocked one eyebrow and smiled mysteriously. "Have you had martial arts experience?"

Sunny blinked in surprise. "No, but I had a class in self-defense from the police department. Sometimes a nurse keeps odd hours and, as they say, nothing good happens after midnight."

"Ah, self-defense training is excellent," Miss Lillian said. "I had hoped for someone with that kind of experience."

"But why?" Sunny asked, gazing out at the garden beyond the tall arched windows. "It looks so peaceful here, and you have people around." She saw the gardener, Gopher, bumping a wheelbarrow full of black mulch across the pebbled path to a flower bed.

Lillian Stirling's face darkened. "Strange things are happening, and I don't know what to believe. Some people think my mind's going. That woman thinks I ought to go to one of those *homes*, like my sister Zoe, who has Alzheimer's."

Sunny nibbled on a cheese straw. Yes, Miss Lillian had said something about "that woman" in the hospital. "Miss Lillian, I can't see why anyone would think you're anywhere near to dementia."

"You haven't met my son's wife."

The killer daughter-in-law. Sunny waited to hear more.

Miss Lillian sipped her tea thoughtfully. "Alex is, at heart, a good man. But his wife wants me out of the way, and she has him by the—oh, dear, I hate to be crude. You know."

Sunny knew, and she shifted uneasily. Where was the daughter in all this? Didn't she have something to say about her mother? But maybe they were estranged.

"Do you . . . have any more children?" she ventured.

"None that can help me," Miss Lillian snapped. "What about *you*? Do you have children? Anything that would make you miss work?"

So Miss Lillian was evading talking about her daughter. Why? Sunny decided to answer truthfully, for the most part. "A fifteen-year-old daughter. She's capable of looking after herself." Sunny crossed her fingers for a moment.

Miss Lillian paused and then said, "Would you two consider living in? Harris has the apartment over the garage, but I have a guest house out back with two bedrooms."

Moving house twice in three months didn't seem like a good idea at all. "Just for six weeks? Avery's finishing her school year, and that would be complicated. I could be here whatever time you need in the morning."

Miss Lillian gazed off into the middle distance. "Perhaps," she murmured, and then she faced Sunny, intent. "Can you act? Were you ever in a play?"

Was Sunny falling down a rabbit hole? Was Miss Lillian going to turn into the Queen of Hearts and shout, "Off with her head?" Maybe Sunny had been too quick to dismiss dementia. She cleared her throat. "Miss Lillian, I'm a good actress. In high school I played Cecily in *The Importance of Being Earnest*. My teacher told me I had natural talent." The next year, she'd been promised a part in *A Midsummer Night's Dream*, but that was the year her whole life got upended. No sense in telling *that*.

Miss Lillian gazed at her, lips pressed together, sizing her up. "I'll be frank. I told my son that I'd get a distant cousin, one he doesn't know, to come live with me so they'd stop the retirement home nonsense. I'm temporarily out of action, but my mind isn't going."

Curiouser and curiouser. "Then you want me to work only until your cousin comes? How long—"

Miss Lillian waved her hand dismissively. "My cousin will have a lot to deal with. I trusted Alex—my son—to look after my business affairs after my husband died. But there is that woman—Kiki." Her eyes grew hard and she sniffed. "I was very fond of his former wife, Catherine, but she left him because of Kiki."

"Oh, please, you don't have to tell me all this," Sunny said.

Miss Lillian dabbed at her nose with a lacy handkerchief. "Kiki wants me out of the way." She rapped her cane on the floor, startling Sunny. "I told you, she's trying to kill me."

Sunny sat back in her chair. She'd had experience with dementia before; the person could seem sane and reasonable one minute, and the next come out with something completely off-the-wall. Still, Miss Lillian's gray eyes seemed lucid and clever.

She'd better go carefully here. "What makes you think you're in danger?"

Miss Lillian pushed her cast straight out. "This ankle! She tripped me up at the top of the stairs, dear. Swan dive to oblivion was her plan. I managed to grab the railing and hang on. Except when my hands slipped and I landed, my ankle snapped like a twig."

O-kay. Maybe a little osteoporosis. Obviously, Miss Lillian hated the daughter-in-law, who probably felt the same way about her. This job prickled with thorns among the roses. She finished her tea, wishing she could slurp the sweet puddle at the bottom.

Maybe she could stand it for a few weeks. She and Avery needed the money for the move. "All right, Miss Lillian. Just until your cousin comes. But I can't live in."

"That's all right. Now, I'd better tell Harris you're coming. I want you two to get acquainted." Miss Lillian picked up her cane and began to pound its tip on the floor.

Sunny edged away. "Miss Lillian?"

"There's a buzzer under the rug. I never can quite find it," The older woman poked again with the cane and in a few moments Harris appeared at the door.

"Miss Iles will do nicely, Harris, and I want her to begin work tomorrow. Please show her the ropes when she comes, and tell Odessa I have someone now."

Harris bowed somewhat, a snide look on his face. "Very good, Miss Lillian." And then he left.

"I don't think he likes me. He complained about me coming to the front door," Sunny said when Harris was out of earshot. And who was Odessa?

"Oh bosh," Miss Lillian said. "He's just proper, that's all. But do come around to the back tomorrow. It will be more convenient for you, truly." She gazed at Sunny, up and down. "What size clothes do you wear?"

"Oh, I have my own uniforms, if that's—"

Miss Lillian interrupted. "Just answer the question."

"Eight," Sunny said. No need to be rude, even if now she was really a ten, or maybe even a twelve. The break-up with Troy and leaving the hospital had played havoc with her appetite—she was scarfing Chunky Monkey one day, sipping chicken broth the next.

"Nonsense. You won't have to live in at first. We'll see if I can manage with just Harris and you. Odessa, his lady friend, who's been helping me temporarily, can go home and get back to her practicing. She's a singer and this isn't really her cup of tea."

Sunny wondered what on earth she was getting into, with all this family drama. At least it wasn't for long. She gazed around the sunroom, at sun winking through the long venetian blinds, dappling the seagrass rug. The house smelled of lilies and sandalwood and orange oil, and its colors and textures oozed with a comfort she'd rarely known. She'd already given her notice to the landlord that they were leaving at the end of June. "When is your cousin coming?"

Miss Lillian smiled blandly and tucked a stray hair back into place. "You're going to be my cousin, dear."

CHAPTER THREE

Neil McEvoy's gut tightened as he watched the boat, sun glinting off its white prow, take a course toward his dock. He wasn't expecting anybody. All he wanted was to be left alone—why couldn't people understand that? That trip to Atlanta to see Lillian in the hospital reminded him of why he stayed on Issatee Island, why he never wanted to leave. It was because he loved this place with a ferocity, loved each wave and sand dune and loggerhead turtle, and because he could live here and bring up his son among their closest and best memories.

The boat drew closer now, and he relaxed. It was only Harlan, with his mail and supplies. The old coot was a day early, and he must have given that old tub a refinishing. Neil walked down to meet him.

Harlan grinned. "Hey, Cornelius!" He drew alongside and tossed a fat orange rope. Neil caught it and lashed it fast to the cleats.

Harlan clambered out of the craft, wiped his brow and mustache with a handkerchief, and replaced his captain's cap on his damp white hair.

"Think I've got all you want here." He gestured back to the boat.

"Lost your calendar?"

Harlan grinned. "Can't come tomorrow. My baby's getting married. Got to leave for Macon early in the morning."

"Well, I'll be damned!" said Neil. "So Sharon's finally tying the knot with Meathead."

Harlan hooted, reddening his cheeks further. "She says I have to call him Nick now. He's going to be the father of my grandchildren one of these days."

"Well, I wish them the very best," said Neil. "I want to send them a present. She was always trying to talk me out of my alligator skull, and maybe I'm ready to let it go."

Harlan looked at him. "She wanted to send you an invite, but I told her you wouldn't come. When's the last time you've been off this island? Before you went to see the old lady last week, I mean. Hell of a thing to happen to her."

Neil gazed off into the distance, not willing to meet Harlan's shrewd eyes. "Last time I was away for a longer time was three years back, when Julie's father died. They asked me to be a pallbearer and I couldn't very well refuse."

Harlan nodded. "You heard from Miss Lillian lately? How's she doing?"

"Good news," Neil said, smiling. "She called me to tell me she hired some long-lost cousin to look after her. She said it would take more than a broken ankle to keep her down."

"So she broke it in a fall, you said? Miss Lillian ain't the kind to fall. She's nimble as a goat."

Neil didn't want to tell Harlan that Lillian claimed she was pushed down the stairs by Alex's wife. He shrugged. "We're all getting older. You'll see her next week, by the way. Says she's coming here and bringing that cousin—somebody I haven't met."

"Hallelujah! She's been gone too long. Ain't my place to say anything but I'm glad Mr. Alex ain't coming."

"But it's damn odd. I thought I'd met all Julie's cousins at our wedding, but I draw a blank at somebody named Sunny Iles."

"Hah! She's got the right name. Do you suppose she's a looker, like Julie?"

"I don't care what she looks like, Harlan."

Harlan cleared his throat, spat into the water. "It's none of my business, Neil, but you been living like a hermit. It's been five years now since Julie passed on, and you ain't but what? Forty-five or so?"

Neil ignored him. "The problem is, it's hard to meet anybody."

Harlan grinned. "Actually, Neil, you got to step off the island."

Neil snorted. "But then I'd come back, and very few ladies want to live here. Hardly worth the effort to make their acquaintance."

Harlan spat at the ground. "Humph. You're going to become a dried-up old hunk of salted squid, Neil."

Neil bristled. Harlan should mind his own business. He reached down to the dock and picked up a length of rope, coiling it. "Part of me was buried with Julie. My dreams."

Harlan shoved his hands in his pockets and scuffed his toe on the dock. "Not your heart, Neil. You ain't dead yet."

"This is the life I want." He stared down at the sparkling water, the waves slapping against the piling, the smell of salt marsh sweet as perfume. It took a special kind of woman for this life, and he hadn't met one.

Harlan was quiet for a minute, studying him.

"Anyhow," said Neil, "I'm not alone. I've got the animals, and Angus in the summers, and those researchers and writers Lillian cultivates." And he had something else too—something he'd never told anyone about.

"Seems I remember one of those lady professors." Harlan's eyes narrowed. "You liked her, as I recall."

Neil watched the bend in the creek, where a crane lifted off with a ponderous wingbeat. Water sloshed against the pilings. "Not enough."

A huge orange tabby cat, lion-faced, sauntered onto the dock and up to Harlan. Then he sat, tail twitching, outsize paws together, alert for the chance of a handout.

Neil shrugged. "I've got Rambo."

Harlan raised his eyebrows. "Not exactly a cuddly cuss."

"He and I get along."

"I don't know what I'm gonna do with you, man." Harlan gave a dismissive wave. "I'd best be gettin' on. Linda Faye's got a hundred honey-dos before we leave." He stepped into the boat, opened a storage hatch, and drew out four tote bags filled with food and supplies. He handed them up to Neil. Next, he shoved a cooler onto the dock and took an empty one from Neil, along with another set of bags.

"Know you'll be glad to see Angus when school's out. How old's the lad now?"

"Sixteen," said Neil. "And already looking into a summer job on the mainland. Damn."

"Well, you can't keep them to home forever." Harlan stepped into the boat and leaned toward the rope. "Wish you could."

"Give my best to Sharon," Neil said, untying the knot and handing the rope to Harlan. "Tell her I'm expecting her and Meathead—excuse me, Nick—to come see me."

"I'll do that," said Harlan. "Oh, wait a minute. Can't forget the mail." He ducked below and came up with a pouch, which he handed over. Then he grinned and went to start the engine, waving as he sputtered away. Neil watched him round the bend in the tidal creek and then jerked his head toward the cat. "Come on, Rambo." He shouldered the cooler and tucked the pouch under his arm. "I've got bait shrimp back at the house."

On the back porch of the wooden lodge set in a grove of palmetto, he tossed the mail pouch on the table, tossed Rambo a few of the promised shrimp and came back for the bags. He'd save the mail for after dinner.

When he'd unloaded and put away all the supplies, he stared out the window at Julie's small garden. The lettuces were producing and the cherry tomatoes were ramping up their vines. The squashes were still in flower, while the beans stretched their tendrils toward the string cages.

Julie's hardy shrub roses in the sunny border alongside the porch were bushy and full-blown, almost shoulder-high, and in her cutting garden, zinnias and snapdragons pushed up through the sandy soil, loaded with tiny buds. He walked out the back door and cut rose branches with his pocketknife, then he headed back to the small graveyard and laid the flowers on Julie's rough tabby gravestone. He'd cast it himself, building the frame from wood, oiling it, then mixing lime and sand and oyster shells to pour into the frame. He hadn't gone the way of the Indians and burned shells for the lime, but used ready-made. When the gravestone was half set, he'd inlaid it with some of his choicest shells—perfect pink scallop, speckled olive, and bleached sand dollars.

Her father's stone was nearby. Lillian had insisted on a chunk of carved marble for him.

Neil hunkered down by the grave, sweeping off the sand that had blown over it. Lord, how he missed her. She'd been so daring, so full of life.

Like picking a scab, his thoughts returned to that last day. He'd seen her on the shore waving him away, telling him to bring more beer for the picnic, her sun-streaked brown hair blowing in the wind, her slim figure backlit against the gentle grey-green waves, kicking up just a bit.

The truth was, Julie had drowned trying to rescue Kiki from her own stupidity. He wished she had just let Kiki go.

He swallowed hard. Then he got up, brushed off his hands, and walked to the house, wanting a drink of water—or maybe a cold beer—to ease the lump in his throat. Rambo shinnied up the tree next to the house and perched on the shady roof in his vulture pose.

He grinned up at the cat. "Don't pounce."

Rambo liked to tag along while Neil went to check the turtle nests, as long as he didn't have to get his feet wet, though he'd been known to try and swat a fish out of a tidal pool. He knew to stay away from the gators. The turtle eggs would hatch in about six weeks, and Neil wanted to keep the baby turtles safe from predators such as the feral pigs and raccoons.

Neil needed to start getting the place in shape for Lillian. When she'd hired him to be the island naturalist because he was going to marry her daughter, she never dreamed he was going to be the death of her. Yes, it was his fault, by not being there when she needed him. Going for beer.

If only that weekend had never happened. Why had they even tried to make Alex and Kiki see the beauty of the island? It was just like Julie to attempt to win them over rather than fight them. To show them how destructive their resort scheme would be to the natural ecology of the island and its home to descendants of African slaves.

The island was barely big enough for a luxury resort, Julie insisted, and he'd agreed. The family had enough money in trust to keep Issatee, or so Lillian had assured him. But Alex and Kiki thought it had to "earn its keep." Did beauty always have to earn its keep the way those two thought, or did it earn its place in the scheme of things just by existing and giving people an experience of transcendence? Beauty was for the soul. Pleasure was for the body.

Whoa—where did those philosophical thoughts come from? He'd been alone too long.

He walked into the house, got a cold beer, and walked out to the shed in the back. He could spend a couple of hours in there and get his peace of mind back.

CHAPTER FOUR

"Mom, what the heck is that smell?" Avery balanced on her crutches in their doll-sized living room, eating an apple. Her tight black leggings, Sunny supposed, were the latest fashion, along with a fancy embroidered tunic that showed far too much budding cleavage. One of the leggings was tied just below the knee. Avery hated to wear her prosthesis at home, saying it was uncomfortable. She needed a new one, and that might be a problem, given the state of their finances. After Sunny started the new job, maybe.

"What smell? You mean the cedar?" Sunny stifled a comment on Avery's outfit, heaving two black plastic trash bags and one small white one into the living room onto the carpet she'd found at a roadside sale. The backing was already turning into some sort of powder.

"I was kind of hoping you'd brought me a hamster and some cedar shavings for the cage." Avery finished the apple, licked her fingers, and pitched the core toward the trash can, hitting the swinging flap. "What's in the bags?"

"My new uniforms." Sunny began to untie the top of one.

"Mom, quit the BS."

Sunny gave her daughter an ironic smile. "These are hand-me-down clothes I'm supposed to wear on the job. My new boss had them bagged and ready, sitting in a cedar-lined closet." Sunny told Avery about the interview. "I'm supposed to pose as her cousin to make her son think I'm one of the family."

Avery erupted in a fit of giggles. "Mom! How freaking! You'll be terrible at it."

"I will not."

"Oh, heck, yes, you will. You are *so* not devious, Mom."

"I *did* act in high school."

"So why are you supposed to be one of the family?"

"They want the good lady to go to assisted living. They think she's losing her mind. I don't think she is. She's convinced them that she has a long-lost cousin that needs a job."

Avery's eyes narrowed. "Go on, open the bags and let me see. You said she was enormously rich?" Avery made her way to the orange upholstered sofa and flopped on it. She laid the crutches on the floor and propped her short leg, the one that ended below the knee, on the back of the sofa. "I hate this sofa," she said. "Why don't you buy something with style?"

Sunny pressed her lips together, ignored Avery's needling, and struggled to untie the bag corners. She'd tied them too tightly. "I might need scissors. Let's go ahead and have supper. You did fix it?"

Avery shrugged. "Spaghetti's boiled, sauce and meatballs thawed and heated, salad tossed." Her voice sounded brittle and careless, unlike her.

"Avery, what's wrong?" Sunny asked.

"Nothing."

Sunny dragged the bags over to the side of the sofa. "Then let's eat."

Facing her daughter across the one good table Sunny had saved from her disaster of a marriage, Sunny ate spaghetti and listened to Avery chatter on about what kind of nail polish she wanted next time they went to Target and why Eva said that black lipstick was the new thing.

This wasn't like her. "What are you not telling me?" Sunny asked. "Did something happen at school?"

"Don't ask me about school," Avery burst out.

Sunny thought a minute. "That Devereaux boy?"

Avery glumly stared at her plate. "What about him?" She picked up her fork and twirled her spaghetti into a ball that grew larger and larger. Dev Wilson was her study buddy, who hung out with her in the library, and who texted her for advice. The advice was about other girls.

Sunny knew she'd scored. "Okay. So don't talk about him. I'll tell you about the fabulous house I'm going to work in, and about Harris, the butler."

"Oh?" she perked up. "Is he anything like Carson on *Downton Abbey*?"

"If Carson had come from the Caribbean. He speaks the King's English with a lilt. I think he's Jamaican or something."

While Sunny described the swimming pool and the garden, Avery calmed and listened, mopping the last of the spaghetti sauce off her plate. "Sounds great. Ice cream, mom? I'll get it."

"I think I'll have an apple." She reached into the bowl on the table, took one out, and polished it with her napkin.

"What?" Avery scraped back her chair. "You're the one who bought the Cherry Garcia."

"I'm not that hungry." Sunny was thinking about all those size-eight clothes in the bag.

Avery heaved herself up. "I'll get mine. You never give me enough." Sunny took a bite of her apple and watched her daughter plop a fat scoop of pure calories into a bowl. The kid was what? Size two? She never put on pounds, but then again she hardly ever stayed still, as if to prove losing half a leg couldn't slow her down.

After the dishes had been washed and cleared away, Avery hunkered on the floor near the bags, untying the plastic rabbit ears with no trouble.

She dragged out wool pants, sweaters, skirts, a camel-hair coat, inspecting the designer labels as she laid the clothes out. The second bag held casual clothes—khakis, polo shirts, jeans.

The garments looked flat and creased, as if they'd been packed a long time. Sunny picked through each shirt, blouse, and sweater, re-folded them, and stacked them on the sofa in order of desirability. They had a youthful air that didn't suit Miss Lillian, so they were a daughter's clothes for sure. Sunny sighed. The daughter in the wedding picture with the hunk? She had to put that dude clear out of her mind. Which was hard.

Avery inspected one garment after another, humming along, TV tuned to reruns of Project Runway. Just to bug me, Sunny thought.

"Ick," said Avery finally, having finished her appraisal. "Total preppy. Five years out of date, at *least*."

Sunny unfolded a pale aqua Brooks Brothers V-neck sweater. "They're classic."

Avery indicated the *Vogue* magazine on the coffee table. "You should let me give you fashion advice. You are so not preppy. "

"But you don't like my usual clothes," Sunny pointed out.

"Will you please throw out that green suit that bags in the butt?"

"But it was such a great deal," Sunny said. "Seventy-five percent off."

Avery rolled her eyes. "Dear Jesus, help my mama to know what a bargain really is."

"I think Jesus is too busy to worry about my shopping habits." Sunny turned the sweater inside out, looking for moth holes. "Avery, I can't do it. How could she think I could pass for the relative of a Buckhead woman? My hair will never get straight. I wonder if she picked me because I was the right size. Sort of." Sunny stroked the soft cashmere. "This is a pretty sweater . . ."

"You're afraid."

Sunny picked up a cotton Ralph Lauren V-neck pullover, a deep, rich purple that would go so well with her hair. "Hell, yes!"

"Mom, watch your mouth, like you're always telling me."

Sunny laid her hands in her lap. "The situation's complicated. I hope I'm not getting in over my head."

Avery gave her such a look, such a grimace. "Well, maybe you shouldn't have quit your job, Mom."

Sunny tightened her lips. Okay, so she had been rash, impetuous, and emotional. So she had put their health insurance at risk. But she had pulled a rabbit of the hat, hadn't she? "In six weeks we'll be heading to North Carolina, where I have a good job with benefits waiting for me."

"I'm not going to North Carolina."

"Avery, we've been through this—"

"I'm *not* leaving my friends."

Avery's complexion reddened, and Sunny's jaw tightened. It was Dev she didn't want to leave. Dev who would never see her as anything but the crippled kid he wanted to be nice to.

"We'll have more money," Sunny entreated. "You'll be going to college. North Carolina has great colleges."

Avery's expression would stun a toad. "I want to be a designer, Mom. How can I do that in some golf resort?"

"Pinehaven has good public schools, Avery, and North Carolina has great state colleges."

Avery shook her head, swinging her hair. "Number one. Here, the kids are used to me. Number two. I need to go to New York to design school, or at least stay here and go to SCAD."

Yes, and how would they afford a private college or school? Scholarships were hard to come by, especially for something like design. Sunny grabbed a stack of clothes and ferried them upstairs to the bedroom. When she came back, Avery was stroking the fabric of a slithery dress of blue-black, and for the first time that evening a smile spread across her impish face. "Now this is fabulous. You can go to another ball, Mom, and this time look great!"

Sunny's stomach clenched at the memory of that evening. "I doubt I'll be taking the good lady to any balls, with that ankle. Anyhow, ball season is over until fall." Sunny took the dress from Avery and held it up. "Whoa, low-cut."

"Wow," Avery breathed. "If that nasty Troy saw you in that, he'd be sorry he dumped you."

Sunny whirled to face her, nearly dropping the dress. She laid it carefully over the back of the chair. "What do you know about that, young lady?"

Avery lowered her eyelashes and fingered the silky fabric. "Only what I could pick up from the way you were moping around and dropping stuff and quitting your job and planning to haul me off to the mountains to perish . . ."

Sunny turned toward the window. A porch light glowed across the street, and two boys chased each other on bicycles, laughing and yelling. "He was a player. I should have known. The next time I see his face, I hope it will be waxy and made up to look natural."

Avery took this in. "Wow," she said. "You really hate him." She paused. "Did you hate Dad that much?"

Sunny marveled at Avery's ability to make quantum leaps in thought. "Let's not talk about your dad right now."

"I don't hate him," Avery said. "I miss him."

Sunny leaned down and picked up clothes, stacking the folded garments on chairs, and fought the urge to shout, "He's responsible for your leg."

The accident had happened five years ago, when Avery was ten. Sunny and Kyle Magee had already separated, on the path to divorce, when he'd come back to their Atlanta suburb from Nashville to pick up Avery for a trip to the beach. He'd moved to Music City trying to become a star, and by this time she was sick of the whole drinking, late-night, groupie culture. Being famous wasn't pretty, as she'd read in a poetry book she'd found in a laundromat, and she wanted out.

Sunny wished she'd listened to her gut and found a reason for her daughter to stay home. She didn't think the beach trip at a borrowed condo was a good idea, but a clash with Kyle always left her weepy and sleep-deprived, with stomach pains, so she'd packed the suitcase.

She'd watched her long-legged, spunky daughter get into that muscle car. She remembered how her gut had clenched when they'd squealed around the corner at the end of her street. That was the last time she would ever see him alive, and Avery whole.

Why had he tried to outrun that sheriff's car on the back road through South Carolina? Just to prove he could do it? Some throwback to his backwoods, shine-running ancestors?

"Mom," Avery was saying. "Are you listening to me?"

"Sorry."

"I heard you talking on the phone to Aunt Sherry." Sunny's older sister still lived in North Carolina, where they'd lived when their mother was alive. Her father had been gone from their lives for years. Sherry, who'd married early to escape the family situation, had been surprised when Sunny told her she was coming back to her home state.

"My little Big Ears," Sunny said to Avery. "So?"

"That's how I know The Troyster dumped you for somebody named Sydney."

Sunny felt her face flush. "She's a socialite with a personal trainer, a $400 haircut, a boob job, a dermatologist, underwear from Neiman's . . . get the picture? Oh, and I forgot. She's also Lady Sydney. She's divorced from a baron or something like that."

"Oh, cool! How do you know about the underwear?"

"I'm guessing."

"What's a socialite?"

"Somebody who spends her time going to luncheons and parties and occasionally does something for charity."

Avery's eyes sparkled with possibility. "What if you run into her somewhere while you're taking the rich old lady around?"

Sunny glared at Avery. "My employer's name is Mrs. Stirling, and I don't think they go to the same kind of events. Don't you have any studying to do?"

Avery shifted her position just a trifle. "Has this Sydney person ever met you?"

"Avery, please, let's drop it."

But Avery leaned forward. "Why is that Troyster so important that you have to drag me into the hills? Is it going to be easy for me to get around there? Nothing is flat!" Avery burst into tears, hopped up from the sofa, and propelled herself out of the room as quickly as her crutches could take her.

Sunny let her breath out in a long sigh and delivered the rest of the clothes upstairs. Maybe she was wrong to take Avery away from the city, where she'd already built up a support system and had friends who liked and accepted her.

But for Sunny, Pinehaven was a new beginning. The job did pay well, and she'd heard there were lots of well-heeled men up there. Plus her new boss, Roger Humbolt, was eager to have her work for him. And it was a long way, in more ways than one, from where she used to live in a mobile home park in the flood plain of a creek.

So Troy Bentley had played her for a fool. Okay. Time to get over it.

She set a stack of polo shirts on the bed and went back for the khakis. Then she hung the dresses from the top of the closet door. She fingered the midnight-blue silk. The ball . . . ha! Then her wall of defiance almost crumbled. She had wanted to be Cinderella. She had wanted Troy to scoop her up and take her to his kingdom, that high castle on the hill, far away from the dank wet valleys of her childhood.

But the wicked stepsister had got him.

CHAPTER FIVE

Sunny drove to work the next day wearing a purple polo shirt, khaki slacks, and her swirly-print nurse clogs. Avery had shrieked with horror and told her that she needed some classic loafers or at least some respectable-looking walking shoes to complement the outfit, but Sunny was adamant. She'd had enough of ill-fitting hand-me-down shoes when she was growing up. One of the bags had held classic brown loafers, too long and narrow. Sunny was returning them today.

She urged her old blue Corolla up to the big stone castle on the rise, admiring its landscape of grassy lawn, drifts of flowering azaleas, and tall magnolias. Her heart lifted. Take that, Troy Bentley, Prince Not-So-Charming. She was going to work *here*.

Still, was there really a daughter-in-law problem with Miss Lillian, or was it oncoming dementia, as her son claimed? It would become clear, she felt. All she had to do was impersonate a cousin who was impersonating a caregiver, and she had qualifications on both counts. How hard could this job be? She pulled around back and parked in a paved courtyard beside the garage. Duck soup.

She'd just entered a covered walkway, trailing her fingers over a huge terra-cotta urn under a stone arch, when a movement to the left caught her eye.

She glanced in that direction, but didn't see anything except the pool area. A quick check of her watch told her that she had a few minutes, so she walked over to the ivy-draped pierced brick walls that enclosed the pool.

Sunny pushed back a rope of ivy and peered through an opening. Instead of gray-white concrete, the pool was paved all the way around with lovely honey-colored stone. The water shimmered deep green. Pink geraniums and lavender petunias spilled from decorative planters in the sun, perfuming the air, while the shady area under overarching trees resembled an enchanted woodland glade. She'd never seen any pool so lovely, and yet—it was *water*. She shivered. Deep water was something that terrified her. Dark water. Water that was rising, rising, up to her chest, hands that clawed at her, dragging her down . . .

Shrubbery rustled behind her, and, catching her breath, she whipped around, but no one was there. Maybe it had been a squirrel—a very loud squirrel.

She couldn't get spooked now. She headed for the back door. She was sure she heard somebody pattering back down the driveway, and she wheeled around to see only empty tinted concrete.

She shook her head and walked firmly to the back door.

Before she could press the buzzer, Harris opened the door, looking down his nose at her. "Come in, Miss Iles. She's already anxious. I'll show you where to put your things."

"Were you expecting anybody else?" she asked.

"Don't be impertinent, Miss Iles." Harris harrumphed and frowned.

"No, I mean, really!" Sunny gestured behind her. "I thought I heard somebody out there."

Harris shrugged. "Probably some child. They're hooligans these days." He led the way to a small sitting room off the kitchen. "You can take your breaks here. There's a washroom, and help yourself to coffee and tea. I'll be available if you have any questions." Then he was gone.

Sunny thought she'd better concentrate on work. She hung her sweater in the closet and put her bag on the table, and then she inspected her make-up in the mirror. She tugged a comb through her hair, curly strands hopeless as usual. Troy had loved to touch her hair, loved its tangled sandy wisps. Wear more white, he said, and look like a ministering angel.

What a load of crap that sounded like now. She wondered if Sydney Fairfield wore white and what kind of ministrations lurked in her Louis Vuitton bag.

She jammed the comb back into her purse. She was NOT going to think about him.

She found Harris in the kitchen putting away the breakfast things. "I don't know if Harris is your first name or your last—"

He held up a hand. "You can call me Mr. Harris," he said. "And I will call you Miss Iles."

She opened her mouth to speak but decided it would be best to close it again. Six weeks, and then she was off to North Carolina.

"You'd better go on up," he said. "She's been like a caged tiger ever since she broke that ankle, and she's ready for her morning swim."

"Morning what?"

He raised his eyebrows. "You heard me, I think."

"But I can't—"

He broke into an evil grin. "Can't swim? Then this might be your last day on the job."

"Nobody told me there would be swimming!" Panic seized her and threatened to choke her. She gasped for breath, and then the old-fashioned intercom on the wall crackled.

"Is she here, Harris?"

He pressed a button and spoke into it. "She's on her way."

He nodded to Sunny. "The back stairs are just past that alcove. Have a pleasant morning, Miss Iles." He smiled, showing perfect white teeth, and if it hadn't been for his sinister look, he would have resembled Uncle Ben on the rice box.

She closed her eyes and took a deep breath. She could do this. Yes, she could. One step at a time. The back stairway disgorged her just beside an upstairs linen closet, and she could hear some kind of music coming from down the hall. Screeching high notes. Geez, did Lillian Stirling like opera?

She knocked on the half-open door.

"Is that you, Sunny?" The voice was sprightly, eager.

"Yes, ma'am."

"Oh, good. Come on, time's a-wasting," she said. "I should have been in that pool an hour ago."

Sunny walked into the room, done up in softest shades of cream. Miss Lillian, holding a pencil and pad, was propped in bed on mounds of silky pillows, the sheets a froth of lace. A newspaper lay on a bed tray, pushed to the foot. An operatic aria soared from a Bose system on the dresser, something Sunny had heard in a movie once, that film with Helena Bonham Carter and the naked men in the swimming hole.

"Do you like that, dear?" Miss Lillian asked. "*Mio babbino caro*?"

Sunny bit her lip. "It's . . . nice. You didn't say I'd have to swim."

"Didn't I? It's the world's best exercise. One of your jobs will be lifeguarding me."

"But Miss Lillian, I can't swim. I really can't."

Miss Lillian sighed, her shoulders rising and falling. "I must be getting old, dear. I forgot to ask. Come here; let me see you in that outfit."

Sunny walked over and shifted uncomfortably while Miss Lillian looked her up and down, nodding approvingly. Were her eyes misting up?

"They fit you so well. So you can't swim? Why not?"

She couldn't explain what had happened when she was a teenager to Miss Lillian, the terror. That would be too much. She took a deep breath. "I suppose I never had the chance to learn, ma'am. We moved around a lot." The standard excuse she always used.

Miss Lillian tapped her pencil on her pad. "But there are public pools, surely. Or are you from the country? I thought country children learned to swim in lakes, rivers, and streams."

Yes, they had lived near a river. "Not all of us," she said.

"We'll just have to teach you," Miss Lillian said brightly.

Sunny felt herself go pale and her knees weaken. "No ma'am. Please. That would be a horrible idea." Miss Lillian, oblivious to Sunny's discomfort, went blithely on.

"Of course. I'll pay for the lessons, if that's what you're worried about. Hand me the telephone, there's a good girl."

"But your cast," Sunny said, grasping at straws. "Your ankle."

Miss Lillian snorted. "Good Lord, girl. You should know that the ankle is immobilized and I'll have a waterproof cover." She waved her hands in elegant frustration. "The rest of me needs the exercise. Can't live without it."

Sunny tried to keep her composure, but she couldn't. Tears began to leak from her eyes, and she sniffed. She grabbed a tissue from the box in an elegant holder by the bed. "I can't do this," she mumbled into the paper handkerchief.

Miss Lillian gave her a long, penetrating stare and tapped her pencil to her cheek. "Why?"

"It's complicated." How could she tell Miss Lillian? Could she say, Well, Miss Lillian, you see there was a flood that wiped out the trailer park I was living in, and it threw my mother into even more of a depression, and she was drunk all the time and lost her job at the GoReady Bait Mart and Burger Stand, and then she started taking up with all sorts of scruffs and jerks, and they fought, and once she pulled the knife she used for watermelons. Nobody got hurt, but still. I couldn't wait to get out of there when I was seventeen and I even read a story like that in high school, ripped from the pages of my life.

No. She could not say that. The images were jumbled in her mind, that night of terror, when the flood came and the water was rising, and her mother was drunk as usual, near to passing out. The stuck door. Sunny kicking the kitchen window, trying to pop it out. The water rising, rising up to her chest. Strange things floating around the mobile home, swirling in eddies, band-aid boxes and colorful scarves and pill bottles and banana peels and beer cans. The window finally out. Trying to get through the window first so she could pull her mother through. Her mother clawing at her, trying to hang on.

Miss Lillian gazed at her thoughtfully, as if she could read her mind. "All right. If it's too painful to tell, don't tell me. But we have to rise above our slings and arrows if we're to get anywhere. Are you a quitter, my girl?"

That's just what Avery had accused her of. Sunny blinked and drew herself up. She had stuck with her mother until she had to leave, and with Kyle until it became impossible to live with him, and she had stuck with her nurse's training even through some ramen-noodle months, and she had done her best to raise Avery alone. But getting dumped by a wolf was the last straw. That wasn't quitting, that was moving on. "No, I am not a quitter, Miss Lillian."

"Well, then." Miss Lillian wiggled her fingers, beckoning. "Telephone, please?"

Sunny went over to a bedside table, picked up an elaborate French-style phone with a golden dial, and handed it to the older woman, who started punching numbers. With all her money, Miss Lillian could surely afford a smartphone, but here she was with an antique-looking gadget with no other function than to talk.

"Lilly Stirling. Let me speak to Flip," Miss Lillian said, then covered the phone and gazed at Sunny. "Please take that tray out."

Sunny picked up the tray and scooted down the back stairs to the kitchen, where Harris glanced up from filling a pepper grinder. "Settling into the job?" he asked.

She laid the tray on the counter, sunk in gloom. "She's going to make me take swimming lessons. I don't know if I can do it."

"Oh, you must." Harris spoke nonchalantly. "I was getting nervous about her swimming in that cast, even if she is strong in the water. Luckily the senator found out about it and told her she had to have somebody at the pool with her—and he's the one person she listens to."

"The senator?" Sunny perked up. This might be interesting.

"A family friend," Harris said. "He's coming to lunch today so she can show you off."

"Show me off? That's a laugh. Can't you swim?"

Harris sniffed indignantly. "I can swim quite well. I grew up in that sort of place. Still, I refuse to wear trunks on duty. It's not proper." He appeared to be considering his next sentence. "She's rather—reckless, you know."

"No, I don't know," Sunny said, though she'd had just such a fear. She swallowed. "Enlighten me."

The intercom crackled. "Sunny, get up here and get me into my suit! Flip's had a cancellation and he can come over for a lesson in half an hour!"

She cast a despairing look at Harris and headed for the stairs.

After she'd helped Miss Lillian into a flattering deep purple sarong suit, Lillian adjusted the straps and said, "Look in that drawer where you found the purple suit and get yourself the red one. So we don't lose you in the pool." She was serious.

Sunny put on the competition suit in the dressing room, and then she saw herself in the mirror. The basic Speedo hid none of her figure flaws. There was that cellulite on her hips, and the little midriff pudge that turned into a muffin top in tight jeans, and the thunder thighs, and this suit had no support whatsoever for her big old boobs, and . . .

Miss Lillian put her finger to her chin. "Oh, well. No one will see you but me."

"What about Flip?" Sunny wailed.

"Oh Flip doesn't count," Miss Lillian said. "He's seen it all."

He was still a guy, wasn't he?

Standing on the honey-colored stones by the pool, Sunny dreaded an encounter with a studly beach boy. But Flip arrived with a squint, the physique of a muscular weasel, and hair like a toy polar bear. All business, he did not stare at her chest. She relaxed and let herself enjoy the warm sunshine and the riot of flowers in the stone urns.

"Come on in," Flip called. She tiptoed to the edge of the pool, closed her eyes, and eased herself into the icy water, shivering. Her stomach clenched and nausea rose at the remembered smell of sewage and floodwater, and then the chlorine stung her back to reality. Breathe, she told herself, but it was hard.

Miss Lillian, wearing an inflatable boot over her cast, stroked laps with the rhythm of a Mississippi steamboat while Flip worked with Sunny in the shallow end. After thirty frustrating minutes, he told her. "You know, you don't have to be a sinker. It's all in your head, kid."

"I thought it was my abs of steel," she grumbled, her nose and sinuses burning from the chlorinated water. She wondered if her hair was going to turn green. It was cheap dye she used for the highlights.

Flip didn't hear her. "I'll see if I have any arm floats in your size in the van," he said.

"Oh, this has been refreshing," called out Miss Lillian, swimming over. "Can we do this again tomorrow, Flip?"

Flip pasted on a grin. "Maybe Thursday, Mrs. S. I've got a class at the Y tomorrow."

"Oh? Maybe Sunny could join."

Flip kept the grin. "Love to have her, but the class is for three-year-olds." Sunny didn't like his tone, which said *and they can swim better than you*. Plus, she had the uncomfortable feeling that someone was watching her through the pierced brickwork.

She was almost positive she'd heard someone sneeze.

Sunny got her chance to look behind the wall after she'd rinsed chlorine out of the suits, squeezed them dry, and hung them on the line behind the pool house. She searched the ground, hoping she'd see a footprint, anything to tell her she wasn't crazy, but there was only springy Bermuda grass. A silver flash proved to be a gum wrapper, and she picked it up out of her innate sense of neatness and put it in her pocket.

"Whatever are you doing, Miss Iles?"

She turned to see Harris. "Oh, just tidying a scrap of trash. What do I do with the wet towels, Mr. Harris?"

"You may leave them in the laundry room. Lunch will be served at twelve-thirty in the dining room. You'll be expected to join Miss Lillian and the senator."

Oh God, please deliver me. If there was one thing that made her more uncomfortable than water, it was politicians. "What's his name, this senator?" she choked out.

Harris's lips curved in a sinister smile. "Senator J. Wesley Blackshear. A state senator. He and the late Dr. Stirling were old friends."

"Her late husband was a doctor?"

"A very fine orthopedic surgeon, Miss Iles. I'm surprised you hadn't heard of him. Providing you really are a registered nurse?"

Sunny gritted her teeth. "Mr. Harris. Now that you mention it, the name does sound familiar. But I didn't meet him at my hospital, Westbury."

"Perhaps," said Harris, "you may have heard of the Julia S. McEvoy Pavilion—"

They were interrupted by a piercing shriek from above.

Harris nodded. "I think she's ready for you now."

He gestured to Miss Lillian's upstairs window; she was leaning out, two fingers between her lips.

"She's rather proud of her whistle," Harris said, nodded, and walked away down the pebbled path.

Sunny helped Miss Lillian dress for the luncheon with the Senator in a vintage lavender pants outfit with legs wide enough to fit over the cast. "But I didn't bring any nice clothes with me," Sunny said, looking down at her slacks, polo shirt, and nurse shoes. "Are you sure you want me to join you?"

"Of course," said Lillian. "Young people dress any old way nowadays. Of course, in my day I would have expected you to wear a suit and hat, or at least an afternoon dress."

Sunny was not sure what an afternoon dress was, or whether Miss Lillian was joking. "I don't know if I can do it, Miss Lillian. I don't know if I can be your cousin."

Miss Lillian gave her an exasperated glance. "Just call me Aunt Lillian and I'll take it from there. Cousin Lillian sounds so old-fashioned."

Sunny could see herself drowning in a sea of talk. "But who are my parents? Where do I come from?"

"Oh yes, and you have a little bit of country in your speech," Miss Lillian said. "Let's work on that. Just don't say much, dear. Say you've traveled a lot." She paused. "Your mother is my cousin Weezie, who ran off to France with an artist back in the sixties and got cut off from the family."

"But I can't speak French!" Sunny wailed. "What if he asks me a question? And did he know my . . . mother?"

"Oh, Wesley doesn't speak French either," Miss Lillian said. "And there are some books on art in the library." She gestured vaguely downstairs. "Monet and such. Just read up when you can. I don't think Wes would remember Weezie. Well, he might. He makes it his business to remember people. Still, don't worry. I'll do the talking. Go on, I don't need you right now. I'm going to write letters and email on my computer."

"Your computer?" She thought of the antique phone and wondered what the computer looked like.

"I have a little lavender MacBook. Amazing what they come up with! I'll show you later. Get me settled in my room, my boudoir, I like to call it. Did you know that boudoir really means a place to pout?"

Boudoir, thought Sunny. Cinderella would have a boudoir in her castle, to pout when the prince didn't let her have her wish. Princes were that way, she thought, and then she went downstairs to learn something about art.

The library was stacked floor-to-ceiling with books, unlike some "libraries" Sunny had seen on TV and in magazines, where the shelves were filled with strange pottery or model cars or photographs. Here, the pictures hung on walls or were displayed in silver frames on tables. And there were lots of them.

The handsome man with gray temples, distinguished in a three-piece suit, was obviously Miss Lillian's husband—the doctor, Duncan Stirling. Then, an outdoor picture of a sailboat and a long-legged, sweet-faced, healthy-looking girl, who was surely Miss Lillian's daughter, the one in the wedding picture she'd seen in that sitting room. Yes, this photo was of the same young woman with the guy from the hospital parking lot, the dreamboat who'd been in the wedding picture. So Miss Lillian had at least two pictures of her daughter on display, but no mention of her so far.

Now Sunny's attention was caught by another wedding picture, on a side table in a silver frame. She lifted it to get a better look. This was a different wedding with a different man, who looked more like the doctor. Ah, this one must be the son. And this must be a second wedding, because the couple looked older, and the bride wore a white sheath and tiny saucer hat with a chic pouf of a veil. He looked about forty-something, beginning to put on a little weight, almost good-looking, with a pasted-on grin that said he wanted to get the damn pictures over with.

His bride, elegant with high cheekbones, dark hair glinting with auburn highlights, faced the camera with a triumphant, heavy-lidded gaze, one that said she had bet her stake and raked it in. Was this bride Kiki, the woman who was trying to kill Miss Lillian? No, better not think that. Nothing had been proven.

Sunny knew there must have been another bride sometime, the first wife. Hadn't Miss Lillian mentioned one, and said she'd liked her? Sunny looked around, but the only other wedding picture she saw on the wall was a faded color photo of Miss Lillian herself, looking gorgeous in a satin gown with a bouquet of white roses.

Sunny's attention was caught by a studio portrait near Miss Lillian of two adorable little girls. Whose children were they?

Sunny returned to gaze again at the picture of Miss Lillian's daughter. Pretty, healthy and athletic-looking. Where was this daughter, and why was Miss Lillian giving away her clothes? She must be living with that good-looking guy somewhere, maybe on a beach with that sailboat, and that's why she wasn't in town looking after her mom. And why would a daughter send her husband to the hospital to visit instead of coming herself? Sunny would keep her ears open and maybe learn something. It wouldn't be polite to ask any further.

Well. Thanks for the clothes, cousin.

Sunny looked for art books, found a whole shelf of them, and settled down with one about Edgar Degas, because the woozy woman on the cover with a green drink in front of her reminded her of her mother.

CHAPTER SIX

Neil relaxed in a cane chair on the front porch toward evening. It was the time he liked best, the air filled with the sounds of insects and the sigh of the wind, the sky glowing with sunset colors. The overhead fan riffled the pages of a letter he'd just read. He set it on the side table and took a sip of beer. That old snake, Harlan, had seen it in the mail, hadn't he? That's why he'd mentioned the "lady professor."

Oriana Welles had written that she'd like to come to the island to do some birding and get a few more shots of the wildlife for her book on island wildlife before summer classes started. She'd be prepared to make a generous donation to the conservation fund, or pay for room and board. She wouldn't presume on their previous friendship.

Friendship, was it? He was glad it was hard to reach him by phone. What were her motivations in coming? Was it strictly business? Even so, he wasn't sure he wanted Orrie here. Harlan was right. Neil did get lonely, but whenever he tried to get unlonely, it seemed to open up a can of worms.

It was a little more than a year ago when Orrie, a college instructor and nature photographer, had appeared along with a grumpy curmudgeon of a journalist with a thick thatch of salt-and-pepper hair. They were working on an article about Issatee, the least known of the Golden Isles, if you didn't count St. Catherine's, which was owned by a private foundation. Neil had wondered then if there might be any involvement between the two. He liked Oriana's looks—in some ways she reminded him of Julie—but he wasn't about to make any moves.

He'd dodged their questions when they asked where to find the artist M. Cornelius, who'd done such gorgeous watercolors of the island. He said the artist had moved on, leaving no contact information, that the painter liked to remain private and let his art speak for itself.

The island was Neil's private retreat, and he only wanted to share it with people he liked. Should he let in the world, with all that implied?

He didn't want to share that with this photographer, no matter how attractive she was. His paintings would not go in her book.

Then early one morning, when Neil had gone to check the turtle nests, Orrie had risen early to go with him, just the two of them. While he'd been stooping in the sand, she'd stroked the back of his neck, making all his neck hairs tingle, and before long they were close together on the beach, talking about baby turtles, while the dawn broke over the sea and sunlight spilled toward shore.

Oriana had come back to Issatee a month later, this time alone, and she and Neil had explored other natural wonders together. He found that she was a vegetarian except for the occasional fish, espoused all the environmental causes, and hiked with the Sierra Club.

And they were good in bed together. Yet he'd been left with a vague disappointment afterward, gazing at a water stain on the ceiling beam, wishing he had a cigarette, but he'd given up smoking after his teenage years. His soul still felt at sea.

He'd never let her go inside his shed—there would be no point in it. She'd be excited; she wouldn't be able to keep quiet. It would raise all kinds of interest he didn't want. She'd tell her journalist friend, and there would go all his privacy. He'd let her think the ramshackle building was an old toolshed, and so it was. In that shed he kept all the tools he needed to keep him sane.

The relationship had fizzled when it became clear there was nowhere for it to go. Living on the island full-time was something she'd never consider.

They hadn't parted on the best of terms, and now, here she was extending an olive branch. Maybe nothing had changed, maybe everything had changed. He wasn't sure he wanted to find out.

He picked up a letter from Lillian, addressed with her signature blue-black ink in her famous swooping handwriting. Reading her letters always made him feel better. Crazy, wasn't it, to feel good about your mother-in-law?

He tore it open and scanned the lines, detailing her oncoming visit. She would be accompanied by somebody called Sunny Iles, whom she called her assistant and distant cousin. Harris would put them on the airplane to Brunswick, and they'd rent a car that Sunny would drive to the marina. Lillian asked him to phone her when his reception was good to let her know his schedule, and to please arrange for Harlan to meet them with the boat.

Neil pondered the requests. Lillian would come for her weekend, and maybe he could schedule Orrie for the weekend after that. He'd make the letter to her impersonal, and see if photography was really all she wanted.

He hadn't deliberately tried to keep the affair with Oriana a secret from Lillian, but he'd seen no need to mention it. He didn't know how his mother-in-law would take it when—and if—he became really involved with someone else. In any case, he looked forward to seeing the old girl. But who was this improbably named Sunny Iles? Julie's cousin? He was sure Julie had never mentioned her. He would've remembered a name like that.

Tomorrow morning he wanted to go to the shed, load his brushes and supplies into the jeep, and drive out to the beach where a sun-bleached wrecked dinghy lay. It was the first time he'd felt an urge to get it down on canvas, because it was too close to the spot where Julie had drowned. Maybe he was beginning to move on, after all.

Sunny watched with her full attention—as if she were attending a demonstration on surgery—while Miss Lillian presided over the luncheon table. She noted the snowy white cloth, cloth napkins, and white lilies and greenery in a silver bowl that made up the centerpiece. At one end of the long table, Miss Lillian sat at the head with the tall senator on her right.

Sunny perched at her left, supposedly to assist, but Miss Lillian had no problem with anything aside from getting into her chair. Sunny saw no sign of memory loss today, or any dementia. Thank goodness, she hadn't mentioned anything to the senator about her daughter-in-law trying to kill her. So far.

Harris served them from platters with silver spoons and tongs: shrimp Newburg on rice with asparagus and a butter lettuce salad with orange slices and poppy seed dressing on the side. He placed a hot yeast roll on each bread plate.

Sunny gazed longingly at the chilled Sauvignon Blanc Harris poured, a wine she'd learned about from Troy Bentley and loved, but she didn't feel right about drinking on the job. Harris raised his eyebrows when she told him she'd prefer iced tea, but he brought it with a crystal dish of lemon wedges.

The senator fixed her with a politician's eye and rumbled on with a story about how long he and "ole Dunc" had been friends; in fact he'd met him when he'd been a young country lawyer down around Saint Simons, and they'd wound up in a golf foursome together.

When the senator finished telling the results of the golf game to Sunny, he turned to their hostess.

"Look here, Lillian," he said. "You know how I love Issatee, and you love it too. I know you're worried about what will become of it. Why not make a deal with the state?"

Miss Lillian looked taken aback for a moment, but she recovered quickly. "I can't say I wasn't expecting that, Wes. In fact, I've even considered it. But it's out of the question."

"What's your reason, Lil? You think this crowd won't be good stewards?"

Issatee Island. Where was that? Sunny was fuzzy about coastal geography. Once, a long time ago before her daddy had gone to jail and disappeared from their lives, he'd taken them to Jekyll Island, the state park. That was the last happy time she remembered with her family.

As if Miss Lillian had read her thoughts, she said, "Look what's happening with Jekyll. There's pressure from developers. Look at Cumberland, all that hoo-ha about the horses that're tearing the place up. Got to please the public and their romantic fantasies, you know, while visitors who really appreciate the wilderness walk around stepping on road apples. Oh, we'll fix that with dune buggies. Can you imagine all that roaring! There's hardly any place at all that's quiet anymore. How can anybody think?"

She paused to let that thought sink in. "The best way to preserve Issatee is to keep it in private hands."

"I've done what I could to keep your taxes down, Lillian," Wesley said. "But there's just so much I can do, and I won't be around forever. That representative they elected—Smutz—is pro-developer, toes the party line. The county needs more money, too, for social services. Pressure from both sides of the aisle." He paused. "They can squeeze you. Even Alex thinks I have a point."

"Don't talk to me about Alex," she said. "He's resurrected that resort idea again."

"It's not a bad idea," Wesley said. "A lot of estates have had to admit paying customers to stay viable," he said reasonably. "Biltmore—"

"Do I have a stately home, Wes? No, no, and no! I remember Hilton Head when it was scrub pine and palmetto. I know what can happen. We only have the lodge, the Big House, and the kids' dorms. They're talking about using the whole island, selling lots and having a grand clubhouse! Where would the Geechees go?"

"We could turn the island into a wildlife center—"

Miss Lillian's face pinkened. "You've got Ossabaw," she pointed out. "Would there be enough money to fund another center in this political climate? I've got my own wildlife center, and we do contract work for the University. Neil's there. If only Julie had lived, she would have—" She took a deep breath, sipped her wine, and appeared to steady herself. "Julie's buried there. And Duncan, in the family cemetery."

Sunny felt as if she'd been smacked upside the head. Julie? Was that the daughter? Dead? She was wearing a dead girl's clothes? She stared down at the purple polo as if the garment might be haunted. She looked at Miss Lillian with a new understanding. The poor woman had her grief to bear, and the island was tangled with her daughter.

When she looked up, the senator was patting Miss Lillian's hand, looking at her tenderly. Sunny felt her neck becoming warm and bit her lip. Miss Lillian should have told her about Julie. It wasn't an insignificant fact. She knew, posing as family, she was supposed to know about the island, and about Julie.

"What do you think about all this, Sunny?" asked the senator.

She gave a tight-lipped smile. "I agree with Aunt Lillian, of course."

"Yes, I suppose you would," he said, rearing back in his chair. "You probably have fond memories of the island, when all of you cousins got together. I spent a lot of time there after I met Duncan. I'm surprised I never met your parents."

She trod carefully. "Well, Mama and Daddy were probably living out of the country by then—"

Miss Lillian broke in on cue.

"Poor Weezie," she said. "She never came to the island after my uncle disowned her because she ran away with that artist. It was very sad." Miss Lillian lowered her eyelashes. "I didn't see why this poor child," she gestured at Sunny, "should have to suffer. It was time I took her under my wing. And, of course, I needed help as well."

"Oh, of course, of course," said the senator approvingly, smiling.

Lord, thought Sunny, hoping beyond hope he didn't ask where she had lived. She didn't know squat about France, except there was an Eiffel Tower there, and how could she miss that, with little replicas all over Walmart.

"Tell me about this political situation, Wes," Miss Lillian said. "Is there anybody I can bankroll against Smutz?"

"Save your money, Lil," the senator said. "Barring some scandal, he's got the county sewed up."

"Scandal . . ." Lillian said thoughtfully.

"Lillian, I don't like that look on your face," the senator said.

Sunny was relieved to see Harris come in with dessert, a yummy-looking chocolate cake, and his excellent coffee. That coffee beat anything that Troy Bentley had ever made in his fancy machine. She sipped on it while she ate her cake, and there was no more talk about the island until the last crumb was gone. Then the Senator placed a hand on Lillian's. "Think about my idea, Lil. You don't ever go down there any more, do you? I mean, it's not as if the family still uses it, and Neil's not blood—"

Miss Lillian withdrew her hand and her gray eyes flashed. "I'll claim him," she said. "He's the father of my grandson, and that counts for something. And yes, I do enjoy going there. It was very lonely at first without Duncan and Julie, and this ankle business has cramped my style, but now that I've got Sunny, she'll go with me."

Sunny, sipping her coffee, sputtered with horror. She dabbed furiously with her napkin, hoping no one noticed.

The senator regarded his empty cake plate. "You're going next week?"

"I think Sunny can learn to swim by then," Miss Lillian said, and the senator's face grew sober. His searching glance made Miss Lillian draw back, poker-faced, and she straightened the fork on her dessert plate. When she spoke, it was lightly and casually. "You know, Wes, India and Julie were such friends. She's unattached now, isn't she? Why not bring that daughter of yours down to the island sometime?" Miss Lillian glanced over at Sunny. Some information for her, Sunny guessed.

Wes didn't seem to notice. "Well, Lillian, she finally called it quits with that stockbroker, and I'm glad. But—"

Miss Lillian's eyes twinkled with delight. "I've got it! I'm planning a party for my birthday next month, and you and India are invited. How I wish Mary Lynn was healthy and could come, too. I'll open up part of the Big Lodge, and we'll have a crab boil on the grounds, picnic at the beach, board games afterwards in the lodge. Wouldn't that be fun?" Her expression was pure innocence. "Mary Lynn wouldn't mind if you two come, would she? I'll make sure to visit her before we go. We four had such good times."

"I miss those times," the senator said.

Sunny watched. There was no glance from Miss Lillian. Mary Lynn must be the senator's wife, and in bad health.

The older man's wiry gray brows tangled. "Oh, no,Lil. Oh, no. I see the wheels turning in that devious pretty head. You're thinking India and Neil?"

Miss Lillian leaned forward, her fingers laced together, her eyes sparkling. "Why not? India used to love Issatee. Remember when we all used to go and take all the kids? What fun we had!"

Wesley Blackshear reared back and snorted. "Matchmaking won't work, Lil. India won't listen to anything I have to say about men, because I was right about the last one. Contrary, she is." He paused and looked at Miss Lillian. "Lil, I'll be frank. Neil hasn't got a dime, has he?"

Miss Lillian shrugged. "Neil wouldn't be interested in India's money. He earns his pay as island naturalist. All he cares about is that island and the work he does there."

Sunny didn't miss the implication. So India had money, probably from some dead relative, and probably due to inherit more. Yes, Miss Lillian was probably interested in it, because it would be good for the island. Wow, this was fascinating, just like those English dukes with huge estates looking for rich American wives to keep up their ancestral homes.

The senator sat back and twiddled his thumbs. He knew what was what.

"Just expose them to each other and let nature take its course," Miss Lillian said. "It's worth a try." She wasn't going to give up easily.

"Come on, Lil. India likes to help people. Children." He paused. "The island she cares about is Haiti."

"But we have people on the island. The Geechees. I can take her over to meet them! She'll fall in love, Wes."

The senator shook his head. "Maybe so, but I believe they're a proud sort who don't want too much help. And will she fall for Neil? She'll be more careful now. That phony she married last time got a Beemer in the divorce, but I had to pay through the nose to make sure he didn't get much else."

"Oh, Wes. India's a sweet girl, and I'm concerned about my son-in-law's happiness. It's not good for him to live alone. Angus is growing up, and all Neil has for company is that dreadful old cat and those horses. Well, he does have the Geechees, but he needs someone in his life. A helpmeet."

He gave her a mischievous grin. "You and your King James Bible. This isn't 1656. You live alone, Lillian, and as I understand, you're fighting to keep it that way."

Her eyes narrowed. "I have my friends, and an active social calendar—even with this." She pointed to her ankle. "I'm going to a bridal luncheon tomorrow."

A bridal luncheon? That hadn't been mentioned. Sunny felt a little knot of fear tighten in her gut. Would she be expected to go too? What she liked was looking after people, and at a luncheon where she knew absolutely nobody she would sit, a knot on a log, while happy wedding chatter went on all around her.

At last the talk between Miss Lillian and the senator drifted to old friends Sunny didn't know, so she let her mind wander, mulling over the possibility that there might be a prince in North Carolina, until she noticed that the table conversation had tapered into contentment and smiles, and then it was time for the senator to take his leave.

Wesley Blackshear walked Miss Lillian to the door, and Sunny lingered in the dining room so the two could have some privacy. She'd seen the warm way he grasped Miss Lillian's hand and the kiss he placed on her cheek, a little too close to her mouth. She wondered how long he had been in love with her.

Miss Lillian summoned her after the door had clicked shut. "I'm exhausted, Sunny." She swiped theatrically across her forehead with her hand. Sunny glanced out a side pane to see Senator Blackshear striding to his car, a jaunty spring in his step. Miss Lillian looked far from exhausted—she positively glowed.

"Why not have a nap?" Sunny suggested.

Miss Lillian smiled dreamily. "Yes, I think I will. Please wake me for my appointment with the hairdresser. By the way, we'll have to do something about your hair."

Sunny touched her locks, now a mass of frizz after that dip in the pool. The strands felt dry and brittle. "I think the chlorine has turned it a little green."

"One of Laszlo's girls can give you a special shampoo and then a hot oil treatment."

Laszlo? This was probably some posh salon. She had to be firm. "Miss Lillian, I can't afford—"

"I'll take care of it. Part of the job." Miss Lillian waved her hand. "Wesley has a sharp eye for deception, and I think he didn't quite believe you were one of the family. I'll get you a good cut and color."

Sunny's stomach lurched for the second time that day. Sure, she knew she could use some help, but there was no way her hair would turn sleek and chic, like Julie's. But she steeled herself. She was playing a role, and she'd do what it took to carry it out. After all, she had taken on the duty to protect Miss Lillian, and if a cut-and-dye hair job was what it took, by gum, that's what she'd do.

She walked Miss Lillian to the tiny elevator by the kitchen, installed her, and then marched upstairs to help her off. The job was for six weeks. That's all. She could stand it for six weeks. But if she was going to play this part, she needed more information.

"Miss Lillian . . ." she began, when she helped Miss Lillian out of the elevator and into the upstairs wheelchair.

Miss Lillian held up a finger. "Later, please. Take me to the boudoir."

Sunny wheeled her into the little room next to the bedroom, all done up in pink and cream chintz, a restful room with comfortable button-back chairs and a lavender-and cream-striped chaise longue. The writing desk looked delicate, with curvy legs and a fancy drawer handle, and a crystal vase of roses perfumed the air. A small, elegant, laptop reposed in its lavender clamshell on the desk.

She helped Miss Lillian out of the wheelchair, walked her in, and lowered her into the chaise.

Then Sunny stepped back and folded her hands. "Miss Lillian."

"Yes? Did you enjoy meeting the senator?" The older woman examined her nails and dusted imaginary specks off her blouse.

"Miss Lillian," Sunny said firmly, "the senator was fine, but I need to know about Julie. I'm wearing her clothes, aren't I?"

Miss Lillian lowered her eyelids. "I know I should've told you, dear. But you know, my mind." She glanced up and tapped her head. "So muddled these days."

"Your mind is perfectly fine, Miss Lillian." Sunny waited, hands together, the very picture of patience. "That is my professional opinion."

"It's hard for me to talk about Julie," Miss Lillian said, her voice catching. "She was the loveliest girl, the best daughter. I miss her every single day." Miss Lillian heaved a deep sigh, and Sunny felt the silence grow and lengthen. Finally, Miss Lillian broke it. "Maybe I can tell you more another time, my dear. I'm really very tired, and my ankle is throbbing."

Sunny immediately tucked two pillows under the cast to elevate it, once again the nurse, not the poor relation. She liked the nurse role so much better. "Please relax just like that. Do you need something for pain?"

Miss Lillian nodded. "Perhaps I'd better."

Sunny administered the dose along with a glass of water. "Is there anything you'd like me to do while you nap? Straighten your closet?"

"Oh, no, dear, I had a professional organizer set it up and it practically keeps itself straight. Maybe you could go down to the library and find some books about the islands."

First art books and now island books. She wished she could use the computer to look things up on Wikipedia, but she had a feeling she shouldn't ask. "This island, Issatee," Sunny said dully. "You really want me to go?"

"Of course," Miss Lillian said firmly. "You'll love it."

Sunny nodded. She took a handwoven afghan off the back of the chaise, spread it over Miss Lillian's legs, and then drew the silk draperies. She turned off the silk-shaded table lamp and walked downstairs to the library.

Rather than look for island books, she wanted to browse the photo albums. After scanning the shelves, she found them stacked neatly in a low cabinet. She picked one at random that turned out to be mostly Julie: Julie in a wedding dress with a bouquet of orchids, Julie with a giant loggerhead turtle, Julie as a child, sifting sand. Julie in a prom dress, standing beside her father. Julie shaking hands with Jimmy Carter.

The next two albums contained people she didn't recognize, more photos of gardens, and more photos of golfers. Stacking the ones she'd perused on the coffee table, she noticed an oversize art book—watercolors of the Georgia barrier islands.

She settled with it on the sofa and opened it. She found an inscription *To my good friend Duncan Stirling*, signed with the energetic, slanting signature of Jimmy Carter, who had written the foreword. She leafed through the pictures, begrudgingly admiring the beauty portrayed there. Three of the paintings had something different from the others—they seemed to catch the mist, the light just so, and she could almost feel the heat and the breeze and see the Spanish moss swaying. And in each of those paintings there was a wild creature—a bird, a lizard, an alligator. She looked for a signature, like Troy Bentley always did when he'd taken her to art galleries. He only bought pictures by known artists and liked the weirdest things.

She couldn't read the scrawled name in the right-hand corner—Cornel or Carmel, trailing off, and some squiggles. She didn't care whether the artist was known or not, all she knew is that he (or she) painted pictures that prickled the hair on the back of her neck. She closed the book and walked into the kitchen, where Harris was sitting at the table, reading a Walter Mosley novel and eating his own lunch.

He set his book face down on the table and looked up with a frown. "Yes, Miss Iles?"

"Mr. Harris," Sunny said. "What happened to Julie?"

Harris lost his look of irritation. He gently set his fork on his plate. "She drowned," he said.

CHAPTER SEVEN

The day after the salon visit had not begun well. Avery had agonized over her school outfit so long that she missed the bus and Sunny had to drive her, barely having time to choke down a cup of coffee, much less breakfast.

"Thanks, Mom," Avery said at the curb in front of the red-brick building, dragging her book wheelie out of the car. "By the way, you look weird in that get-up. Nobody from the hospital would recognize you, not even the Troyster."

Sunny felt the new hairdo was flattering and chic, and chalked the comment down to Avery's age and general snarkiness. She kept her opinion until she was at work, when, on her way downstairs with Miss Lillian's breakfast tray, she passed a big gilt mirror and got a load of herself wearing the green polo, the pink slacks embroidered with little palm trees, and the blond preppy haircut—straightened, tamed, and toned. Who *was* that person? She stumbled, almost dropping the tray. Maybe she could pass, after all.

In the kitchen, Harris was off buttling somewhere else. The coffee smelled divine, and Sunny's mouth watered at the three strawberries and slice of untouched toast left on Miss Lillian's bone china plate, along with a tiny crystal bowl of fig preserves. Why waste good food when she was so hungry?

She poured coffee into a plain, serviceable mug and let it cool while she finished the strawberries and spread the toast with the preserves. She took a big bite, and almost choked when a woman's face appeared at the back door. The back doorknob rattled.

Sunny took a quick sip of coffee and swallowed. She recognized the looming face from the wedding photo. The hair had been given even more bronze highlights, until it was almost striped, and was now cut short, sweeping over her brow and back behind her ears, exposing diamond earrings. Kiki Stirling wore a tight red jacket, an olive green tank top, and enough gold necklaces to choke King Tut.

The woman smiled broadly and gestured for her to open the door.

"Mr. Harris!" Sunny called in panic. Harris appeared, wearing a canvas apron, with a duster in his hand. The woman called, her voice faint through the glass. "Harris! Open up!"

He glided over and unlocked the back door. The woman strode in, black pointy-toed heels clicking, a leather portfolio in her right hand.

"Good morning, Miss Kiki," Harris said, nodding. "I wasn't expecting you today."

"Good morning, Harris." The woman tilted her head, examined Sunny, and kept smiling. She said, in a voice smooth and deep, like a noir babe sitting on a private eye's desk, "I don't believe we've met."

Sunny reluctantly rose and smiled in return. "Sunny Iles. Miss Lillian's . . . ah . . . assistant."

Kiki Stirling's eyes crinkled in amusement. "Sunny Iles? How delightful."

"It's my real name," Sunny said automatically, wondering what else she was supposed to say. Was she really in the presence of the enemy? The woman seemed pleasant enough, if a little cold.

"Miss Kiki, Miss Iles is Miss Lillian's young cousin," Harris supplied, his professional poker face giving nothing away.

Kiki's eyes glittered. "I thought that's what my husband told me."

Kiki. The daughter-in-law. The potential murderess. Sunny kept her own smile going. Best to find out all she could and not make an enemy.

"From California," Harris added for good measure. Sunny stared at him. Did Harris know something she didn't? Weezie was living in California, not France?

Kiki's smile wavered and she pursed her lips. "Funny, Alex never mentioned having a cousin in California."

"I'm a black sheep," Sunny said, improvising, trying to mimic Kiki's manner of speaking. "No one mentions me."

Before Kiki could ask another question, a terrible racket commenced outside, like someone bouncing on squeaky bed-springs. Kiki shrugged her shoulders and gave Harris a pleading look. "Oh, dear. Poor Muffin hates being cooped up in the car. You don't suppose—"

Harris held up his palm. "Miss Lillian hasn't changed her mind, Miss Kiki. The dog is not allowed in the house. Those needlepoint pillows it ruined were irreplaceable heirlooms made by her grandmother, and it cost hundreds of dollars to get the odor out of one and the other rewoven."

Kiki opened her hands. "Now, Harris, I've taken her to training, but . . ."she trailed off with a long, exasperated sigh. "Never mind. I need to see Mother Lillian. I haven't been able to reach her."

"She's been rather busy," Harris said. "And with that ankle . . ."

"Yes, yes," Kiki said. "It's hard for her, isn't it?" She seemed genuinely puzzled that a broken ankle might put a cramp in one's social calendar.

"I'll go see if she's dressed," Sunny said quickly.

"Very well," Kiki said. Out of the corner of her eye, Sunny saw her reach in her bag and pull out a packet of sugar-free gum. Sunny remembered with a jolt the gum wrapper she'd picked up from the driveway. Had this woman been lurking around, spying on her and the swimming lesson?

"Oh, *merde*," said Miss Lillian, perched on a vanity bench at her dressing table, a powder puff in her hand. "I don't want to talk to her. It gives me a headache. Why should I make myself sick? Why should I give her the opportunity to kill me?"

Sunny was glad she'd had professional training to remain expressionless. She replied, "Your daughter-in-law doesn't look so dangerous. Killer fashionable, maybe." Avery would approve of that outfit. Still, there was that packet of gum. The wrapper was still in the pocket of the pants Sunny had worn that day, in the laundry she hadn't had time to do.

Miss Lillian frowned at her. "Kiki knows I'm going to that bridal luncheon today. She'll be there too."

"Maybe she just wants to give you a ride."

Miss Lillian swiveled toward Sunny. "Heavens no, I won't ride with her! She may crash the car on purpose."

"Well, then she would be dead too," Sunny observed.

"She would cut my seat belt," Miss Lillian said. "The air bag on my side would be jammed."

Sunny began to organize the jars on Miss Lillian's dressing table according to size. "If you don't talk to her now, she'll corner you at the luncheon with whatever she has on her mind. You don't want that, do you?"

Lillian returned the jars to their previous locations. "She would have the bad manners to do that. It makes me furious my son sends her to do his dirty work instead of talking to me himself. He wants to be the good guy." She straightened her shoulders. "I'll see her. But not without my eyebrows. Help me do them, dear."

Miss Lillian handed her a Chanel eyebrow crayon. Sunny gulped, took the crayon, and hoped for the best. They didn't teach eyebrow management in nursing school, and she'd always done her own with a #2 pencil. "Close your eyes, Miss Lillian."

When she'd finished, Miss Lillian smiled. "Not bad. I suppose Harris has plenty of coffee left?"

Sunny nodded.

Miss Lillian picked up a mascara wand. "I'll do my lashes. Go see that Madame Kiki has a cup in the morning room. Then come and help me into my old suit and this ridiculous thigh-high stocking. I'm sick of palazzo pants!"

The "old suit" turned out to be a perfectly nice classic St. John knit, fuchsia and white with silver buttons. It came just below the knee.

Sunny turned to go. "And Sunny," said Miss Lillian, "you have fig preserves on your face. It's fine—you're welcome to eat whatever you find here."

"Yes, ma'am," said Sunny, blushing furiously. She grabbed a tissue from the dressing table and slashed it across her lips. No wonder Kiki had stared at her. How many blunders would get her thrown out of here? She thought of all those moving expenses that her new boss had not offered to pay for.

And what was *merde*? She must ask Harris.

Sunny paused in the door of Miss Lillian's morning room, near the kitchen, where Miss Lillian liked to entertain women friends, read, discuss schedules with Harris, and watch women's tennis and Netflix classic films.

Kiki had already set herself up on the flowered chintz sofa with a cup of coffee, a folio open beside her. She held an iPad, on which she was trying to jot notes while talking at it. Light glinted off her diamond earrings and designer wedding ring.

"Darling," she was saying, "I know, I know. What else can I do? When does your flight arrive? What if she says no? Wait.

Someone's coming." Kiki looked up at Sunny and closed her hand over the device. "Yes?"

Sunny played over the conversation she'd overheard and memorized it for future reference. "Miss Lillian's on her way. She said to have some coffee."

"Harris saw to that, thank you, dear." Kiki gave Sunny a cheerful smile.

Dear? Sunny turned to go back upstairs. "Alex darling," she heard, "I love you, and so does Muffin."

Somehow Sunny doubted Muffin loved Alex, or vice versa.

Sunny went up to report that Kiki had coffee and was talking on the phone to Alex, who seemed to be arriving in town shortly and knew she was here.

"I might have known," Miss Lillian grumbled. "Conspiring against me. I think I've changed my mind about what to wear to that luncheon. Maybe I shouldn't show off my cast." Half an hour and three changes of clothes later, Lillian was back in the St. John knit and pearls. "Let them all see the results of Kiki's efforts!" she'd finally announced.

Sunny at her side, Miss Lillian rode the scooter into the morning room, elephant-headed cane tucked behind her. Muffin's incessant yipping reached their ears. "Chewing on my grandmother's pillows," Miss Lillian murmured under her breath. "All that needlework."

"Hello, Kiki," Miss Lillian said warmly as if she were happy to see her. Kiki came over to air-kiss her mother-in-law, and then Sunny helped Miss Lillian into the chair at the corner of the sofa. She propped the cane beside her. Miss Lillian turned to Sunny. "Would you bring us some fresh coffee, please?"

Sunny headed for the door to get the pot and tray. Kiki was saying, "Alex sends his love. He's on his way back from Geneva."

Sunny reached the kitchen but Harris wasn't there. The fancy Chemex coffee maker was steaming, and a plate of pastries beckoned from a silver tray trimmed with lacy cotton napkins.

She peered out the back window. Harris stood outside in the driveway, gesturing at two young men standing beside a white van with a lightning bolt painted on the side. Nobody looked happy. Some kind of electric company, or comic strip action hero? She shrugged and got back to work.

She poured the coffee into a waiting silver pot, placed the heavy tray onto a cart, and trundled it into the morning room, where she parked it near Miss Lillian. "Is there anything else, Aunt Lillian? I'll pour coffee and leave you two to talk."

Miss Lillian raised her eyebrows. "You'll stay right here. And get yourself a cup."

Kiki's brows knitted ever so slightly, but she kept the sugary smile. She couldn't quite keep the vinegar out of her voice. "But, Mother Lillian, this is a family discussion!"

"Sunny is family, and I need her." Miss Lillian smiled sweet-and-sour as well. "Since you're under the impression I'm losing my memory, I'd like her to take notes. I see *you* have a notebook, dear." She leaned over and stroked Kiki's leather iPad folio. "I don't know how I've survived all these years without one of those."

Kiki realized she was being mocked and set her lips in a thin line.

Sunny declined coffee, found pad and paper in a drawer as instructed, and perched, pen ready, in a yellow chenille chair across from the two women.

Kiki's eyes darted to Sunny and then over to the window, where the edge of the white van peeked from behind a large boxwood. She cleared her throat. "It's about the island."

"Oh, good," Miss Lillian said, arching her eyebrows. "I wondered when you were going to get around to it. Now we won't have to waste time on idle chit-chat." Miss Lillian turned to Sunny. "Sunny dear, I'll fill you in on what you need to know later. Just take notes for now."

Kiki darted another glance in Sunny's direction, then apparently decided to ignore her completely. "Alex has found a major, *major* investor who'll make a substantial donation to the wildlife center . . . and is a really big name in resorts . . ." Kiki let her voice trail away in implication.

Miss Lillian folded her hands. "In exchange for?"

"A wonderful resort development," said Kiki. "In the best of taste. It'll blend with the surroundings. Very exclusive. The best sorts of people."

"How big?"

"Well, we need to talk about that. To get maximum profitability, we need to use as many buildable lots as we can."

"How many houses do you propose? And where do you intend to put them? I suppose there will be clubhouse, marina, spa, pool, nail salon, the works?"

"Well, you can't expect that caliber of people to rough it." Kiki made a few stabs on her pad.

Miss Lillian leaned forward and picked up her cane. "Buildable lots? Where? On the other end of the island? What about the Geechees? Esther and her family? They own their land."

"But Lillian," Kiki went on, still mellifluous and throaty as ever, though her left foot twitched with a mind of its own. "We can buy it from them. Maybe trade for land somewhere else. Maybe over by the wildlife center. The club, the spa, and all that—they'll have jobs. You do realize, don't you, that taxes and expenses are eating away at the trust fund?"

"I have plenty for Caesar and the wildlife both." Miss Lillian banged her elephant-topped cane on the floor for emphasis.

Kiki winced. "Alex just wants to make sure you have enough for any unforeseen outlays, such as . . . ahem . . . that is, he's afraid of dipping into capital if you should . . ."

"Nursing home expenses?" Miss Lillian snorted. "Less for you two when I fly away home, as they say in the gospel song."

Kiki's tense jaw quivered. "Oh, Mother Lillian," she cooed, "don't talk like that. You know we have your best interests at heart."

Miss Lillian gave Kiki a gray-eyed stare. "Then why does Alex keep stalling when I ask to see the books? I was content to let his father take care of our finances, but I made a mistake in not asking to be informed. I want to know what's going on with my money."

"Well, it's complicated . . ."

"You seem to understand it very well."

"Well, I'm in the business, you know."

"That's what I'm afraid of," said Miss Lillian. "But hear this. I'm not going to develop the island. I'm not going to have a resort, no matter how exclusive, and I'm not going to interfere with the Geechees. I'm keeping the island wild as a memorial to Julie and Duncan. That's what they would have wanted. I want Angus to have the island one day as it is, and as it was."

Blood rushed to Kiki's cheeks. "Angus! He doesn't care about it, Lillian. He's told us that he wants to join the military." Her façade was beginning to crack. Perspiration glowed on her brow.

Miss Lillian remained firmly upright, cane in hand. "Angus is too young to know what he wants now, and one day he'll want that island."

"But Lillian, it's changed since you were a child, you know. Change is natural. Young people embrace change."

"No," Miss Lillian said. "It's his childhood home, and he's got to get away for a while and learn who he is, see other ways of living. And then, he needs something unchanging to come home to. A rock."

Sunny understood. Miss Lillian's daughter was gone—buried far away on an island she loved—and Miss Lillian was going to keep what was left. She was willing to let Angus, the grandson, pull at the chains that bound him to that small world, wanting to see a bigger life, but she intended for him to come back and take his rightful place.

Sunny longed to tell Miss Lillian and that smug Kiki about Avery, about herself. Talk about wanting a bigger life! But she was just the hired hand. It wasn't her business. She mustn't confuse her role with reality.

Kiki was leaning forward. "Alex says that you always favor Angus. You have two granddaughters, you know. Aren't you concerned at all about their future?"

At the mention of the girls, Miss Lillian's face hardened. She carefully took a sip of her coffee and settled the cup back on the saucer before she spoke. "The girls can always come to me for instruction and advice, which they need more than mere money. All they've done is make those strange people on reality TV look like choirgirls. I'm not throwing cash into that black hole."

Kiki sighed deeply. "Their therapist says—"

Miss Lillian banged her cane on the floor. "Therapist! Alex should've let them stay with their mother. Catherine wanted them. She loves them."

Kiki rolled her eyes in exasperation. "Then why on earth didn't she fight for custody?"

Miss Lillian looked hard at Kiki and shook her head. "That talk is for another time. The subject of the island is closed now, but I'm sure I haven't heard the last of it from you two." She paused and motioned for Sunny to hand her a tissue, and, whisking it to her nose, she blotted carefully. "I've already made one decision. I'll go to Issatee next week and see how Neil's managing the place. While I'm there, Neil will help me plan a grand party to celebrate my seventy-ninth birthday next month. I'll be expecting all of you, of course—girls included. Time for you to appreciate the island as it is meant to be."

Kiki shivered, opened her mouth to speak, and then closed it. She pulled herself together with iceberg calm. "But will you be well by then? Isn't that too much . . ." Her voice was tight.

Miss Lillian's voice didn't quaver. "My ankle is broken, not my head. I'm perfectly able to plan a party."

Sunny scribbled furiously on her pad. Party? Island? Next month? Maybe she would be well off to North Carolina by then. OMG. She had to get out of going to this island next *week*. She would die. She might have a panic attack. But how could she avoid going and still keep this job?

Miss Lillian nodded to Sunny and then turned to her daughter-in-law. "Thank you for coming by, Kiki. I've got to make some phone calls before the luncheon. I'll see you there." She nodded at Sunny, and Sunny stiffly laid down her note pad and walked over to help Miss Lillian out of the chair. Kiki rose, walked over, and air-kissed the older woman's cheek good-bye.

"I'll let myself out, Mother Lillian," she said, edging off toward the kitchen. The dog's yipping had never let up.

After the sound of both yipping and the car's powerful engine had died away, Sunny was following the scooter toward the elevator when Harris appeared, cool as ever. "I sent those people away, Miss Lillian."

"Sent what people away?"

"The so-called electricians," he said. "Mr. Alex hired them, they said."

"Electricians, you say? Why were they here, and why did you send them away?"

Harris sniffed. "Because we don't need any electrical work. Mr. Alex noticed the sun room's ceiling fan wasn't working last week. He decided the house needed the wiring checked, and those gentlemen said they were here to do it. Mr. Alex never informed me he'd called anyone, so he didn't know I'd already repaired the fan myself. In any case, the doctor updated the whole 1950s wiring system when he got his first computer. Mr. Alex should have known that. He should also know that maintenance is my job."

Miss Lillian raised an eyebrow. "Why did you say *so-called* electricians?"

"Most electricians I've met have an air of competence. These didn't seem to know their amps from their joules, in a manner of speaking."

"Maybe they didn't know English very well," Sunny offered.

Harris's disdainful expression didn't change. "They struck me as pretending not to know English. I'll bet they were planning a robbery. Getting the floor plan. Finding where the valuables are kept. Casing the joint, as they say."

Silence hung in the air, and a strange look came over Miss Lillian's face. "No," she said slowly. "They weren't coming to rob me. They were coming to kill me."

Uh-oh. Kiki did have a bad effect on Miss Lillian. One aspect of dementia, she knew, was to seize on a certain delusion and not let go, whether it was space aliens talking through a hidden antenna on the roof or assassins in the guise of electricians. "There might be any number of explanations," Sunny insisted.

"No. Mine is the most logical explanation," said Miss Lillian. "I'm glad you didn't let them in, Harris. Next thing, we might have all been electrocuted in the shower." She glanced at her antique Bulova watch and turned to Sunny. "I need to dress for the luncheon, and I'm glad that my sister's granddaughter is having it at the Swan Coach House. There, Kiki can't poison the food."

"Oh, Miss Lillian, that's silly," Sunny said. "She couldn't poison your food at a party."

"No? How would you like to be my taster, like kings had in the middle ages?"

Sunny grew sober. Would she be willing to be the taster, or not? Did Miss Lillian have dementia, or did she have insight? Kiki was outwardly nice and pleasant, but was there something ruthless and stony underneath?

Well," Miss Lillian said. "No matter. I can't wait for you to see Issatee! We'll prepare for our island visit. At least she can't try anything there."

Sunny nodded slowly. Surely there was nothing to these accusations. Still, she needed to keep her eyes wide open.

That night, she did laundry. In the pocket of the pants she had worn the day she'd first come to work, she found the wrapper for sugarless gum.

CHAPTER EIGHT

The Swan Coach House luncheon passed without incident. Or so Miss Lillian said. Luckily, the good lady had been seated at one of the big round tables with friends of the same generation, several tables away from Kiki. "Honestly," Miss Lillian said, "I'm finding these bridal luncheons a bit tedious. I think I've attended too many in my life, with people having so many weddings. Not like when I was a girl."

"Now, Miss Lillian," said Sunny. "Don't you like seeing friends?"

"I suppose so, but I'd rather be sitting on the patio having a drink with them."

Sunny bit her lip and helped Miss Lillian out of her luncheon suit and into the caftan she liked to relax in. Bad luck that Miss

Lillian was in that kind of mood. How could she tell her boss there was no way she could go with her to that island?

Maybe she should tell her before the next swimming lesson, which was that very afternoon. She gazed out the window at the nature-inspired pool lurking below in all its jungle ambiance, its deep green water concealing murky depths. If there had to be a pool, she liked it bright blue, the kind where you could clearly see the horrid drain on the bottom that was sure to suck you down if you weren't careful.

"Sunny, I'm waiting!"

"Sorry." She helped Miss Lillian onto her chaise longue. Miss Lillian looked up at her quizzically. "Sunny, you seemed to be solving the problems of the world just then. What's your recommendation for the latest crisis with Russia?"

Sunny blinked and then said firmly, "I'm sorry, Miss Lillian. I know you're counting on me going with you to the island and all, but you know I have a daughter. When I took this job, I didn't know there would be travel involved."

Miss Lillian pointed a manicured finger at her. "Don't be silly. We can make arrangements for your daughter. Are you trying to get yourself fired? It won't work. I'm not ready to give up on you, young woman. You have a lot to offer and it's not going to waste if I have anything to say about it."

"But, Miss Lillian . . ." Heat crept up Sunny's neck. No one had ever talked to her like that—certainly not her mother, who'd let Sunny muddle through life without much of a compass, making it up as she went along.

"About your daughter," Miss Lillian was saying. "Thursday to Sunday, while we're gone, she can just move in here, into Julie's room—that is, the blue room. She's fifteen, did you say? I can find somebody who'd spend the night and keep an eye on her, and Harris would be around to feed her."

Sunny fell silent. Miss Lillian was volunteering to shelter Avery, and had shelled out for swimming lessons, as well as a hair styling session. In return, she, Sunny Iles, was supposed to go to an island surrounded by water? The thought numbed her.

"Let me—let me think about it."

Miss Lillian nodded. "You do that. And get a hold of yourself, girl! Now I'm going to have a little rest before we swim, and while I'm resting I'll tell you a little about Issatee." She leaned back and closed her eyes. "Well, sit down! Stop hovering."

Sunny eased herself into the chair beside the desk. She took a pencil and note pad, just in case.

"There's no history written down," Miss Lillian said, "just family lore. Neil keeps saying he's going to write one, but I haven't seen a word."

Her great-grandfather, she told Sunny, had acquired Issatee as payment for a gambling debt from a Yankee industrialist back in the late 1800s. He'd sold a good bit of timber off it, and then decided he'd like to have a fishing and camping retreat, nothing fancy, as Issatee was small, barely ten miles long. He'd fixed up the Yankee's big house for the family and guests, and he'd also built a small lodge for the caretaker of the property.

Neil and Julie took the caretaker's lodge. The big house, now simply called the Big House, had fallen into dilapidation during the Depression and had only been partially restored. A couple from the Geechee settlement—descendants of freed slaves—looked after it.

Later, in her father's time, as the family grew, a dormitory was built for the children and their friends.

As the eldest of three daughters, she inherited the island along with her two sisters, and after she'd married Dr. Duncan Stirling, she found that he loved the island more than she did. Together they'd bought out her sisters' shares, and the sisters were only too happy to sell. They'd always hated the isolation, the "primitive" conditions, and the upkeep of the buildings, and would much rather spend time at the more civilized St. Simons or Sea Island, which featured golf and tennis and social life.

Once Miss Lillian started talking, Sunny thought, it was hard to stop her. Sunny wished she'd get around to Weezie, but she'd started in on her son.

Alex, much to Miss Lillian's disappointment, preferred city life and resort life like his aunts, and had no inclination for the medical field. He'd gone into real estate. But her daughter Julie had loved Issatee, and she was drawn to medicine like her father. But in her pre-med courses at UGA, she'd met her husband Neil, studying to become a marine biologist. Of course, she'd brought him to the island, suggesting that he could become the island naturalist.

"Then," Miss Lillian said, "nothing else would do but for her to become a naturalist too and marry Neil! Let me tell you, her father was fit to be tied. The boy was on a full scholarship and didn't have two nickels to rub together."

Quite right that they should oppose the marriage, thought Sunny. Poor mixed-up Julie didn't know what she was doing. Here she was in Cinderella land already and she was going backwards. She bit her lip, reminded of Troy Bentley and his betrayal. How could she have mistaken him for a prince?

Kyle too—he had promised her the moon, him, and his guitar. He was going to be a star, showering her with dreams of Nashville glory—he, too, turned out to be no prince in froggy disguise, but just a regular frog.

Miss Lillian was looking at her quizzically. "Where are you, girl? Am I boring you?"

"I'm sorry, Miss Lillian." Sunny picked up the suit Miss Lillian had worn to the luncheon, inspected it, and seeing that it didn't need cleaning, walked over to hang it in the closet. "What you told me about Neil and Julie was so different from my own marriage, which wasn't so happy. It ended six years ago." There was no point in telling her about the wreck.

"I'm truly sorry," said Miss Lillian. "Duncan and I were wrong about Neil. He and Julie were so in love, and he turned out to be a dedicated steward. He truly loves the island. Together, they wrote articles about nature and cared for the wildlife. They did some conservation work for the state and, of course, I paid them as well."

Sunny felt skeptical that everything had been as rosy-posy as Miss Lillian made out. Sunny knew that doped-out feeling of love didn't last. Julie had probably scrubbed and worked her fingers to the bone, wishing she was back in the castle. This Neil was probably just like Kyle and let Julie do all the scut work while he went looking for crabs or seaweed or whatever biologists did.

Miss Lillian looked sad and far-away and Sunny wasn't going to say anything against this son-in-law Miss Lillian obviously adored. Sunny was anxious to change the topic. "Have you thought about clothes for the trip?"

"Yes. I'd like to take some caftans," Miss Lillian said, breaking out of her pensive mood. "No shorts. There won't be anyone but us; still, I believe that after a certain age, Sunny, there are things which must be concealed if a woman is to keep her mystery and glamour." She smoothed a hair back into a spike.

Well, Sunny thought, this advice was wasted on Miss Sunny Iles—she'd never have mystery and glamour. On the other hand, she'd seen some pretty awful legs sticking out of shorts at the mall. She decided to keep the advice in mind.

Miss Lillian was a good old bird, even if she was a little nutty. No, Sunny remonstrated herself. Don't start thinking like that. It's disrespectful, and wrong.

"Sunny, hand me that mirror on the dressing table," Miss Lillian said, sitting up. "I'm thinking about a new haircut. These spikes have been fun, but now the shock value is over."

Sunny handed over the mirror and looked at Miss Lillian skeptically. "If you'll pardon my saying so, Miss Lillian, there isn't much to cut."

"Mmm, yes. Maybe I should let it grow a little first." She put down the mirror. "Well, how about it? What about your daughter? Can she stay here?"

Sunny cleared her throat. "About my daughter."

"Yes?" Miss Lillian glanced in the mirror once more, but she was watching Sunny keenly. There was a small golden clock on the dressing table whose second hand was ticking around, ticking around. "Well? Nobody's forcing you to go, dear. But I'm going, and I'd like you to come with me. I'd hate to let you go and find somebody else, because I like you, Sunny. It's good to have you around."

Sunny swallowed. Miss Lillian missed her daughter. "I think maybe Avery can stay with a friend," she said at last. "There's this boy she likes, though."

Miss Lillian looked at her severely. "And you're afraid he'll take advantage while you're gone. Listen, Sunny. If you expect them to behave badly, they will."

"But I can't just close my eyes," Sunny said.

"No," Miss Lillian replied. "Set limits, and then expect the best. Tell her you're counting on her. And be sincere."

Had she ever done that? Or had she vacillated between coddling Avery because of her—her—*limitation* and screeching at her that if she didn't mind her mother, she'd end up *just like her father*? Projecting her anger at Kyle onto Avery. She shouldn't do that.

"It's just fear," Miss Lillian said softly. "Don't let it sink its fangs into you. Now let's put on our bathing suits and get ourselves ready for the great wide ocean."

Great. Wide. Ocean. Sunny said a silent prayer and went to get the suits. Miss Lillian's fearlessness reminded her of Avery, actually. Now, all she had to do was convince Avery to stay with Mariela, the friend who had the strictest mother of all.

For some odd reason, she wanted to keep this job.

CHAPTER NINE

The motor gave a roar, Harlan's ferry accelerated, and Sunny, thrown off balance, gripped the rail. Cool salt spray misted her face. She shut her eyes tight, even though she longed to stand and look at the island as they approached; but vast expanses of water surrounded her. If she fell in, she'd surely 1) drown, 2) be eaten by sharks, or 3) be stung to death by jellyfish.

Miss Lillian, across from her with her cast-bound foot stuck out, wore no scarf or hat, blissfully allowing the sun to pound her face and the breeze to whip her white hair into a bristly froth.

Sunny squinted against the sun, curiosity mingled with dread. Memory catapulted her back inside the flooded trailer, water rising, closing over her mouth and nose, while she pounded and kicked on the stuck door, the stuck windows. With a mighty blow she'd finally popped a window open so she could drag her drunken mama out, both of them gasping and choking, the water stinging her nose. She towed her helpless parent over to a tree limb, where they clung until the Rescue Squad paddled up in a raft, almost when she'd given up hope. Her daddy was safe in jail by that time, on high ground, far from attack by the kitchen knives.

She shuddered. And Kyle, her so-called loving husband, who knew about her ordeal because she'd let herself tell him one night after they'd had a few beers, had wanted her to go to Myrtle Beach so she could "face her demons." She was so in love she hadn't seen *his* demons.

And because she'd been under the spell of that big South Carolina moon, so crazy for his kisses and the sound of his singing, she'd let him sweet-talk her into the water. Then he'd pushed her under, saying he was going to drive the fear out of her. He'd let her go and laughed when she'd come up dripping and gasping. She had never trusted him again.

Beaches held nothing but bad memories for her.

But, man. If only she could tough this job out. All she'd promised was six weeks, and now she was down to four. She'd already put a deposit on an apartment that Roger Humbolt had found for her, and she'd looked into moving herself by U-Haul. She knew a couple of guys from the hospital she could hire to load the truck.

"Sunny! For heaven's sake, look!" Miss Lillian shrilled.

She blinked her eyes open and saw that the boat was cruising down the tidal creek, through the reeds, and great white birds were rising and flapping across the glittering blue-gray water.

"Aren't they breathtaking!" exclaimed Miss Lillian.

Sure, if you liked honkin' big white birds that guzzled fish. But Sunny couldn't say *that* to her boss. In front, the bearded captain hummed a little tune, almost drowned out by the roar of the engine.

The engine slowed, approaching the dock and boathouse, and they slid alongside with a series of bumps. On the dock, a grubby man in a khaki shirt with rolled-up sleeves and a baseball cap leaned over, grabbing the line the captain threw him. A dark-skinned boy about twelve took the line and tied the boat fast to the dock.

The grubby man, hugely grinning, extended one bronzed arm to Miss Lillian to help her out. "Hello, Neil!" Miss Lillian kissed him on the cheek. "And hello, Reggie," she said to the boy.

Sunny felt herself go numb. *The man from the parking lot.* Would he recognize her? She'd known him at once, even though his khaki shirt was dirty and stained and he was all sweaty. The cap was grubby. Well! He knew Miss Lillian was coming, his own mother-in-law, and he might have made a little more effort. She seemed unconcerned about his possibly fishy hands on her nice coral linen jacket. And then he extended a hand to Sunny.

When her eyes met his, she felt a sharp jolt, as if they'd known each other somewhere in a different universe instead of meeting in a dark, echoing concrete parking lot. He didn't seem to remember her, though. There wasn't that light, that spark in his eyes. Just curiosity. Watchfulness.

Neil helped her onto the dock, and she wrinkled her nose at the oniony tang of sweat. Her tolerance for dirt had been bred right out of her by nursing school; and her late ex-husband, despite his faults, had been a nasty-neat man.

Miss Lillian made introductions, identifying the boy, Reggie, as Neil's assistant. "I call him my apprentice," Neil said, giving Sunny a cockeyed smile. "You know, I thought I'd met all of Julie's cousins. Welcome to Issatee, Sunny Iles."

"It is my real name," Sunny said pre-emptively.

"You bet." Neil's amusement rankled her, and she moved away from him.

The captain, whose name was Harlan Fish—which Sunny thought was just as proper as Sunny Iles—tossed their bags up to Neil and Reggie, and they loaded them into a cushioned cart big enough to carry Miss Lillian. Miss Lillian hadn't wanted to bring her folding wheelchair, saying it wouldn't work well on sand or shell paths. She'd get by with crutches and help.

They trudged to the lodge, Neil leading the way and Harlan pulling the cart. Miss Lillian sat snugly between the ice chest and the supplies. Sunny tagged along behind, bumping her one nice duffel-on-wheels behind her. She breathed in the fresh sea air, feeling the packed sand beneath her feet, looking to the right and left to take it all in. The wide path led through an overgrown tangle of seaside undergrowth up a gentle rise. Neil looked back at her, and she realized she was lagging behind. She hurried to catch up, now aware of her appearance. She would be so embarrassed if this Neil recognized Julie's old clothes. But then again, she felt that he was not a man to pay attention to clothes.

Miss Lillian piped, "Tell me, Neil. Tell me everything that's going on here. So you have that photographer coming?"

Sunny could have sworn Neil blushed, but maybe it was just the heat. "Oriana Welles," he said. "She and that guy want to turn that article about Issatee into a book on bird life and other wildlife in the islands, and she wants more pictures. They've already covered Little St. Simons."

Miss Lillian shrugged. "I don't mind being included," she said. "But more exposure means more requests for visitors, and we're not set up for that."

"I got calls and letters after the article appeared in *Southern Living*," Neil said. "I had to tell them all no."

"There are plenty of other places for island-hoppers to go." Miss Lillian waved her cane for emphasis.

Yes, Sunny had seen a shelf full of island books in the library back at the house. Why did the world need another one? But now they were arriving at the lodge, rustically built of cedar. Sunny took in the plain weathered construction, the faded rattan furniture on the spacious front porch. She expected the cushions to smell of mildew.

Miss Lillian appeared disgustingly happy to be here. How could she like this primitive place? All Sunny had wanted was to get out of places like this, and into places loaded with gleaming bathroom tiles, warm soft fabrics, and shiny, sturdy furniture that didn't give you splinters or smell like old socks.

A huge orange cat bounded off the front porch to greet them and wound around Neil's legs. Sunny jumped back, startled.

"Hey, Rambo," Reggie said, grinning.

Rambo eyed Sunny distrustfully, walking all around her and nosing at her shoes.

"Is he tame?" Sunny glanced at his switching tail.

Neil laughed. "Depends on what you mean by tame," he said. "I've taught him a few tricks."

"Tricks?"

"That creature," sniffed Miss Lillian.

"Wait right there." Neil plunged his hand into the ice chest on the cart. He came up with a raw shrimp and held it high above Rambo's head.

Rambo leaped into the air and swiped the shrimp away with one pass of his claw, then hunkered down and gobbled it, leaving only a few remnants of shell. Reggie grabbed a shrimp and repeated the act.

"Aren't you worried about getting scratched, young man?" Sunny said, glancing from Reggie to the beast. "Cats' claws carry all kind of germs."

Reggie laughed, and Neil chimed in. "We're immune to all the resident bacteria by now. Anyhow, he doesn't miss."

"But—"

"You'll understand when you've been here awhile," Neil said kindly.

Sunny's face flushed. He was patronizing her, and she didn't like it one bit. If only she could tell him she was a registered nurse and not some impoverished relative in need of charity! She bit her lip and watched Rambo finish his snack, leap atop a fence post, and observe Neil and Reggie carry the luggage up the three wooden steps onto the porch and into the lodge.

Once in the front room, she was surprised at the lodge's pleasant woody smell, which blended with aromas of the salt air, the marsh, and seagrass. The stone fireplace with rustic pots on the hearth charmed her.

But did it ever get cold enough here to light that fireplace? Inside the lodge, out of the breeze, she felt as if she'd been wrapped in warm absorbent cotton. A gnarled-stick sofa and chair looked awfully rickety, but the coffee table made from a tree trunk and a glass top was solid. A seagrass rug lay on the varnished pine floor, and the lamp bases were—what? Some kind of signal light?

"Hope you don't mind staying in my son's room." Neil said over his shoulder. "Right here." He indicated a small, white-painted room to her right.

"Not at all." As long as it was *clean*—

Neil set Miss Lillian's bags in a room across the hall, where a handmade quilt bloomed with appliqués of purple lilies, then he walked back to the kitchen, where Harlan was unloading the groceries and gifts. Miss Lillian was supervising nearby from the sound of it.

Sunny gazed at a watercolor painting on the wall of the island, of the purple shadows in the path through the jungle. Was it done by the same artist she'd admired in the book? She couldn't read the signature from this distance. "Hey!" Sunny heard Neil say. "Lillian, thanks for the fig preserves."

"Oh, Harris must have found another jar," Miss Lillian said. "I thought I'd eaten the last of them."

"Good old Harris," Neil said. "He always knows what I like."

Sunny went into her assigned room and set down her duffel at the foot of the dark pine bed. She dropped her handbag onto a canvas folding chair. Shelves were filled with shells, driftwood, and books. There wasn't a TV set! Why, even Avery had her own TV set. Sunny realized she was going to miss her favorite shows for *three nights running*. And as for Avery, she'd reluctantly agreed to stay with her friend Mariela. Sunny knew Mariela's mother would keep her promise to ride herd on the girls. Now to find the bathroom!

"Everything okay?"

She whirled around to see Neil standing in the doorway.

"Ah—" she began.

"Through there," he said, pointing at a small board-and-beam door, "if you want to freshen up. When you're ready, meet us on the porch for a tour."

She nodded, embarrassed that he'd read her mind, though he was probably just being a thoughtful host. She didn't like the knowing twinkle in his eye. He had no right twinkling at her like that.

She visited the necessary room, washed her hands, and tried to smooth her windblown hair back into its straight bob. Tucking the comb back into her bag, she spotted a picture on the dresser of Julie and a small boy. He had to be their son, Angus, Miss Lillian's grandson. Julie shone slim, toned, and radiant, while Angus was blessed with the same crinkly hair as his father, along with the skinny arms and belly pudge boys get right before they go through a big growth spurt.

Five years since his mother drowned. He was sixteen now, Miss Lillian had told her, so the tragedy had happened when Angus was eleven. The same year of Avery's accident, when she was ten.

Unsettled, Sunny stalked onto the porch, her bag slung over her shoulder out of habit.

"Time for the tour!" Neil announced. He nodded at Sunny. "You won't need that. There's nothing to buy out there."

She gave him a withering look. "I hope you have a handkerchief if anything makes me unhappy." She couldn't stand smart alecks.

Reggie walked up from the back of the house. "Want us to drop you home?" Neil asked him.

"Nope, Cap'n," Reggie said. "I'll go up to the Big House and see if Daddy needs me."

Neil cheerfully shrugged and helped Miss Lillian into the front seat of the Jeep. Sunny climbed into the back, with her bag, before he could assist.

He drove them first to the biological station, where Miss Lillian insisted on going in.

"I think you should stay in the Jeep," Sunny insisted, touching Miss Lillian's arm. The lady had had a long, exhausting day.

"I've been sitting for hours." Lillian turned to Neil with a look of desperation. "Neil, please! I need to see."

To Sunny's amazement, Neil picked up Miss Lillian and carried her in, setting her down on a bench where she could prop her ankle. Sunny scurried along behind. In the front room she took in the displays of flora and fauna, of fossils and shells. There were skeletons of island animals on display, and a huge stuffed alligator hung from the ceiling; for educational purposes, Neil said. He did not collect trophies. He pointed out the shell of a loggerhead turtle. "Hit by a speedboat," he said with a grimace.

In the second room, animals were recovering or held for observation. There was a baby alligator in a cage, soon to be released, he said, and an injured turtle in a tank, waiting to be transported to the Turtle Center on Jekyll Island. Sunny was used to unpleasant smells, but Miss Lillian wrinkled her nose, winced, and didn't ask to be shown around further.

Sunny recognized that wince. "Is your ankle hurting, Miss Lillian?"

"It's nothing. I need to see those records."

"I can bring the account books and logbooks back to the lodge," Neil said.

"Can't you go over those books later, Miss Lillian?" Sunny asked. "I know you have things to do, but the more you rest, the quicker you'll heal."

Miss Lillian frowned, but Neil said, "Tomorrow morning when you're fresh, Lil. Why don't you let me drive Sunny around this side of the island and then we'll go back? I'll take you to Turtle Point tomorrow."

"How's Esther?" asked Miss Lillian, smiling.

"She's fine." Neil grimaced. "Feisty as ever. Asked me if Harris was coming. She's never forgiven her brother for running off to the mainland."

Miss Lillian shook her head. "Kids and grandkids okay?"

Neil's brows pulled together. "Sure. Keziah comes over and helps me out some. Helped me clean house for you all."

"Pretty girl," Miss Lillian remarked.

"Yes," Neil said. "I don't know if she'll stay on the island. Boys come over in boats to see her."

"I think she's always had a crush on you," Miss Lillian teased.

"Esther would have put the kibbosh on that." Neil clamped his lips together, and Miss Lillian beckoned for Sunny to help her up.

They bumped along the rutty path through a tangle of jungle—over a wooden bridge where reeds grew in the shallows and a blue heron waited for fish. Sunny's heart wanted to encompass the island's light and shadow, its colors and movement, its breezes and colors, its jungle tangles and its wide, wide sky. She wanted to see more, to know more. Too bad this place was surrounded by waves and water.

Neil slowed and pointed to a multicolored bird that looked like a Disney creation. "Painted bunting." It rose up from the scrub and flew away.

Miss Lillian clapped her hands. "I love it! Don't you, Sunny?"

"It doesn't look real," Sunny said. Birds were supposed to be dun-colored, weren't they? All the ones she usually saw in the city were.

"Tomorrow we can take the bird scopes," Neil said, encouraged. "I'll show you lots of birds, colorful ones. Or we can go out in the sailboat."

Sunny stiffened. Didn't the man know poor Miss Lillian needed to keep her leg up? How was she going to heal at this pace? Yet Miss Lillian was saying, "What a splendid idea."

"I think Aunt Lillian needs a nap now," Sunny said firmly. Sunny herself hadn't slept much the night before and would welcome a little shut-eye.

"After we finish our drive," Miss Lillian said, "and that's final." They completed the circuit of the island.

They were approaching the lodge, Sunny watching the scenery intently in order to keep from dozing off, when she noticed a padlocked shed not far from the house. "What's that place?" she asked, wondering what could be so valuable on this island.

Neil shrugged. "Just an old toolshed."

"You have to lock up the tools?"

Neil leaned over and looked her in the eye. "Actually, it's where I butcher the hogs I kill. It's not a pretty sight."

Sunny let out breath. He was kidding, of course. Wasn't he?

Sunny was dozing on the lower bunk, lost in a dream of Avery on a raft in the pounding surf, going out farther and farther. A knock at the door popped that nightmare, thank God. She opened her eyes, disoriented. Where in heck was she? Oh, yeah. On an island pretending to be someone she wasn't, surrounded by deep, scary water.

The knock came again, more insistent.

"Come in." She scrambled up just as the door inched open, and banged her head on the top bunk. "Ow!"

Neil eyed her through the crack. "Lillian wants you. You okay?"

"Fine," she said, rubbing the knot on her head. She glanced at the bedside clock. She'd been sleeping for an hour, and she'd only meant to take ten minutes! What would he think of her, sleeping on the job?

She found Miss Lillian out on the porch watching birds. "Look, Sunny," she said, passing her a pair of binoculars. "Right over there, you can see a flycatcher."

Sunny tried, but didn't see anything, so she said "pretty."

Miss Lillian took back the binoculars. "He's flown away."

"Do you need anything?" Sunny papered over the gaffe with her best caregiver mode. "Can I bring you a drink?"

Miss Lillian pointed to a gin and tonic on the table. "Neil's fixed me up, and I'm in hog heaven right here," she said. "You could go help him with dinner." She looked over her glasses. "He'll say he doesn't need any help, of course, but insist."

Sunny nodded and made her way back to the cramped kitchen. On the table a tangle of red crabs lay on sheets of newspaper. She nudged one—cold and dead. She remembered taking Avery to see *The Little Mermaid*. What had been that animated crab's name?

Neil ducked in through the door, freshly showered. He'd changed into clean khaki shorts and a green Hawaiian shirt. Whoa. His tan was awesome, and he cleaned up *good*. He was grinning. "Hi. I cooked those earlier today. They've been on ice until time to pick them."

"Pick them?"

Neil gave her a grim smile. "Are you one of those airy debutantes who thinks crabmeat grows in cans?"

"Of course not," Sunny said, coloring. "My mother was . . . allergic to seafood. And thrifty." Crabmeat was damned expensive at the store, she knew.

"Oh, that's right. Lillian said your mother fell out with the family. I hope you're not allergic."

"I don't know." Sunny had never eaten crabmeat in her entire life, and eating one of these creatures—with all those legs—did not seem appetizing, to say the least. Seafood, when she was growing up, meant tuna casserole with potato chips or a filet sandwich from the golden arches.

But Weezie, her presumed mother, was artsy and sophisticated, a regular bohemian, so said Miss Lillian. A bohemian's daughter wouldn't flinch at a pile of crabs. She looked at him and smiled the way she'd seen Ethel Kennedy smile in the Camelot documentaries. "Why don't you show me how it's done?"

"Sit here." He pulled out a chair facing the pile of crabs and she wedged herself in. He stood behind her and leaned over. "It's easier if I show you like this," he said. She caught the scent of his body, fresh from the shower, soapy and unmistakably male.

No, no, no, she told herself, cursing at the butterflies in her gut, that familiar sweet unease, that creeping warmth. That would not do. For one thing, he was still married to the woman whose eyes gazed at them from all over the house. There was even one of those pictures right here in the kitchen. Julie beamed at them from the sideboard, holding a wire whisk and a big pottery bowl.

"Sunny, are you listening?"

"Oh, sorry, I thought I heard Miss Lillian. You were saying?"

"First you flip the crab over on its back."

Sunny's hands were familiar with human bodies, but crustaceans were another matter. She turned the crab over and stared at the creamy ivory underbelly.

"Now." He handed her the knife, and she thought about the time she had to dissect a frog in biology class.

"No, not like that," Neil said. "The object is to get the meat out in large chunks." He showed her how to pry up the shell and discard it; pointed out that the heart and fat were good to eat. He cracked the shell neatly in two. His arms were around her as he picked out a chunk of white meat that smelled of the sea.

He held it to her lips. "Go on, I know you want a taste."

Sunny couldn't admit she'd never had crab, but she was not going to allow him to feed her. She took the chunk from him between thumb and forefinger and popped it into her mouth. Oh . . . gee. The crabmeat tasted like—like—really fabulous sex.

"Thanks," she said, stunned, but he'd gone to the sink to wash greens.

"This is some of the first lettuce from the garden," he said, dropping it into a spread-out clean dishcloth to dry. "Sorry my tomatoes aren't ready, but we'll have to make do with these from Florida."

He set a pot to boil and measured rice. "Julie was a hell of a cook," he said. "I've been learning as I go, but she taught me a lot about what was healthy."

With the mention of Julie, Sunny was jolted back to Earth. She concentrated on the crabs, picking and picking. She could hear music coming from the porch. "What's that?" she asked.

He grinned. "Lillian and her opera," he said. "That's Madame Butterfly. You haven't seen it?"

"It's not my favorite," she hedged. The daughter of an artsy bohemian would have known opera, right? There had been that weird film *M. Butterfly* she'd seen on TCM or somewhere, but she didn't think that was what he meant. "What are you going to do with all this meat?"

"I'm planning to just toss it with some butter and lemon juice in a pan and serve it over rice." He turned and saw the white meat piled in a bowl, the claws off to the side. "Hey, those claws are good. You can suck on them," he said.

"Suck on them?" She glanced at him to see if he was being crude, but his face was friendly, not snarky, not flirtatious.

"Like this." He took a nutcracker and cracked the claw, deftly pulled off the pincers, and showed her the delectable morsel clinging to the cartilage.

"Now watch." He slipped the meat from the cartilage with his mouth. "Now you try it." She did, and licked her lips with the briny sweetness. Her heart began to pound.

"Better with a little sauce." His smile was infectious, and her brain felt weird and buzzy, as if she'd downed a double martini. What a waste, this good-looking man stuck down here on this island, pining his heart away, but hey, if that's how he wanted to spend his life, who was she to stop him?

She was going to make a new life in North Carolina.

Almost as if he was reading her thoughts, he said, "So are you in it for the duration?"

Into what for the duration? "What do you mean?" Her heart raced faster.

"How long are you planning to stay with Lillian?"

It was time for truth. She took a deep breath to calm herself. "Just four more weeks," she said. "I have other plans after that."

"Getting married?" His tone was casual, but there was something else there—something beyond polite conversation.

She flushed, then took another crab claw and cracked it loudly. "Why do you ask?"

"Just curious why you're bailing out so soon."

It wasn't soon. Maybe he had some different idea of why she'd been hired. "So soon? She'll get well, the ankle will heal, and then she won't need me." Sunny sucked out the meat. Yum. She was blissing out.

Neil watched her for just a moment too long and then spoke. "Lillian may act like she's tough enough to chew nails, but she won't admit she's not young any more. I feel responsible for her. I want to make sure she's well looked after, and I can tell she likes you. You'd be a great assistant for her."

"I may be just a poor relation, but I'm a competent—" she almost said "nurse," but changed it to "assistant," since that was what Miss Lillian chose to call her. She said lamely, "I've had CPR training, and first aid. And self-defense."

"Self-defense? I'd better watch out, then. "

She gave him a sideways look. "Miss Lillian liked the idea. She thinks she's in danger."

"Yes, I know about what she thinks. And I have to admit, there's no love lost between her and her son's wife. Kiki's . . . not one of my favorite people." He looked off into the distance for a moment and Sunny thought there might be something he didn't want to say. Then he turned back to her, the moment gone. "I hope this thing will blow over. But I feel Lillian will eventually need someone long-term, someone committed."

Sunny shrugged. "Well, she's basically a healthy woman, and I can't take the place of—" she broke off what she was about to say and looked down, flushed and flummoxed. She almost wished Miss Lillian *was* her mother. The mother she'd never had.

"Sunny?" He was looking at her, "You meant to say *a daughter,* didn't you? Or did you mean to say *Julie?* Julie's not unmentionable in this house."

She swallowed, met his eyes, and threw herself into the role she was playing. "Sorry. I'm going to level with you, Neil. My life is kind of at a crossroads right now. I love Aunt Lillian, and I'd like to stay with her, but I need to move on." She became quiet.

Neil gazed out the window. Was he thinking *if only Julie had lived?* Julie was all around her, she knew. It was Julie who'd decorated this house; Julie who'd planted the garden out back; Julie who'd been the light of his life. Now extinguished.

"Sunny?" Lillian called from the porch.

Sunny gratefully scraped back the chair. "Coming, Aunt Lillian!" She washed her hands, dried them on a dishcloth, and scurried out to the porch.

"The birds have gone into hiding," Miss Lillian said when Sunny burst through the screen door. "Come on, I'm tired of sitting here. Let's set the table."

They'd planned to eat at a picnic table under a spreading live oak out back, and Lillian's contribution was in telling Sunny what to carry out—red-and-white checkered tablecloth and white plates rimmed with blue stripes.

Sunny placed the settings, conscious of Neil in the kitchen. It was hard to remain cool when she helped to bring out the food and wine, and when the three of them sat at the table.

The sautéed crab and buttered rice and fresh green salad were to die for. While they ate, Neil and Lillian talked about island business, while Sunny mulled over the spark that had passed between her and Neil, wondering if he would remember her from the parking lot. *Then* Miss Lillian would have to tell him the truth.

But her hair had been different then, and the light had been dim, and he was concentrating on seeing Lillian. She tasted the Alsatian Riesling that Harris had loaded in the basket, and found it beat the heck out of cheap Californian in a box. She was afraid her time with Troy Bentley had spoiled her for the two-buck variety.

Neil wouldn't let her help with the dishes, and she sat out on the front porch with Miss Lillian while a fresh evening breeze floated over them, the fan turning lazily overhead The sun was slowly sinking into the thatch of marsh reeds, so splendiferous a sight it took her breath away. At that orange-red moment she almost didn't hate the beach.

"I didn't nap well, and I'm exhausted," Miss Lillian said, breaking the spell. "I think I'll turn in early and read a bit. You're not uncomfortable with Neil, are you?"

"No, of course not," Sunny said. "He's very . . . nice. Why don't you tell him who I really am? Why pretend I'm Julie's cousin?"

Miss Lillian shook her head. "It's better if he doesn't know, and then he can't slip up around Alex and Kiki. Like most men, he tends to be forgetful when it comes to women. In any case, I'm going to need to spend about an hour with him in the morning going over the books. You'll be bored, I'm sure."

Bored? Yes, she would be! No TV, no books, no magazines! But Miss Lillian was saying, "He'll be glad to take you down to the beach in the Jeep before he and I get to work. You did bring a bathing suit? Maybe you'd like to jog?"

The last thing Sunny wanted was to go to the beach, but she knew she didn't have any choice but to make herself scarce. She swallowed. "That would be fine."

"You don't sound very enthusiastic. You could ride one of the horses."

"No, thank you," Sunny said. Horses were another thing that terrified her. Motorcycles she could handle. "The beach, I guess. Maybe I can walk there."

"Whatever you like," said Miss Lillian. "Now, if you'll help me to bed and dole out my meds—" She pushed herself forward in the rocker, reaching for her crutches, and Sunny hurried to help. She could hear the dishwasher chugging in the kitchen. So Neil didn't frown on all modern conveniences, after all.

"Lillian!" He pushed open the front door. "Angus wants to talk to you." Now her face brightened. "Aren't you glad I got you that satellite phone?"

Miss Lillian glowed as she talked to the boy, and Neil couldn't hide his pleasure. It was clear that this grandson was her darling. No wonder she wanted to save the island for him.

Sunny grudgingly admitted that the island was a wonder, and she found herself hoping it could be saved. Watching Neil's face as he talked to his son, she saw the love there, the same kind of love she felt for Avery.

After Neil rang off, he caught her elbow. "How about joining me on the porch for a glass of wine after you get Lil settled? I'd like to know what makes Sunny tick."

Sunny swallowed. "Sure." Oh. My. God.

CHAPTER TEN

Neil leaned back against the door frame, breathing the sweet night air. He was going to find out all about this cousin. She looked vaguely familiar. Where had he met her? How long ago? Maybe at the wedding?

He racked his brain to remember all of the relatives in the Stirling and Alexander families, and came up with no one resembling Sunny. He headed to the stable to check on the horses, Rambo trotting after him. His strawberry roan, Archie, snorted, while Shalimar, Julie's old white mare, greeted him with a whicker. He rubbed her nose and filled the hay racks and water troughs while Rambo patrolled for rodents. Neil didn't see his tame crow, Blackjack, who usually spent nights in the barn. The bird and Rambo had made peace with each other.

Satisfied the horses had all they needed, Neil returned to the lodge, poured two glasses of his best Pinot Grigio, and settled in his comfortable porch chair with a sketch pad and soft pencil. Wine was an indulgence he'd gotten used to, he thought ruefully. He hoped the budget didn't get cut too much, for wasn't that why Lillian was looking at the books and asking all these questions? The satellite radio poured out lively ballet music.

He turned to the sketch he'd made earlier of a blue heron. Birds were tricky, with their skinny legs. He drew in a few cattails. Now if he changed the creek bank slightly—

The screen door banged shut and Sunny appeared. "Wow," she said. "What do you do here every night, fella? Just sit out here and listen to the crickets and the opera while you doodle? Let me see."

He looked up, narrowed his gaze, and closed the pad. "Private notes," he said, appraising her with an artist's eye for cheekbone angles, the tilt of the nose, the bow of the lips. He didn't see any family resemblance to either Julie or her brother. And opera wasn't playing, for God's sake. He shrugged. "I enjoy God's creation—the sounds of nature, the breaking of the waves, a little Shostakovich."

"Is that some kind of vodka?"

Neil tucked the sketch pad and pencil underneath his chair. "The composer of the music you're listening to. Or are you making a joke?"

The look on Sunny's face, that panicked expression, told him what he wanted to know. Lillian's family were all musical. He couldn't imagine a cousin of hers not knowing a famous composer—but then he didn't know how she'd been raised. Maybe barefoot on the beach, or in a commune where they all sang Arlo Guthrie folk songs. "Never mind. What kind of music do you like?"

"Oh, all kinds," she said blithely.

He would let her off that hook—for now. "Cheers," he said, picking up his glass of wine, and she did the same. He took a sip. "Do you ride?"

Sunny tasted her Pinot Grigio thoughtfully. "Horseback, you mean?"

"No, elephant." He watched her.

"You're teasing me," she said airily. "Mama and Daddy were artists. They couldn't afford to keep a horse. Certainly not an elephant. Daddy painted and Mama, well, she did sculpture." She raised her glass and sipped slowly, gaining time, and Neil could almost see the wheels turning. "I did ride a pony once. At some kind of festival. When I was little."

Neil pushed ahead. "I'll bet you'd like to do it again. Want to ride around the island with me tomorrow?"

"Tomorrow?" Did she sound a bit panicky?

"Sure. How about it?"

"I didn't bring any jeans," she said. "Or boots, for that matter. I do have a pair of cowboy boots, but I didn't think to pack them."

Neil shrugged. "Maybe you'd prefer to go sailing. I have a great boat. The *Jolie.*"

"*Jolie?*"

"It's French. Means pretty. Lovely."

"Oh." Like Julie was pretty. Lovely. Once again she took her time over her wine. "I'm tempted," she finally said, "but I can't go off and leave Aunt Lillian for very long. It's hard for her to get around here."

Neil was determined that she wasn't going to weasel out so easily. "Maybe Lillian would like to go sailing, too. How 'bout if I ask her?"

Sunny shook her head. "You know that's not a good idea. Not with that ankle. If anything happened, she'd find it hard to save herself. "

"Sunny, you're selling her short. Yes, I can see the cast might be a problem, but did she tell you she's a champion swimmer? She's competed in the Senior Olympics before, 400 meter IM. She won a silver medal in her age group and was furious it wasn't gold."

"Wow. I can believe it." Sunny glanced in the bottom of her empty glass and sighed. Neil could swear she looked a little green around the gills. "What do you do for fun here?" she said. "There's no TV or computer or anything."

Neil was tempted to leer at her and say something suggestive, but he didn't take the bait. "What I've just been offering is fun," he said. "Riding and sailing are fun." He swept his arm in an arc, pointing toward the glittering moonlit sand, the lush green dark of the forest. "Hear the rattle of the wind in the reeds? Smell the marsh? I live in Paradise, Sunny."

She listened to the far-off sounds of wind and water and picked a blade of grass from between her toes. "But isn't it lonely?"

Lonely. Neil wished he could pick up his sketch pad, but he took a sip of wine. This girl wasn't his type at all. Too bad, because she tugged at him in a weird way, and she was easy to be with when she wasn't defensive and prickly. He raised an eyebrow. "Nope. Not lonely. Lillian allows students and professors from the university to come here to study. Writers. Photographers. Artists. Natural resources folks from the state. Anthropologists looking for Indian artifacts. There are Geechees living at the other end of the island. And there's my son, Angus. He's away at school but he'll be home soon."

He saw interest spark in her face. "What does he do here, your son? I can't imagine my daughter without her smartphone and iPad."

"He does whatever I do," Neil said, "or did. This summer he wants to get a job on the mainland. Maybe working at the marina, maybe being a fishing guide." And then he'd go to college, and Neil would watch him leave the island. He was counting on his son to come back and take over some day.

He needed to keep needling Sunny and see if she'd crack. "Didn't you ever come here as a kid? Julie said they used to have all these big family reunions, up at the Big House. Were you bored? I don't think so. No cable TV, and a radio that would pick up only a few stations. Remember all those board games and puzzles for rainy days?"

Sunny bit her lip, as if she was thinking hard. "But things were simpler then. The world's changed."

"The fundamental things apply." Neil finally looked directly at her. Under the porch light her fair hair gleamed, curling from the humid air. She had pinned a gardenia behind her ear, and she looked, well, *jolie*. And she was blushing.

He lowered his gaze. He sure didn't need any lovely women, especially women who lied through their pearly whites. He'd heard about unscrupulous caregivers who were con artists. Sunny Iles might be plotting to steal Lillian's jewels, siphon off her money, or wreck his son's inheritance. He'd play it straight and keep his eyes open, but he found himself wishing like hell that she was telling the truth.

"Let me tell you something about the work here," he said. "We'll start with the sea turtles." Usually he could figure out a lot about a woman by how she felt about sea turtles. "If one turns up dead, I try to find out what happened to it."

Her eyes shone with interest. "How?"

"I'll do a necropsy."

"You will?" she asked. "Have you had medical or veterinary training?" Funny, she didn't ask him what a necropsy was, like most women.

"A couple of years of grad school biology." He picked up his wineglass and reached for Sunny's. "Refill?"

She shook her head, and he put his glass back on the table. "Sea turtles. I've learned from experts, and I've studied. Sometimes it's easy to tell what killed them. You just pull the plastic bag out of their gullets."

"People are so damned careless," she said, with a vehemence that surprised Neil. "Carelessness nearly cost my daughter's life."

Something twisted inside Neil. Whose carelessness had killed Julie? Had it been his own? Had it been hers? Or had it been the carelessness of her brother's wife? Careless people, Kiki and Alex, like Tom and Daisy Buchanan. He didn't want to take that too far.

Sunny had noticed his face, and hers took on a concerned, softer look. "Did I say something wrong?" she asked gently. "I'm sorry." She laid a hand on his arm, and her touch was unexpectedly comforting. She got up and picked up her empty glass. "It's been a long day. Good night." She walked back inside.

Neil picked up his sketch pad and pencil from beneath the chair. He hadn't asked her any of those direct questions he'd intended. Maybe because she seemed as if she really cared about Lillian. But the key word was *seem*. Tomorrow, he'd try to sketch her when she wasn't looking. Sometimes the sketch can reveal what the eye refuses to see. And with her hair curly from the moist air, she'd looked even more familiar. He just couldn't place her.

Dawn had passed into early morning when the slanting pale beams of light woke Sunny. She peeked out into the hall and saw that Miss Lillian's wooden plank door was still closed. Breakfast noises were coming from the kitchen—the sizzle of sausage, the clank of pans—and there were smells of coffee, oranges, and something sweet and bready. Naaah. The man didn't bake.

She washed her face, dabbed on lipstick, and pulled on a white shirt, khaki shorts, and a pair of Julie's Merrill flip-flops, which Avery had told her cost seventy dollars new. She thought that was scandalous. Her first pair, garish coral rubber, had cost her seventy *cents* at the K-Mart.

She reached for her only good jewelry, a pair of gold hoop earrings Kyle had given her, and slid them in, clicking the wires closed.

She walked into the little kitchen. Neil turned and grinned at her. "Good morning, Miss Sunshine." She winced, because she'd heard that a lot; even so, she swallowed hard. Gosh, Neil ought not to be so good-looking, early morning clean, sun-browned skin, his nut-brown hair tinged with sunstreaks. And that grin, and the way his muscles rippled when he lifted a chair and moved it to the table. She knew what was happening to her. She was walking toward the edge of a cliff three hundred feet above the sea, surf crashing over jagged rocks below.

"Smells good," she said, eyeing the batter-encrusted mixing bowl soaking in the sink.

"I've learned to make a passable whole-wheat banana muffin," he said.

"What? No biscuits?"

"What? All that hydrogenated fat?"

"You're cooking sausage," she said.

"One hundred per cent natural," he said. "I make it myself. There are still a few wild hogs here we haven't eradicated. My solution is to eat them."

"Eating your problems sounds okay to me." Everything and nothing was okay about Neil.

"Julie grew quite a garden," he was saying. "I've tried to keep it going. Those strawberries came from my patch. Or if you'd like some preserves, I'm afraid I'm low right now, but Harris sent those figs." He gestured to the jar of preserves on the counter.

The strawberries in the bowl on the table weren't large, but they were bright red and perfectly shaped, glistening with freshness. "The strawberries will be lovely," she said.

"Have you ever had a loquat? They're pretty good." Outside, in the space he'd cleared for a garden she could see the trees with their long, dark green leaves and knobby fruits.

Loquat? Sunny was about to ask him when she heard her name being called.

Miss Lillian wanted to wear a red-and-white striped cotton wraparound blouse, white linen full-legged capris, and one white sandal, because it was obvious she wasn't going on any nature walks. Sunny was glad Miss Lillian had decided to go the Judi Dench route with her hair instead of the gelled spikes.

By the time they arrived in the kitchen, Neil had set out plates and mugs on the painted wooden table.

"Oh," Miss Lillian said, "the breeze is so nice on the front porch and this kitchen is so tiny. Let's have our breakfast out there on trays."

"Fine with me," Neil said. "But you'll have to contend with Blackjack and Rambo."

"Rambo, I know," said Sunny. "But who's Blackjack? Do you have a dog?"

"You'll see," Neil said, smiling mysteriously.

"Oh, Neil," Miss Lillian declared. "Don't tease her." But she didn't enlighten Sunny, who was setting out the light bamboo trays everyone seemed to have and lining them with paper napkins.

The porch felt fresh and mildly humid, the ceiling fan whisking early-morning bugs away. Sunny tucked into a buttered muffin and strawberries, and took a bite of Neil's homemade sausage. It was *dee-vine.* She spooned a dollop of the fig preserves on her plate and took a second muffin from the gingham-lined basket.

Rambo, keeping lookout on the roof, peered over and down, then yowled. A large black crow was flapping, heading for a fence post. The crow alighted, cawed, and eyed them, making a clicking noise.

"That's Blackjack," Neil said. "You have to watch him. I rehabbed him after he'd gotten in a skirmish with a hawk, and he doesn't want to go back to the wild. Now he knows where the food is, he'll take it right off your plate. Be careful."

"He wouldn't dare," said Miss Lillian, clearly delighted. She waved her handkerchief. "Shoo."

The crow didn't move, but flapped his wings and gave three caws. He settled down, rustling his wings.

Miss Lillian turned to Sunny. "What would you like to do this morning while Neil and I talk family matters?"

"I think I'll walk on the beach," Sunny said. She had to face it sometimes. Maybe she could make good memories of a beach crowd out all the bad ones.

"It's about a mile or so from here," Neil said, "I'll drive you, unless you'd rather take the Jeep yourself. Or you could walk. There's a short cut I'll show you."

Before Sunny could answer, Blackjack lifted off from his fence post, dive-bombed, and snatched her fig off her plate. Startled, Sunny jostled her tray and the plate crashed to the floor.

"Goodness!" said Miss Lillian.

Rambo yowled from above.

Mortified, Sunny leaned over and picked up the two halves of the plate, but Neil was watching Blackjack, laughing. The bird returned to his perch and, thrusting his beak upwards, gobbled down the fig.

Neil grinned. "What did I tell you?"

"Very clever, Neil, but I've spilled my coffee," Miss Lillian said. Sunny hastened to take Miss Lillian's tray, where the coffee had soaked the muffin and preserves.

"I'll take care of it, ladies," Neil said. He took the tray from Sunny, placed the broken plate on it, and walked into the house.

The crow began to caw loudly, flap his wings, and then he fell off his perch to the ground. He began to regurgitate, slinging his head from side to side.

"Neil!" called Sunny. "Neil!" She rushed to the crow and saw that the bird was in distress. She had no idea how to do CPR on avians. "Help!"

Neil banged the door behind him and ran down the steps to Sunny's side. He knelt, picked the crow up, and cradled it gently.

He looked back at Miss Lillian. "Don't eat those figs," he said. "I'm going to put Blackjack in a cage and force some water down him." He took the crow in the direction of his nature center.

"She's tried again," said Miss Lillian slowly.

"Who tried what?" asked Sunny.

"Kiki," Miss Lillian said. "Remember when she came to the house before we left? Was she ever alone in the kitchen? She must have slipped this jar of figs into the pantry, and Harris put them into the box to bring down here."

Sunny shook her head. "Oh, Aunt Lillian. That sounds like some detective novel. Maybe it was just one bad jar. A bad seal or something. Botulism."

"No," Miss Lillian said grimly. "We're going to send those figs off to be tested. There's probably arsenic or something. And I believe I'm through with breakfast, Sunny. Lost my appetite. But do bring me more coffee."

"Yes, ma'am," Sunny said. "Did you get any on your clothes?

But she hadn't. The white slacks were spotless.

Miss Lillian, despite feeling angry and jittery, insisted on sticking to the day's plan for going over the books. She refused to eat, refused to lie down, and told Sunny to go on to the beach.

Sunny unfolded the new black suit from her suitcase and gazed at it. Before coming to work for Miss Lillian, she'd never owned another bathing suit after the red bikini she'd worn to please Kyle that horrible day at the beach. Cleaning out after the divorce, she'd stuffed the bikini in the garbage. On the rare occasions when she'd been invited to a pool or lake party, she'd dressed in shorts. It was perfectly understandable for a woman not to swim at certain times, and she'd been considered just unlucky.

Now she shimmied out of her clothes and slipped into the black suit Miss Lillian had bought her in addition to the red Speedo for lessons. She had to admit this one was flattering, emphasizing her curves, and alluringly low-cut.

There was no way she was going to swim in the ocean, however. She took out a big white boyfriend shirt for a cover-up, pulled on a pair of hot pink nylon shorts, and slid her feet into the hand-me-down Merrills.

But when she stepped out onto the porch, Neil's attention was on the crow in the cage he was bringing from the nature center. He hardly noticed her when he told her to follow the Jeep track straight to the beach, and when she saw a narrower track leading off to the left, take it—it was the footpath to the beach.

"Okay," Sunny said, a little disappointed at his inattention to her skimpy outfit. "How's the bird?"

"I hope he makes it," Neil said, frowning. "I'm going to keep him close by me today." Sunny nodded and walked on.

"Wait, Sunny," Neil called out, and she stopped, her heart standing at attention. But he said, "You're not going to wear those flip-flops."

Was he commanding her? How dare he? She turned, frowning. "I'm not? Why?"

"Look," he explained. "You're not prepared. There are sandspurs, sharp shells, and hot sand. Get some sneakers for the walk. Carry the flip-flops if you like, and take some sunscreen and bug spray. Wear a hat. Haven't you been to the beach before? In California?"

"We didn't live near the beach," Sunny said. "And my folks liked the mountains and the desert." She was ad-libbing like crazy. She hoped he didn't ask Miss Lillian where in California she was from.

Fortunately, he seemed distracted. "Too bad, kiddo. Make sure you stick to the path."

Kiddo. She scurried back, saw that Neil and Miss Lillian were settling in the front room, and swapped the flip-flops for her trusty

Nikes. She picked up a broad-brimmed straw hat she'd found on the back porch, along with bug spray. She didn't see any sunscreen. Oh, well. She wouldn't stay out that long.

Holding the hat in her hand and smelling to high heaven with the spray, she walked down the back steps and set out past the lodge. She saw the boy Reggie heading to the nature center. She guessed he had duties there.

Walking the jeep track, she found a trail to the left and followed it to a small bridge over a creek, and she found herself overlooking a marsh high with the grass Neil had called spartina on their first tour. She walked past flat land, grass stretching off toward the horizon, and then passed beneath huge live oaks and a tangle of yucca plants and vines. Shells crunched under her feet, and tiny flies buzzed about her head.

This must be the long way to the beach, and who cared if she ever got there? Wow, it was hotter than she thought in the shade. And then, abruptly, she was back in the sunshine and the sand was getting hotter too. She wiped away a trickle of sweat from her neck and thought about those cool mountains of North Carolina; she couldn't wait to get away, start that new life. The fly in the ointment was Avery, of course. Stay put for her? No. The girl imagined she was in love, but that boy, Dev, was just using her to do his homework so he could stay on the football team.

She dodged a pile of road apples surrounded by hoof prints. So Neil rode this path, too, through the lush landscape of grasses and leaves and sand, through the dappled shade. A flash in the long grass beside the path caught her eye. Expecting another gum wrapper, she stooped to pick it up. This was no gum wrapper, she realized dumbly. It was a diamond stud earring. She picked it up and wiped the sand away. Cubic zirconia, probably. But wait—she'd seen Kiki wearing diamonds just like this.

Maybe it was one of hers. Or Miss Lillian's. She slipped it into her shirt pocket.

The path converged with the jeep track, and then the dunes were before her, topped with waving sea oats. She scrambled up the blistering sand and peered at the silvery expanse of sea. On the horizon a couple of shrimp boats shimmered like a painted backdrop. At the high tide mark twisted hunks of driftwood lay, like modernistic sculptures.

She started her walk on the softer sand, as far from the water as possible. It proved to be hard going, and dried weeds and stalks of sea oats stabbed at her feet through the holes in her shoes. She gazed at the hard-packed sand near the gentle waves, and then a good distance down the beach, where a boat had washed up a long time ago, leaving a bleached-out hull.

Harris said Julie had drowned. Was it in a boating accident? Had she gone down in that boat?

Sunny felt the boat might have something to say to her, and she wanted to touch it, feel it. By the time she walked there and back, and then returned to the Lodge, Neil and Miss Lillian would surely have finished their business.

Taking a deep breath, she walked just far enough toward the gentle rolling, breaking waves for the footing to become firm. She strolled onward, the sun at her back, all alone on the wide expanse of sand. The Nikes got in her way and she took them off, backtracking to soft sand and stashing them beside a bedraggled chunk of palm.

The wind and the sun felt good, so she shimmied out of the shirt, wrapped the sleeves around her waist, and tied them. Then she slowly made her way to the water and stepped through the chuckling waves, letting the foam tickle her feet. The tide sucked sand away beneath her toes, and she giggled at the sensation.

She settled the hat firmly on her head and ambled on. Her mind lapsed into the dreamy mode it did when she had time to kill, say night duty on a quiet hall. She remembered those daydreams she used to have then: that Troy Bentley would take her off to a garden in Italy, as he always promised he would, and they would wander the hills of Tuscany drinking jugs of local wine and eating grapes and new bread and local cheese. *Pecorino*, he used to say. You must taste pecorino.

She never did get any pecorino. A lump rose in her throat, and then swallowed it in anger. That man shouldn't have the power to hurt her, damn it. He wasn't worth it. If only he hadn't been such fun, playing his guitar, spinning daydreams—no, no, no! How could she have fallen for a guitar player *twice*? She tossed her head. The wind caught the borrowed hat and pulled it away, flying it like a kite. The hat cartwheeled through the air, landed many yards down the beach in the water, and floated out with the tide.

Oh, great. That had probably been Julie's favorite hat. How would she explain losing it? She could possibly retrieve it, but that would mean going in the water. She could swim now, but she was all alone out here. Wait—the tide was coming in, wasn't it? The hat would float back to shore, perhaps by the time she was on the way back from her walk. She furiously stepped up her pace.

The wrecked boat appeared to be very old; she ran her hand over the bleached timbers. It had been there longer than five years, she guessed. Before Julie's accident.

It would make a nice picture. She wished she'd brought her phone with her, but she'd left it back in the lodge. She knew it wouldn't work for calls here.

She started her trek back. Too many things going wrong in this family. That crow. Poisoned figs. She had been about to eat that fig. She ought to quit this job right now. But how could she abandon Miss Lillian if someone really was trying to kill her? And there was Neil. She wished he didn't stir up such confusing feelings. Anyhow, she'd learned she couldn't trust feelings. They could blind you to the truth that was sneaking up on you, giving you all sorts of clues you couldn't see. Neil was impossible, for more reasons than one.

She peered down the beach, and saw that the hat had washed back to shore. She raced toward it and snatched it up, wet and sandy. She retraced her steps, now being dribbled away by the incoming tide, and shook sand out of the hat. The sun had climbed to the noon position. Had she been out that long?

Feeling the heat on her shoulders, she wrapped the cover-up around them. She looked for the place where she'd stashed her shoes, and then realized several chunks of palm littered the high-tide line. The seascape looked the same everywhere, and panic made a sour taste rise in her gullet. How far had she come? Was the path over there, next to that palmetto? Those bushes?

The sun beat down relentlessly. There would be no shade unless she went into the jungle, and she didn't want to go into the jungle without her shoes.

She hurried from one palm to the next. At the eighth palm, she cried out with relief and sank to the sand, dusting off her feet. She laced the shoes loosely and hurried back past the sea oats, past the shells, to the shade of the trees. She took the Jeep track back, and she was coming near a bridge when she saw an alligator blocking her way.

Jaws, sharp teeth, Captain Hook, Tick-tock.

She was fond of her arms and legs and wanted to keep them! Should she run? Would he chase her? Just then she heard a motor, and the alligator ponderously waddled off to the brimming ditch beside the path, sliding into the murky water. Neil pulled up beside her in the Jeep. She realized she was shaking.

"What's the matter?"

She pointed to the ditch.

He grinned. "Sure. They're all over the place."

"Why didn't you tell me?"

"Thought you knew. Climb on in." He gazed at her. "You've got the beginnings of a nasty sunburn. Why didn't you keep on that shirt?"

"The sun felt good," she said lamely.

He glanced down at the wet and sandy hat and said nothing.

He put the Jeep in gear, lurched off, and turned around at the nearest clearing.

"Thanks for going out," he said. "Lillian can concentrate better when she has privacy."

Sunny felt she'd had no choice. Still, it was nice of him to thank her. "Is Miss Lillian all right?" she asked. "I mean, did you talk about the figs? Do *you* think they were deliberately poisoned?"

"Maybe," Neil said slowly. "Maybe not."

"How's Blackjack?"

"Touch and go," Neil said grimly. "Can't get up. Hard to swallow. Some paralysis. I've put in a call to a vet I know, but it seems like botulism to me."

It sounded like botulism to Sunny, too, but she didn't want to seem too knowledgeable. The California boho girl wouldn't know. "So who made the preserves?"

Neil gave a rough laugh. "According to Lillian, her pal the senator gave them to her. His housekeeper made them. Lil's eaten all the other jars. I'm sending this one off to be tested."

Sunny laid her hand on Neil's tanned arm and spoke seriously. "Look, Neil, I don't know this part of the family well. You do. I thought at first Miss Lillian was getting dementia when she started saying that someone was trying to kill her. Now I'm beginning to wonder. She suspects her daughter-in law. In your opinion, is this lady—Kiki—capable of doing something like that?"

Neil was quiet for a minute. "Kiki. I have a problem with Kiki." And then he took a deep breath, composing himself. "Let me tell you this. She's ambitious. She hasn't made the splash she'd like in Atlanta. She's gotten some press in *Jezebel* and other local magazines, and now she'd like to be written up in *Town and Country*. What better way to get publicity than by opening her very own exclusive resort island, a new Jekyll Millionaire's Club? Except, in this case it would be a Billionaire's Club. I wish she'd married that dude with the hotels and casinos. That would suit her just *fine.*"

Sunny knitted her brows. "Very funny, Neil. You didn't answer my question."

"I'm letting you draw your own conclusion," Neil said. "You'll have more time to get to know her. In fact, Lillian is hell-bent on having a little birthday party down here, and she's expecting you to come with her. That should be interesting. With all the feuding parties present. I predict fireworks."

"Do you feel she has any dementia?"

"Lillian?" Neil hooted. "She's the sanest of us all."

They pulled up in front of the Lodge. Miss Lillian was waiting for them on the front porch, cool drink in hand. She waved gaily at them, a huge grin gracing her well-worn, aristocratic face. Her peevishness, her air of worry, seemed to be gone. She looked, in fact, as if she had something up her sleeve.

Sunny had something in her pocket. She felt the earring there, tumbled it between her fingers, felt the bare pin. It was missing its back. She wondered whether to mention finding the diamond.

Now was not the time.

CHAPTER ELEVEN

Sunny wanted to go to Turtle Point with Neil and Miss Lillian, and they wouldn't let her, and it was her own fault, and she was miserable in more ways than one.

"You look like a lobster," Miss Lillian said. "Go out back and pick some aloe. Slather the juice on anywhere that hurts. You'll find a patch right beside the back steps."

Sunny nodded. She knew about aloe. "What is Turtle Point, anyhow?" she asked. "Are there turtles there?"

Miss Lillian told her that Reggie lived in the settlement there. Even though there hadn't been a plantation on Issatee, freed slaves had come over by boat from other islands to work for a Yankee industrialist who'd taken the island as a winter retreat. An abolitionist, he'd given them a chance to buy their own land, and a community developed at Turtle Point.

After Miss Lillian's great-grandfather managed to acquire the house and the rest of the acres in the infamous poker game, he wondered if he'd gotten such a bargain after all, with the houses so rundown.

Neil and Julie's house had been the caretaker's lodge. The Big House, partially restored, was only used occasionally these days, and a couple from the Geechee settlement looked after it, Sinclair and Naomi Walker. Reggie was their youngest son.

"We're going to see Esther," Miss Lillian said. "She's struggling to keep the island community together. Sunny, maybe you can go another time."

"Let me do something," Sunny protested. "Maybe I could start supper."

"Not necessary," Neil said. "We'll grill some venison steaks."

"Those pretty little deer I saw?" Sunny had seen them, half-tame, flicking through the brush.

Neil shrugged. "The bucks have to be culled. They fight and they eat all the vegetation."

Sunny longed for a simple McDonald's hamburger and fries, something uncomplicated that didn't make you think of fairy tales or Walt Disney. But she didn't say so. She might get a lecture from Neil.

"Don't get into trouble while we're gone," Miss Lillian said, as Sunny wincingly helped her into Neil's Jeep.

"Yeah," Neil said, grinning at her. "No telling what she might get into without us here."

Sunny wanted to stick out her tongue at both of them, if they were going to tease her.

After the Jeep had gone, Sunny went out and found the long, fat aloe leaves poking out of a patch near the back steps. She broke off one, squeezed it, and spread the slithery juice on her shoulders and back as best she could. Then she soaked dish towels in ice water and lay on her belly with the poultice on her back and shoulders.

Lying in that quiet lodge, with just the sound of the wind and the calling of the gulls, was boring. She got up and looked for a *People* magazine, but there weren't any magazines at all.

Shoot! She scanned the bookshelves, hoping for a juicy romance, but all she found were books by writers she'd never heard of—who the heck were Laurens van der Post and Loren Eisely? She thought she'd heard of Henry Thoreau. Wasn't he that travel writer? There was a history of the Georgia barrier islands, and a few books on politics. Typical male stuff. She wondered what had happened to Julie's books. Surely she didn't read this stuff.

She pulled out a book by Fanny Kemble, which promised to be about an actress who married a planter a long time ago. It was kind of thick. She put it aside and began to browse Angus's shelf. She found schoolbooks about nature and biology and chemistry, a few classics such as *All Quiet on the Western Front*, some science fiction, graphic novels, and war stories, as well as a paperback copy of Pat Conroy's *The Lords of Discipline*.

Nope.

Rooting around the shelves, she dislodged a well-thumbed copy of the Red Cross booklet *Water Safety*, started to jam it back in, and then thought better of it. Browsing through the pages, she came upon a diagram of a rip current, with instructions for what to do if you were in one. The current goes straight out from shore, she read, and doesn't pull people under. It just pulls them out to sea and eventually dissipates. The danger is that you can exhaust yourself trying to swim in against the current and go under.

She settled herself with the book and began to read. She learned that she'd done the right thing instinctively during the flood that washed her home away. She read about life saving, about *Throw* and *Tow* and *Row* before you *Go*.

Humph. She wouldn't be saving any lives. As she closed the book, a folded slip of paper fluttered to the floor—a certificate that Julie Stirling had passed her Senior Lifesaving test at Camp Willowood.

Julie was an expert swimmer! Julie knew about rip currents! Then why did she drown? Did she hit her head on something? She guessed Neil had asked himself all those questions.

She wished she had a doctor she could discuss it with. Other than Dr. Troy Bentley, of course. Good old Doc Bentley—two years out of her life, two years she couldn't recover. All that waiting and hoping and dreaming and longing, singing and winging and headaches and heartaches, long dark nights of the soul, short high flights to the moon, quarrels and tears and crying in beers—

How did that country song go about getting tears in your ears?

This had to stop. She was going to a new life in four weeks, right? She snuggled into the pillow and closed her eyes to rest them.

She awoke to a painful touch on her shoulder. "Ouch!"

"Sorry," she heard.

Lying on her tummy, she raised her head and peeked through her bangs. Miss Lillian and Neil loomed over her, and she wondered if her cellulite was showing. Miss Lillian smiled. "I hate to disturb you, dear, but I'd like to bathe and change for dinner."

Neil said that he was off to grab a shower and left, Miss Lillian calling after him to not use all the hot water.

"Give me a minute to change out of this suit." Sunny eased herself out of the bunk and pushed gingerly to her feet.

"You should have changed already," Miss Lillian scolded. "Did you use the aloe?"

"Yes, ma'am," Sunny said. "And I'm sorry you had to come and get me." She stiffly walked Miss Lillian to her room and settled her in a chair.

The shower was still running, so Sunny ventured to Miss Lillian's closet. She took the terry-cloth spa robe off the hook on the door.

"It's bad," Miss Lillian said.

Confused, Sunny said, "What's the matter with it?"

Miss Lillian said, "I mean the robe's all right. My mind was on Turtle Point. Someone's been to see the people there, talking about the resort, trying to convince them they'd be better off moving to that wasteland area inland, or even off the island, and sell their waterfront property to the development. They'd have new houses and jobs with the residents, *so they say.* If Miss Kiki ever gets hold of this island, you can bet jobs will go only to the young. Esther was so outdone she threatened to try root on them, but I persuaded her not to even think about it."

"Root? What's that?"

Miss Lillian shook her head. "It comes from Africa. Spells and such. It's never really died out. Oh, those folks are good Baptists, you'll see the little church, but the old ways haven't disappeared, just survived as folk culture. Esther does some healing and some midwifery, when it's needed. Harris, bless his heart, suspects she put root on him."

Sunny couldn't hide her astonishment. "But why?"

"I'll tell you while you help me change." Sunny helped her out of her clothes and into the spa robe, and Miss Lillian continued. "Harris is Esther's brother. She was angry with him for leaving the island, said it was his duty to be the leader after their father died. But he wanted a bigger life. She told him she was going to see that he regretted leaving.

"As it turned out, Harris wanted to marry and courted a number of ladies, but the relationships never worked out. He thought it was Esther's doing. Now he has a new lady friend, the singer I told you about, and he doesn't want Esther to know. So he won't come."

Sunny heard the shower stop, and she visualized Neil stepping out and reaching for a towel. Then she wished she hadn't.

"I'll adjust your water now." She breathed deeply and hurried to Miss Lillian's private bathroom.

"More Pinot Noir?" Neil asked, bottle poised. They were sitting out back at the picnic table while a big egg-shaped charcoal grill sizzled with Neil's marinated venison steaks.

Sunny, now wearing a halter top and flouncy white cotton skirt, knew she probably shouldn't drink more wine because of the dehydrating effect on her sunburn, but she held out her glass.

The Pinot Noir made her sunburn feel much better, so she drank three glasses. The venison steak was a little tough but tasty, and he'd put native mushrooms in the rice pilaf.

She lifted another forkful of rice. "This is great."

Neil grinned sheepishly. "Uncle Ben's," he said, making her think of Harris again. She wondered just how much root Harris really believed in, and whether it was his own fault he'd been unlucky in love. He was awfully stuffy.

"Will Angus be home for my birthday party?" Miss Lillian asked.

"That depends on when we have the party," Neil replied. "If we have it when school's over, no problem." He paused. "Are you asking Blake and Ellery?"

Miss Lillian's nose twitched. "Of course," she said. "But they'll try to find an excuse not to come, mark my words. I'm going to put my foot down."

Whoa, thought Sunny. Just who were Blake and Ellery? She felt like a Martian trying to decipher Earth-speak. She couldn't ask who they were, because Neil would assume she knew, since she was supposed to be family.

"What do you hear from Cathy?" Neil asked. "Does she still write to you?"

And who was Cathy? Sunny bit her lip. Wait—was this the son's first wife?

"Not so often," Miss Lillian was saying. "The last thing she told me was that she was thinking about studying for the ministry. She called a while back, asking me to put in a word to the Bishop. She wanted to attend the theology school at Sewanee and wanted me to contact him for a recommendation."

Neil whistled in surprise. "Wow. Is she all right?"

"She still misses the girls." Miss Lillian sighed, and they looked at each other, and Sunny was bursting to know what the hell they were talking about.

"I always liked Cathy," Sunny ventured, looking sideways at Miss Lillian, because she felt she ought to say something. She hoped they'd pick up this conversational ball and say more, enough to confirm her guess.

But apparently Neil and Miss Lillian felt it would be a bad idea to talk about Cathy. "So you're happy with the way I'm running things?" Neil asked Lillian, changing the subject, and Sunny once again felt herself isolated on Mars. Was the conversation being censored for her benefit? A blackout here, a code there? She assumed an air of patient interest, waiting for a communication in her language.

"Of course," Miss Lillian said. "Everything's in order. Alex and Kiki can't say you've mismanaged anything. The books are straightforward and expenses are minimal. Of course, it would be nice to have a little more income. Are there any paying customers coming this summer?"

Sunny detected a slight flush and a hesitation before Neil replied. "A photographer's coming next week to take a few more pictures for a book she's working on. She'll pay the usual fee for room, board, and privileges. I'm expecting a group of Boy Scouts the last week of June. They'll stay in the dorm."

Miss Lillian didn't seem to notice Neil's discomfort. "Very well. Let's plan my birthday celebration between the photographer and the Scouts. School will be out by then, surely?"

Neil nodded. "No problem."

"Then it's settled," Miss Lillian said. "Two weeks from now, if the rest of the family can come. I want everyone here. I'll work on the details and write to you. Now, let's have a pleasant evening. What do you two say to a game of Scrabble?"

Sunny's hair stood up on the back of her neck. "I'm not good with words. Let me do the dishes."

"Sunburned people don't get to do dishes," Neil said lazily.

"I'm fine. Really." Her shoulders were stinging, but she was sure she wouldn't know all the words that Weezie's daughter would be expected to know. Thank goodness French words weren't allowed.

"Oh, Neil." Miss Lillian waved her hand. "Let's play, and then I'll be off to bed. Both of you can wash dishes later."

Miss Lillian won, of course. Miss Lillian always won at Scrabble, Neil told her later. Sunny asked him if he let her, because wasn't she supposed to be losing her memory? She was the sharpest dementia candidate Sunny had ever had the privilege to know. But Neil objected that he would never do such a thing, and Miss Lillian would hate it.

After the older woman had closed her door, Sunny and Neil stood at the sink: he scraped and rinsed and she loaded them into the ancient noisy dishwasher. She missed her own dishwasher, a sleek and modern machine.

"Play much Scrabble?" asked Neil.

"Don't be cruel." Sunny tried to act nonchalant, but her heart was racing.

"Maybe it was that extra glass of wine." Neil pulled a disapproving face. Was he serious?

"Hey, who's the health care professional here?" Sunny shot back.

"Health professional? Really? " Neil said with surprise. "Lillian told me you were a flight attendant with Oceanic and had been laid off because of the big merger."

Flushing, Sunny wished Miss Lillian would inform her what lies she was supposed to tell. "Sorry," she said, thinking fast. "They gave us CPR and first aid training. That's one reason Aunt Lillian thought I would be able to help her."

Neil nodded. "I can appreciate that." He picked up the wooden salad bowl, dried it, and put it back on the shelf of the yellow-painted hutch. "How about some fresh air? There's a full moon tonight and the beach will look spectacular. Let's ride out."

Sunny hesitated for a moment. "In the Jeep, you mean?"

Neil looked at her slantways. "On the horses. I have two."

"Maybe we shouldn't leave Aunt Lillian." Sunny untied her apron and hung it on a peg. Holy mackerel, how was she going to get out of this?

He folded his dishcloth, hung it beside the sink, and gave her a knowing smile. "We wouldn't stay long."

"I—I told you," Sunny said. "That pony ride was a long time ago. Horses scare me, actually. I have kind of a sensitive nature."

Horses bit you and they trampled you underfoot and you could break your neck falling from them . . .

"Ah yes. Daughter of the artists." He gazed at her for a minute. "Okay. We'll go in the Jeep."

"But I don't think—"

"I have no ulterior motives, if that's what you're worried about." He smiled at her as if he thought it was funny, and she bristled.

Ulterior motives she could handle. It was the interrogation she felt was coming that she wasn't confident about. Maybe she could ask *him* questions, find out more about the family. She sighed. "All right."

Still wearing her pink halter top, white flouncy skirt, and flip-flops, she settled into the passenger side of the Jeep, which smelled of rubber and mildew. The air was warm, sweet, and moist, tempered by the breeze. Night birds screeched, insects chirred in deafening chorus, palm fronds rattled like old bones. She was almost relieved when Neil started the engine. A sound of civilization.

They passed the small shed with the padlock, the horse barn, and then another barn behind it. "What's in the second barn?" she asked.

Neil smiled as they bumped over a wooden bridge. "It's just for storage. A few antique farm implements and the charabanc."

"The what?"

"A vehicle from the thirties. It's like an open-air bus. It was used for house parties, to take people to the beach and to tour the island."

"Does it run?"

"You bet. Julie and I got one of Esther's nephews to tinker with the engine. It runs well enough for short trips, though it's a little short on comfort."

The thought of the charabanc puzzled Sunny. Why didn't Miss Lillian get some decent transportation for her guests? But she was curious. "Can I see it?"

"It's too dark. We never got electricity in that barn. Maybe tomorrow."

The Jeep bounced along the double track through the scrub forest. Wispy clouds scudded across a slate sky, teasing her with glimpses of a full and glowing moon. A loud splash gurgled from the roadside ditch. "There's your gator," Neil said, and laughed.

"Oh, shut up." Sunny playfully tapped his arm, but in truth she was still scared. Suppose he hit a dip in the road and she bounced out? Here would come Mr. Gator, and gators were fast. They'd have to box up the leftovers for Avery to bury. Though she'd been intimate with death in the hospital, she'd felt immune to its sting because her job was fighting for others to live.

What if Avery buried her next to Kyle, in South Carolina? A fate worse than death. Stuck next to him for all eternity, or at least until somebody like Kiki decided to build a mansion on top of the graveyard, and then they'd all be dug up and sent to a plot on the bad side of town. She was seized with a sudden urge to call her little girl with instructions and remembered her cell phone wouldn't work out here. She swore under her breath.

"What is it?" Neil glanced at her.

"Oh, something I forgot to tell my daughter."

"Is it urgent? When we get to the beach I could try my phone."

"I hope it isn't urgent, Neil," she said seriously. "I certainly hope it isn't."

"You're funny, you know?" he said.

"I know," Sunny said. Better to be thought funny than crazy.

Neil pulled in and parked at the weathered viewing platform built for an earlier age. "Come on."

Mindful of the sandspurs, she stepped out carefully into the path. Neil spotted the upscale flip-flops and gave her a look, but didn't say anything.

Holding her head high, she flat-footed carefully as she followed the path through the dunes. And then the beach lay before them, sand a sweep of silvery gray in the moonlight, trees a tracery of twisted black against the sky. Sea oats tossed and softly rattled, and salt smell drifted in to give her pleasant shivers.

And of course, the waves, burgeoning to the shore and sighing back, leaving a fretwork of foam and shattered shells.

The moonlight swept arcs of mercury across the sea, shimmering like the scales of a fish, and Sunny felt an aura of happiness come over her. They walked on in silence. Sunny wished the spell would never be broken, that they could walk along like that forever, a moment out of time. The world would disappear—Miss Lillian, the senator, Alex, Kiki, the planned resort complex—not to mention the idea that someone was trying to kill Miss Lillian.

A fetid stink jolted her out of her reverie. "Phoo!" On the sand a couple of yards ahead lay a dead fish, half as long as herself, half-eaten, half-shining, fully reeking.

She shook her head. "My God, what is that?"

"Looks like a grouper," Neil told her with amusement. "Haven't you ever eaten grouper?"

She thought maybe Troy Bentley had treated her to grouper a couple of times. "Sure, but that doesn't mean I'd know one when I saw it. I've never seen a tuna fish dead and in person either."

"Fair enough," Neil said.

"How'd it get here?"

Neil shrugged. "Maybe it got away from a hook and died. Maybe it fell off a boat. Maybe a barracuda got it."

Sunny glanced down at the peaceful ocean. Barracudas were out there? Weren't they supposed to strip a body to the bone in minutes? Or was that piranhas? Avery had been to the aquarium with her class and had talked about those horrid fish.

They walked, settling down into the rhythm of each other's steps, the silky breeze ruffling her hair. Sometimes they'd step into a washout and bump into one another. Her sunburn tingled at his touch, and the sweet recesses of her body began to stir and come alight.

A few steps past the fish, Neil said, "It wasn't far from here where she drowned."

Sunny touched his arm. Her breath came shallowly. Neil walked on, jaw set.

"How did it happen?" She spoke so quietly she thought he didn't hear her. But then he began to talk.

"That weekend we had lunch on the beach. Kiki and the two girls were here, and Angus."

"Two girls?" Sunny ventured. "You mean Blake and Ellery?" Were they Alex's daughters from his first marriage?

"Of course. Lillian and Duncan weren't here—they'd gone over to St. Simons to play golf with friends. We had chicken I'd cooked on the grill, shrimp, watermelon, all sorts of stuff Lillian had brought down. Cookies and cakes. Having a great time. And after lunch the girls packed it all up and wanted to stay at the beach.

"I wanted to take the leftovers back to the house and Angus went with me to get a mask and snorkel he'd forgotten to bring."

Neil swatted away some kind of monster bug whirring by Sunny's nose.

"I told the girls to wait until I got back before they went in the water, but Julie laughed and said they'd be fine. Kiki told us she was a good swimmer, and the girls were more concerned with working on a tan. You can't tell those kids a thing about too much sun being bad for you. Alex was there, too, in a beach chair under an umbrella, reading the Wall Street Journal, probably wishing he was playing golf too."

Here Neil stopped his story.

Sunny continued walking by his side, a strange feeling in the pit of her stomach, calmed only by the tumble and rush of the sea. She breathed in the salt spray, welcoming its sharp tang, and the clear air. Hair whipped across her lips and she pushed it back, tying it with her bandanna. She knew to be quiet and let him take his time.

Neil finally spoke, his voice thick.

"Nobody saw it happen," Neil said. "Kiki told me that Julie had been ragging her about going in the ocean, proving that she could swim. If you've met Kiki, you know she's not the type to get dirty. She finally got on a float and paddled out, and then she found she was getting carried out to sea and started to scream. There's a rip current here that comes and goes with the shifting dunes.

"Julie went in after her. Kiki is a bit fuzzy about the details, but while Julie was trying to pull the float carrying Kiki back to shore, she crossed the current again and the whole thing went under. The girls heard the screams first and went running to their dad. They loved Julie.

"Alex told the girls to come find me and went out on the other float, because he's a terrible swimmer. They were good kids, then, nine-year-olds, and they came straight to the Lodge. We piled in the Jeep and raced back, and found that Alex had managed to bring Julie back to shore. He was still working on her, trying to resuscitate her, when I got back. Oh, yes. Kiki paddled her own float in."

Sunny felt sick. So it had just been Julie and Kiki out there. And Kiki had survived, and Julie, the one with lifesaving skills, had drowned. This did not sound right. But she couldn't tell Neil that. Not now. "You don't need to tell me more."

Neil looked at her with a sad smile. "You'll understand. Lillian tells me you're a widow."

The sand squeaked under their feet. She wasn't a widow exactly—what do you call an almost-divorced woman whose soon-to-be ex-husband died? She guessed widow would do as well as anything.

"Yes," she said.

"I suppose you don't want to talk about that either," Neil said.

"Miss Lillian didn't tell you?"

"Nope," he answered. "She just told me you were a cousin who'd lost her job, and she needed an assistant."

Sunny realized she had to say something. Not the real story. Miss Lillian wouldn't approve a story about Kyle crashing his car while trying to outrun a cop.

She cleared her throat. If Miss Lillian could make things, up, then she could certainly leave a few things out. "My late husband died in a car crash. I wasn't with him." She paused, dug for a tissue in her pocket, and blew her nose. "I don't like to talk about it." She snuck a peek at Neil, but his face was impassive. Surely Neil wouldn't check up on that story.

"I'm sorry," Neil said. "Has it been hard for you?"

"It's been . . . a challenge." She tried to imagine what it was like for Neil, losing someone he loved. She'd been so angry at Kyle for his drunkenness, lying, and hell-raising, that her sadness at his loss had been for Avery's sake, not her own. And she couldn't shed a measure of guilt for leaving him. Maybe if she hadn't, the accident would never have happened.

"I just wondered," Neil said. "Some people handle things better than others. You seem a little jangly. Has it been very long?"

"A year," Sunny said. This was what Miss Lillian had coached her to say, though Kyle had been under the grass and gravel of Shadyrest Memorial Garden since Avery was ten.

"It takes a while," Neil said. They were walking back now in a companionable silence, broken only by the whisper and rumble of the sea.

Sunny wasn't used to such quiet. Wherever she'd lived had been full of noise. In the mobile home park she'd heard couples screaming, TVs screeching, dogs barking, trucks grinding, and music wailing.

In her neighborhood in the city it wasn't much better: the expressway, the teenagers, the growl and howl of leaf blowers. Inside, the television babbled, the phone rang, the microwave beeped, and on the street, in the mall, the beat went on. In the hospital, an occasional quiet moment was broken by people walking, monitors chirping, patients and visitors murmuring, the low hum of all the effort it takes to hold a soul to life.

Here, there was nothing but a man beside her, and maybe a ghost.

"You're mighty quiet," he said, as if he'd read her thoughts. They had reached the edge where the damp sand stopped, and she dropped her flip-flops to slide into them.

Neil took her elbow to steady her, and she turned to protest that he didn't need to, but he was looking at her in the moonlight, his hair flopping over his brow, his expression serious. She felt as if she glowed in the moonlight like a mica stone, but felt more like butter, in danger of melting—

He bent down and kissed her, soft, lingering.

The kiss was a flowing spring to one who'd been wandering in the desert, and she clung to him and kissed him back, feeling the rush, the heat, the tingle of his fingers on her spine, the crackle of pain on her sunburnt back, the caress of his lips against the tender skin beneath her ear. His body pressed against hers, the moon pouring over them like pale champagne. She had just met this man, and wasn't even sure she liked him, and the kiss went on, and the kiss became strong, and the kiss broke something inside her loose to grow and glow, and within all this glowing she was aware of his scent, the saltiness of his hair, his sweat, the faint musk of after-shave. If she didn't stop now—

She pulled back, gasping. "Ouch."

"I'm sorry. Your sunburn . . ."

"I don't think . . ."

"No. Don't think."

She felt as if she were struggling into a boat after being thrown overboard. She took a step back, and tripped on a hillock of sand. He caught her before she fell. She was panting. Like a dog.

"Thanks." She put her hands to her warm cheeks.

"My pleasure." Neil was grinning.

"Maybe we ought to get on back. Miss Lillian might need me." Sunny willed herself to look at the sand, not at his eyes.

"Lillian's asleep."

"Please, Neil."

Her breath had calmed. He tipped her face up with his forefinger and placed it on her lips. "We'll do this again."

What the hell was happening?

They slogged across the dry sand to the Jeep. As they drove back through the dark forest, an owl hooted somewhere in the distance. Sunny sank down in her seat, away from Neil. That had been a complete lapse of judgment; moonlight and wine were deadly combined.

Neil was all wrong, and they were leaving in the morning.

When Neil pulled the Jeep around to the front of the lodge, Miss Lillian was sitting on the porch in a long silk robe, crutches beside her. Sunny's muscles tensed. She shot an I-told-you-so glance at Neil, but he hailed Miss Lillian.

"Are you all right?" Sunny leaped out of the Jeep and hurried up the porch steps.

"Of course," Miss Lillian said archly, waving her hand in dismissal. "Except that Alex called and woke me. He's back in town, and wants to have lunch the day after we get back. That's day after tomorrow, of course. With Kiki. Unfortunately."

"You don't have to, Lillian," Neil said.

"Oh, but I want to." Miss Lillian grabbed her crutch and pointed it at Neil. "I'm going to have them over to the house, on my turf, and we're going to talk about the birthday party. And then we'll talk about fig preserves, and Sunny's going to watch Kiki's face. I can't wait."

As Sunny was packing her duffle bag that night, the diamond earring she'd found in the sand tumbled out of her shirt pocket onto the floor. It sure looked real, flashing inner fire. For some reason she hesitated to ask Neil about it. He had disappeared after dinner, said he had some work to do at the nature center, and everyone ought to turn in early because they had an early start the next day.

Okay. Just as well. Plenty of time to ask Miss Lillian later.

Sunny wondered how long Alex and Kiki had wanted to turn this island into a resort. Julie would have been their greatest obstacle, she realized.

She felt a chill. Maybe Julie's death hadn't been accidental. She picked up the earring and carefully tucked it into her makeup kit.

CHAPTER TWELVE

Sunny tried to read Harris's expression when he met them at the airport, but it was, as usual, inscrutable. He efficiently collected their baggage, wheeled it out, and pulled the big silver Lexus SUV into the handicapped loading zone where they waited.

Miss Lillian settled in front to have more room to stretch her leg, while Sunny perched in back, feeling like a little kid.

Harris negotiated a smooth merge into Interstate 75/85 traffic. "How was your trip, Miss Lillian?"

"Dreadful," Miss Lillian replied, wiping a speck of dust off her lavender linen blazer. "People wear all sorts of foolishness on planes. There was a time you traveled in hat, gloves, and heels, and got a decent snack to boot." She paused, but Harris waited. "I expect you're asking about the island, Harris. Esther and all your kinfolks are fine, but somebody's been talking to them about selling out."

Sunny, in khakis and polo shirt, was digesting the thought of dressing up to fly. A suit and heels? A hat? Gloves, like Grace Kelly in a mid-century movie with Cary Grant?

"Yes, my sources have enlightened me about the land proposals," Harris said. "I believe Mr. Alex sent an envoy to them earlier."

Miss Lillian straightened. "One of his cohorts, yes. Well. I suppose that's why that son of mine wants to talk with me. Now, Harris, I've been thinking about this luncheon to which he's invited himself and his dragon lady. I'd like to serve scallops and linguine in cream sauce, with whole artichokes and hollandaise. Tomato aspic to start, or maybe poached egg *en gelée*. Something slippery, Harris. And then something crumbly for dessert."

"Crumbly, madam?"

"Of course. Crumbly and creamy and colorful. Blueberry cobbler with ice cream, for instance."

"Are those your son's favorite foods, Miss Lillian?" Sunny asked, looking for a clue to Alex's personality.

"Oh, no," Miss Lillian said happily. "He's the skate wing and arugula sort, trendy gourmet. But you've heard of the power lunch? This is the stealth lunch, planned to make them insecure. I hope Kiki wears silk."

And *this* was a woman with dementia? Ha!

Miss Lillian related the poisoned fig story to Harris as they hit the expressway, and Harris was suitably shocked and horrified. Those figs did *not* originate in his kitchen, he insisted. Expertly weaving in and out of traffic, Harris glanced in the rear-view mirror at her and frowned.

Could she really trust Harris? Maybe he was in cahoots with Alex and wanted a resort? Did he have a grudge against the islanders? Did he really think his sister, Esther, had put root on him?

"Mr. Harris," she asked, "why did you decide to put the fig preserves in the box?"

She saw one of the gray bushy brows lift. "I didn't intend to, Miss Iles," he said carefully. "I knew Mr. Neil had a great affection for fig preserves, and I was sorry we didn't have any to send him. I thought we'd used the last jar. I was searching for a jar of my own peaches to include when I happened on another jar of the figs in the pantry. I thought I'd overlooked it in haste. I packed it, of course, along with the peaches."

"Aha," Miss Lillian said. "Did you leave the room when Kiki was here, Harris?"

"I regret to say I did, ma'am," Harris said. "Miss Iles was in attendance." He smiled his Evil Uncle smile.

"Me?" squeaked Sunny. "After she gave me the third degree, I had to get out of there. I came up to you, Miss Lillian."

"Kiki could have put those figs in the pantry when you were both out of the room, Harris."

"But how did she know we'd take them to Neil?" Sunny asked.

"She didn't," Miss Lillian said. "Neil wasn't her target. It was me. Dear as he is to me, Neil doesn't make the decisions about the island."

Sunny still didn't want to believe this could happen. It was crazy. "Miss Lillian, maybe it was an accident. A bad batch. A loose jar seal."

"Just what Kiki would like everyone to think," Miss Lillian said. "Anyhow, Neil's going to let us know what was in those preserves as soon as the lab tests are back."

"I doubt it was one of the senator's jars," Harris said. "I know his cook, and she is always careful."

"Yes, I agree, Harris," Miss Lillian said. "If the lab finds arsenic, it'll be an easy call. But what if they find botulism? If I say Kiki's trying to poison me, Alex and Kiki will say that's my delusion. A loose jar seal, as you say, Sunny. One more piece of evidence that I'm losing my mind."

Sunny relished the few minutes of quiet as they sped through the canyon of the Downtown Connector, tall buildings disappearing behind them.

Miss Lillian broke the silence. "Harris, I have a brilliant idea. If Kiki comes to the house today, don't let her in. If she calls, say I can't talk." Lillian lowered her voice conspiratorially. "Say I came back from the island sick. Let her think the plan almost worked."

That was all well and good, but . . . Miss Lillian trusted Harris. Should she? Could he be involved in the plot? Sunny was relieved when a red pickup truck with a skinny, gum-chewing driver swerved in front of them, causing Miss Lillian to gasp and Harris to come out with some uncharacteristic swear words. "Excuse me, Miss Lillian," he said. "I need to concentrate on driving."

Miss Lillian said no more, and settled back in her seat.

Sunny's thoughts strayed back to Neil. He was really curious about her background, suspicious, even. Had he believed the stories she and Miss Lillian had concocted?

He'd seemed glad to see the last of them. She'd offered to strip the beds and start the washer, but he'd just hustled them on out the door, saying Esther's granddaughter would think somebody was taking her job. Well, okay, he wanted them to be on the dock and ready when that Harlan Fish came with the boat. But still. There was that kiss to think about. Maybe a kiss was just a kiss.

They were heading toward Buckhead now. Sunny had tried to call Avery in the airport, to tell her they were back, but the silly kid's phone went to voice mail. She hammered out a text, sent it, and then Harris was pulling to a stop behind the house, and she shoved the phone back in her bag.

Now she hauled it out again. There wasn't a return message. Didn't Avery miss her at all?

Sunny began another text to Avery but was interrupted.

"I have an idea," Miss Lillian announced as Harris came around and opened the door for her.

Sighing, Sunny slipped the phone back into her bag and got out herself. She came around to help Miss Lillian negotiate her way to the back door. "What's your idea, Miss Lillian?"

Miss Lillian chortled like a B-movie villain. "We'll catch Kiki at her game. Then Alex will have to believe me."

"Catch her? But how?" Sunny could feel that familiar rabbit hole opening up in front of her. Maybe next she'd start growing, or maybe shrinking.

Miss Lillian's eyes glowed with excitement. "Oh, we'll come up with something, I'm sure we will. Harris, Sunny, this is the best I've felt since I landed on this wretched ankle."

Sunny did not feel good. In fact she could barely breathe. She was expected to help catch a supposed murderess? They hadn't taught that in nursing school. Killer bacteria were gruesome enough.

At last they were in the house. "Just get me settled, dear, and then go on home," Miss Lillian said. "I know you want to see that girl of yours."

Sunny was happy to leave, but when she came back she'd have questions.

In a day or so, the lunch meeting would be held, and she'd be expected to take notes. This time, she'd pin down Miss Lillian about the details of her cover story beforehand, because she was sure Alex and Kiki would want to know more about her. She was sure Alex was suspicious already. How was Miss Lillian going to convince her son he had a cousin he'd never heard of?

CHAPTER THIRTEEN

Neil, with Rambo beside him, plumed tail blowing in the wind, stood on the dock and watched the ferry take the women away. For some reason he was reluctant to turn his back until the boat was out of sight, though he wanted badly to get back to his shed and contemplate the weekend. And he needed to straighten up the lodge, as Oriana Welles would be arriving Friday.

Orrie. Was he reluctant to see her again? Maybe.

How much of this visit was because the book project needed more photographs, and how much was due to unfinished business between them? Or business he thought was finished, but she didn't. The affair, or whatever it was, had ended unevenly, badly, with no clear definition. They'd stopped calling each other after the last big fight—not even a fight. They'd just had a civilized disagreement of the first order, and afterwards, no one had been willing to be the first to break the silence.

He could have found some excuse to refuse her request to come here or challenge her motive for the trip, but he'd taken her words at face value. A working weekend, Friday to Sunday, and then she'd have to be back to prepare for summer classes.

Did he want to rekindle the flame? He didn't think so, but maybe Orrie had changed. Then there was Sunny. What had that meant? Was he falling for Julie's cousin, if that's who she really was? The whole thing sounded fishy to him, but Lillian seemed certain the girl's story was true, and damn it, there was something about her.

He grinned in spite of his misgivings. He liked Sunny Iles' face. He liked her body. He liked her weird ways. It was a pretty elemental attraction. Damn, but it was lonely here sometimes. Rambo nudged against his leg, reminding him that he was not exactly alone. The damn beast seemed to read his mind sometimes. He reached down and scratched the furry head. "Sometimes a guy needs more than a friend, old sport," he muttered.

Sunny had avoided him that morning, but when he was loading their luggage on Harlan's boat, she'd darted a look his way just as he'd sneaked a look at her, and they both had been caught like ninth graders with crushes. What had he seen in her expression? A come-on, or a warning to stay away? He shook his head. He really had been alone too long.

Rambo sauntered back toward the house then stopped and looked back at Neil, as if to say, *come on, it's time to get to work.* Rambo followed him down to the nature center to check on

Blackjack. He found Reggie already there, feeding the injured turtle. Neil knew the boy was bright. What would be his future? Was there any way he would stay on the island?

Friday afternoon, Neil was down at the dock when Harlan brought Orrie. He watched them approach through the tidal creek, the breeze blowing her hair, one hand steadying her bird scopes and tripods in their canvas cases. Across the marsh, a heron lifted off, displaying its grace as if it knew a birdwatcher was nearby.

He'd forgotten how attractive she was: tall, rangy, sun-lightened chestnut hair tied back, long tanned legs in khaki shorts.

His spirits lifted when she stepped off the boat, giving him a dazzling smile. The smile lingered a little too long, making him uncomfortable. Enduring Harlan's knowing wink behind her back, he hefted her gear to carry to the lodge. She hadn't been kidding about working, he guessed, with all this stuff.

"Thanks for letting me come," she said.

Neil hesitated for a moment. "I'm looking forward to the book."

She gave him a cool, appraising glance. "Maybe you can sell it to people that come here."

Neil shrugged. He didn't want to go commercial, with T-shirts and such, but a book might be a good thing to entice potential donors, if it came to that.

While Harlan carried the food totes around back to the kitchen, Orrie stopped for a moment on the porch and gazed at the flower beds, the tabby walkways, and the paths leading to the vegetable garden, the biological station, and the stables.

"It's just the same," she said. From her tone, Neil couldn't tell whether she wanted to sigh with regret or clap her hands in glee.

"No reason to make changes." He opened the screen door and held it for her to pass.

She paused again in the front room to take stock, and then in the hallway, Oriana hesitated in front of the guest room, Lillian's room. She threw a look over her shoulder at him, as if there was a question where she would stay.

Consciously poker-faced, he nodded. "I'll put your stuff here."

She walked in and set her camera bags and tripod in the corner. He squared up her suitcase on a luggage rack.

"So I'm officially a guest?" With a lilt to her voice, she gave him that familiar little half-smile with an edge to it.

Damn. There would be no right answer. "I thought you'd be more comfortable here," he said.

She dropped her shoulder bag on a side chair and went to the mirror. She unbanded her long pony tail, raked her fingers through her hair, and secured it once again with the band. Then she picked an object from a small china dish. "Interesting visitor?"

She handed him a tube of Dior lipstick. The resentment in her tone was almost palpable.

"She'll be missing it," he said, shrugging. "Thanks." He closed his fist and shoved the black tube into his pocket. It had to be Lillian's, but he'd let Orrie think what she would. Maybe it was mean of him, but he wasn't thinking too clearly now. Kissing Sunny had definitely messed with his mind.

He left Orrie to put away her things while he went to find Harlan, who was smoking a cigar on the back porch and drinking a cup of Neil's coffee.

"How was the trip with Lillian yesterday morning?" Neil asked.

"Them two ladies was awfully quiet. Just watching the scenery, not much conversation. When I let 'em off at the marina, I told Miz Lillian I spotted those two granddaughters of hers couple weekends ago, and she was all ears."

"Blake and Ellery, you mean?"

"Them or two girls that looked awfully much like 'em, and one more girl with pink hair. Miz Lillian said nobody told her the girls would be coming down, and she was sure you didn't know they were around."

Neil rubbed his chin. They might have come with their father and stayed on the mainland, some fancy hotel. If Alex and his sideman had been down here talking with the islanders, the presence of the kids would make sense. He'd probably brought them because Kiki didn't want them left at home with her. Lillian was going to be pissed.

Kiki kept her distance from the kids, and those wild kids needed a mother. He knew why Catherine hadn't fought for them—she had her dignity, and she hadn't wanted her mental condition dragged through the courts. Hadn't wanted to risk being denied.

"Was their dad with the kids when you saw them?"

Harlan shook his head and spat. "Didn't see him. They was talking to some hotdogs with a speedboat. When they saw me, they skedaddled. Don't know why, I'm not such a scary fella."

"I'll bet they weren't supposed to be with those guys, and they knew you might tell."

Harlan gave a knowing chuckle. "Yep. I've toted them over to Issatee ever since they were knee-high to a grasshopper. You know, last time I seen 'em they were cute little blonde things, but now they done dyed their hair black and chopped it off. Three years since they been down."

Neil shook his head. "Their stepmama lets them do as they please."

Orrie opened the screen door, saw that they were talking, and ducked back in. "Come on, Harlan," Neil said. I'll walk with you back to the boat." He gave Harlan a warning look so he wouldn't ask why.

"What happened to their mama, if you don't mind my asking?" Harlan asked. The shells of the path crunched under their feet. "She was a sweet lady."

"I just heard that Cathy was thinking about becoming a minister," Neil said. He glanced back and saw that Rambo was following them.

They stepped onto the dock, and the water lapped around their feet. "A lady preacher?" Harlan said. "Lord help us. Why can't she just be content to do good by people?"

"She's a gentle soul. She needs an outlet, I think, for her love." Neil sniffed the salt air and watched a gull alight on a post.

"Well, she better love her own flesh and blood. I feel sorry for those little gals, but Neil, you should have seen 'em. They don't wear enough cloth on their backsides to cover a baby's butt."

Neil nodded. "Harlan, do me a favor. Let me know if you see them again. Alex Stirling has been talking with the folks over at Turtle Point. I told you about his resort plans."

Harlan snorted. "There's a heap of pressure on these islands. There's just too many folks with too much money, that's what it is. The whole world's getting eat up by cement. And the weather is acting crazy. Along comes a hurricane and there goes your fancy-ass buildings. A couple hundred years from now the alligators will own this place."

They both looked out toward the faint shoreline of the mainland, shimmering in the distance. Harlan spat into the water. "See you when I come back to get your lady friend. Monday, is it?"

Neil looked hard at Harlan. "Sunday. Ms. Welles is strictly business."

"Hey, take it easy, buddy," Harlan said, and leaned down to scratch Rambo's ears. Then he saluted Neil and got into his boat.

Neil helped him cast off, and then he walked back up to the lodge, Rambo following, and took a deep breath before he went in.

He found Orrie in the kitchen, putting away the fresh groceries. Was she being a helpful guest, or trying to slide back into her old role? She delved into his grocery bags and set sugar, tomato paste, and spaghetti on the counter. "Thought I ought to earn my keep," she said, eyeing the sugar. He knew she didn't approve of it. "I brought wine and herbal tea. And you will let me pay this time?"

"Afraid so. Miss Lillian said no more freebies."

She frowned. "Keeping you on a short leash, Neil?"

"It's the economy, professor." He reached past her to shove tomato paste onto a high shelf. She was wearing double tank tops, no bra, and he could feel the heat of her skin, perfumed and musky.

Memory stirred and he felt aroused and a little unquiet, but it wasn't the same feeling he'd had toward Sunny. Kissing her had quickened something he'd thought almost dead—not the physical, but something emotional, an echo of some deep plangent chord. How could that be? He didn't even know that girl. She didn't remind him of Julie in the least.

In fact, Orrie was more like Julie—tall, athletic, tanned, fearless, and out there. What you saw, you got. Sunny was pale-skinned, freckled, bottle-blonde, skittish—and a bit of a mystery.

"Earth to Neil. What are you thinking about? Not tomato sauce?"

"Sorry. Lillian was just here, and I was wondering—"

"Ah. The Dior lipstick."

"That's right," he said.

"Why, Neil. Were you trying to make me jealous?" Orrie's voice became seductive. She turned, brushing her breast against his arm, and delved into the bag for carrots, cucumbers, tomatoes. She smiled. "Vegetables. For me?"

"I have lettuce from the garden to add," he said. "We'll have a big salad. I don't suppose you'd like a venison steak?"

"Dead deer," she grumbled. "Did you hit it with the Jeep?"

This time, her heckling rankled him and he didn't reply.

She opened the freezer compartment. "Here's shrimp. Let me make dinner tonight." She seemed to be struggling to stay cheerful. "Vegetable curry with shrimp. You can have your old deer tomorrow."

"It'll be a good change from my dead pig," said Neil.

"What did you feed Lillian?" Orrie's voice took on a defensive, hostile tone. This wasn't getting off to a good start.

"She's easy to please," Neil said.

Orrie tossed her head. "You know, you could be almost self-sufficient here if you got down to it. You could plant more veggies, keep a cow for milk, chickens for eggs, and a couple of donkeys as well as the horses."

"What would I want with donkeys?" Neil laughed. He had to hand it to her. She could keep him off balance, still.

"You could use them if the Jeep broke down," she said.

Neil shrugged. "Harlan does my shopping, and I like it like that. Animals are just more work. What next? Growing my own cotton? Spinning on a wheel like Gandhi? I thought you didn't like island life. I thought you wanted civilization."

Here it came, the argument. Her wanting him to leave the island, come teach somewhere in Atlanta or Athens, closer to her, and his countering suggestion that she move to Issatee. Would he have asked her to come last summer if he'd had the faintest suspicion she might agree?

For his part, leaving the island was not negotiable. He wasn't going to live anywhere but Issatee. Period.

They found themselves out of groceries to put away, and stared at each other for a moment. Orrie shrugged and said, "Well, I've got pictures to shoot while the sun's out. Want to go?"

Neil looked away. "Sorry. I've got a full schedule of chores. I've got to tend the boats." He wasn't sorry to have a good excuse. He liked working on the canoe, the small outboard runabout for fishing and crabbing, and his sailboat, a lovely thing, his pride and joy. It was due for caulking.

"Otherwise I'd have dressed a little better for you." He looked down at his jeans and grubby T-shirt, with only a few flecks of paint here and there.

"I know, Neil." Was there a little sarcasm there?

He tossed her the keys to the Jeep, walked outside, and ambled down the path to the boathouse. Rambo had disappeared somewhere, probably taking a nap.

It was hot and going to get hotter. He'd just stepped inside when he heard a plank behind him creak. When he turned, she was filling the doorframe, backlit. "Neil . . ."

Uh-oh. She touched her tongue to her lips and held his eyes for a long instant. Her breasts strained at the layered tank tops, tips tautening the thin cotton. She reached out her arms to him with that old smile—he'd teased her about the come-hitherness of it once—and he embraced her awkwardly. He didn't want to hurt her feelings, but this wasn't a good idea. Why start something that wasn't going anywhere?

He kissed her forehead. "Hey, remember? We've got work to do."

She sighed and relaxed against him alarmingly. "Neil, it's been so long."

Neil stifled a laugh, pretending to cough. Orrie wasn't a woman to go without a man for months on end. She was probably still involved with her book partner.

Last summer he'd liked her forwardness, bringing him out of his grief and seclusion, even as it had made him uneasy. He'd always been a straight-laced, hold-it-in type of guy. Honor society. He'd planned to become a marine biologist, be the first in his family to become a professional. Then he'd met Julie, fallen in love, and had come with her to Issatee Island. Nope, he wasn't a womanizer.

But now, the fanned embers were kindling. Who had lit those embers in the first place? Had it been Sunny, or only memory and moonlight? He opened his mouth, whether to speak or kiss Orrie again he didn't know, but he never got a chance.

A speedboat roared across the sound, carrying two young people, one a girl with pink hair. Was that the boat Harlan had been talking about? There weren't that many girls with pink hair.

He stepped back from Orrie. "What is it, Neil?" she asked.

"That girl with pink hair—"

"I didn't think you were the type for jailbait, Neil." She flipped her hair.

Ah, the tart tongue. He'd liked that too at first. It had been bracing after everyone's treating him as if he'd been stuck together with spit and baling wire after Julie died. Now he didn't like her tone. "I think she's a friend of my nieces. I wonder who she is."

"Why do you care?"

"Tell you what," Neil said, clenching his jaw. "Why don't you go out looking for birds?"

"Oh, Neil." She pouted prettily. "Don't be that way."

"You said you came here to work." He smiled with his lips but not his eyes, and she nodded slowly, understanding.

A cough sounded from behind the boat and a dark head popped up.

"Just a minute, Reggie," Neil said.

Oriana froze and took a step back. "You did say something about later," she murmured. "I'll be a good girl. For now." She turned and walked up the path toward the Jeep, not glancing back, ponytail swinging.

He shrugged his shoulders. Why hadn't he expected this? The breakup hadn't been clean. There had been too many things not said. Too much taken for granted, too many assumptions. The one thing he did remember was her saying she wasn't Julie and never would be, and why was he clinging to a ghost? He wasn't. Was he?

"Come on, Reggie. Sorry for the interruption." He handed Reggie a new scraper and took his own, bending to the task of scraping out the old caulking of the sailboat. Maybe he'd take Orrie sailing if he got finished. Tomorrow, maybe.

What would Lillian think if he married again? She'd said to him, after they'd finished going over the books, "It's so quiet here now with Angus away at school. I don't think Julie would have wanted you to be so alone."

That remark had surprised him. Had she suspected the spark that had flashed, however brief, between him and Sunny? He didn't think so. He turned on his mp3 player, found a seafaring album, and went back to scraping.

The sun was hanging low in the sky before he was finished with the boat. Reggie had already gone home for supper. Orrie still wasn't back; a small irritation. He hoped she wasn't in trouble somewhere. Maybe he'd better ride out and find her.

He went inside and splashed cool water on his face and hands, washing off sweat and boat gunk. No point in showering before the ride. Feeling refreshed, he went to saddle Archie and found Rambo in the stable crouched, attention fixed on something rustling in the straw. The cat barely flicked his tail when Neil entered and walked to Archie's stall.

Archie, a rolling-eyed roan who didn't like people as a rule and barely tolerated Neil, inexplicably loved Rambo, who often snoozed on his back. That was okay with Neil. A horse who loved him would have been too much.

A donkey to keep ol' Arch company, he thought, when Shalimar goes. He looked over at Julie's dappled gray. He should have sold her long ago, because she didn't get enough exercise. Orrie, he recalled, didn't ride.

They'd go sailing tomorrow. Orrie would like that. And then . . . he'd see.

CHAPTER FOURTEEN

K iki Stirling was wearing a silk shell and jacket combination, the color of old brass, over black linen slacks. And her diamond studs. She cut her pasta with small neat strokes, eyeing the leafy artichoke as if it might suddenly leap off the plate and land in her lap. She cast glances at Sunny, smiling like a movie Cleopatra.

"So you're from what branch of the family?" Alex's voice was as smooth as the butter on his knife approaching a chunk of crusty baguette. "Where did Mother dig you up?" He spread the chunk heavily and bit into it, not waiting for an answer.

"Oh, Alex, be nice to your cousin," said Miss Lillian.

Sunny bit her lip, hoping she could remember the whole story. "Well—" she began, but Lillian toed her under the table and spoke first.

"Don't you remember, Alex dear, my first cousin Weezie? She had red hair, and she was such a belle the year of her spectacular debut at the Driving Club?"

Sunny perked up. She had picked up from Troy that the Piedmont Driving Club was where all the Old Atlanta upper crust gathered.

Alex replied, "Before my time, mother dear." He furrowed his brow. "When would I have met her? I don't remember her."

"They did come to Issatee once in a while, but you were just a little boy when the big dust-up happened. And she came to Julie's wedding. I'm surprised you don't remember her."

Alex blinked. "That was a huge wedding. So what was that dust-up?"

"She ran off with that famous artist, Freddy Roussel."

"What? He lives in France! His wife is French," Kiki blurted. "And must be around Sunny's age."

So Kiki kept up with all the well-known figures of art, Sunny noted. She probably wrote them all down in a black book, followed them on Twitter or something. But Miss Lillian was saying, "Freddy and Weezie divorced some time back. He wasn't famous back then. Weezie met him during her junior year abroad, when she was majoring in art history, and it was *instant* between the two.

"They came back to America to live. I bought quite a few of his canvases to help them out. In fact. There are two of them out here." She pointed to the pair of riotous yellow and shocking pink lilies on the wall. "This wasn't his usual subject. He painted them for me."

Everyone stopped eating to stare at the lilies. Alex forked up linguine and dribbled a little sauce on his tie. Kiki hunched over her plate as if she was protecting it, rather than her silk blouse.

Miss Lillian continued, "In any case, your uncle Hilton was not amused. Mr. Roussel was, according to him, a foreign frog commie, and Hilty cut poor Weezie off without a cent. He thought Freddy had married her for money and would pack her back home once she'd run out. Instead, Freddy packed her off to California, where they lived hand-to-mouth until they started selling pictures and things. Weezie had always wanted to sculpt, and she flourished there. They had a daughter, their only child, and here you see her." Miss Lillian smiled at Sunny.

"Why haven't we heard this story before?" Alex grumbled.

"No reason to bring it up," Miss Lillian said. "You children were better off not knowing. Hilton and Mackie treated her awfully then. That was the real scandal to me."

"What kind of a name is Sunny?" Alex eyed the spot on his tie.

"Well, you know these artsy types. Summer of Love and all that," Miss Lillian said with a shrug. Sunny marveled at Miss Lillian's story. Damn, she was good. Miss Lillian gestured dramatically, piping, "As I was saying, Freddy became famous, the marriage broke up, and Freddy went back to France. Weezie stayed in California and continued to sell her sculpture, but she was too angry with how she'd been treated to make peace with the family."

Miss Lillian fluttered a wink at Sunny, who clenched her jaw so she wouldn't collapse in a fit of giggles. She offered to go ask Harris to refill the tea glasses. Miss Lillian nodded. "My buzzer's not working again."

Sunny left the room as Miss Lillian launched into an explanation about Sunny meeting a doctor and marrying him, followed by the good doctor dying in a car crash while rushing to an emergency, leaving Sunny with one daughter to raise alone. Thank goodness she'd remembered Sunny's invented story.

Sunny closed her eyes and leaned against the kitchen wall, wondering how she was supposed to remember all this. "Are you all right, Miss Iles?" Harris asked.

Sunny nodded, glad to be out of the firing line. She hoped she wasn't supposed to have inherited any art talent. She wondered if there really was a Weezie, and what she would do if Weezie suddenly showed up. No, Weezie was in California, right? She couldn't just turn up out of the blue.

Harris, tea pitcher in hand, was refilling the cut-crystal tumblers when she took her seat again. Alex had apparently found fascination in the faceted crystals of the chandelier, while Kiki sat poised as a squirrel, her trim silk jacket contrasting perfectly with her sleek mink-brown hair with the bronze stripes, cut to fall toward her face with geometric precision. With her pointed nose and shoe-button eyes darting from Miss Lillian to Alex, Kiki quivered with pent-up energy. If she'd had a tail it would have been twitching.

Sunny, her hair frizzed around her head like a saint's halo, felt like a used teddy bear in a yard sale in the face of all this glamour. She breathed a sigh of relief when dessert was served. This agony would soon be over.

She carefully spooned up each morsel of her delicious blueberry cobbler with melting vanilla ice cream, noticing that Kiki just pushed hers around on her plate. Harris appeared and asked if anyone wanted coffee.

"We'll have it in the library," Alex said, and glanced at his mother for approval. Miss Lillian smiled brightly. "I prefer to have it in the sunroom."

"The sunroom? But we always have it in the library," Alex protested.

"Time for a change," said Miss Lillian. "Let's get some light on your ideas, young man."

Sunny settled Miss Lillian into her favorite wicker peacock chair, very much a throne. A white ceiling fan stirred the air. Beside Miss Lillian the tall windows gave a view of the lush garden: pathways and byways, pergola and pagoda, stately lilies and stonework and meandering paths through boxwood and rhododendron. Everything Miss Lillian had poured her heart and soul into. Sunny realized why Miss Lillian had chosen this room. This was her space, and her space only, and provided a view of her handiwork.

Alex plopped a briefcase on the settee. He hemmed and hawed for a moment, as if he was waiting for something. Then he said heartily, "I'm sure Sunny has things she needs to be doing."

"No, she doesn't," snapped Miss Lillian. "I don't know why I have to repeat myself, but as I told Kiki, I want her here to take notes and help me remember."

Alex frowned. "Why, ah, Mother, this is family business."

"She's family," Miss Lillian said, "and that's an end to it."

Kiki's eyes met Alex's.

At that moment, Harris brought in the coffee tray. "Just leave it, Harris," Miss Lillian said. "I'll pour."

As Sunny passed the filled cups around, she wanted to be anywhere but here. She returned to her chair and stared at the walls, trying to relax. No photos in this room, just some antique-looking flower pictures. Was there a picture of Weezie anywhere in the house? She ought to know what her supposed mother looked like. And was there really a daughter? What if she suddenly turned up on the trail of her long-lost relatives, tracking them down on Ancestry.com? Well, Sunny hoped to be in North Carolina before that happened, and Miss Lillian could sort out the mess.

Sunny was in the middle of her second sip of coffee when Lillian fixed her with a meaningful glance. "We might as well begin," she said.

Sunny tucked one foot under her chair and drew out the new black-and-white paisley organizer that Miss Lillian had given her. She opened it to a blank page, smiling brightly. "I'm ready."

Kiki gazed out at the garden, chin on her knuckles. "You know, Mother Lillian, some yellow daylilies would be stunning over by the water feature. And a few more rhododendrons, and possibly some Star of Bethlehem. I can give you some of my bulbs."

"Yes, I know you'd love to rearrange my garden, Kiki." Miss Lillian frowned over her glasses at Alex. "Don't change the subject. All right, son, let's hear what you have to say."

Alex looked up from the papers he was shuffling, cleared his throat, and selected a page. He passed her a chart colorful with blocks and rectangles. "Here," he said, pointing to a tall red block, "I have the expense of Issatee—what it costs the trust to run the place, pay Neil's salary, the taxes, all that." He pointed to a much shorter green block. "Here are payments from the state for use as a wildlife refuge and educational center."

Below the blocks was a rising graph. "Projected costs. You can see they'll go up as time goes on."

Below the rising graph was a falling graph. "After this year, we'll have to dip into capital to meet expenses. And here is what will happen to the capital."

Miss Lillian flapped her hand dismissively. "That is not what your father planned, Alex. The trust was well-funded to keep the place going. I've looked over Neil's books, and he's running the place very efficiently."

"Well, you know what's happened to the markets—" began Alex.

Sunny was lost. She didn't know what they were talking about. Outside, a woodpecker was tapping on a tall pine tree. Lazy clouds floated across azure sky, and the goldfish pond rippled with flashes of sun.

"That trust was heavy in blue chips, and balanced with bond funds," Miss Lillian was saying. "It should have been insulated against too much loss."

Alex looked down and frowned. "We need for the money to grow, Mother. In my capacity as co-trustee, I would have been irresponsible if I hadn't tried to invest for growth."

"What you mean is, you took some risks and lost," Miss Lillian said.

The woodpecker was climbing round and round the tree. Sunny wondered how Blackjack the crow was doing.

"We do the best we can with the information we have," Alex huffed. "My advisers are professionals. Neil's not."

"Don't try to change the subject from your management to Neil's," Miss Lillian said. "He's the father of my grandson, and Angus will inherit Julie's share of the island." She smiled indulgently. "I have a better idea. Be patient. Wait until I'm gone, dear, and work this out with your nephew."

Hearing Neil's name, Sunny snapped to attention. Then she reddened to see Kiki glancing at her.

Alex shifted uncomfortably in his chair and rearranged the charts and graphs. "Angus won't inherit outright until he's thirty, Mother. That's fourteen years from now."

"And Neil will look after his interests until then, as Julie planned. Is that what you're trying to avoid?"

Kiki, eyes shining and soft, leaned across her husband. "Mother Lillian, you wouldn't want to split the family apart, would you?"

"I wasn't aware that there was any solidarity," Miss Lillian shot back, but Kiki's soft, entreating expression didn't change. Alex sat back and exhaled a long-suffering breath.

"Mother," he said. "It's no secret I've advised you to sell Issatee for a long time. It's a burden, a money sink. You could be doing so much more. You could contribute to any number of wildlife projects. You could make yourself much more comfortable."

"I'm comfortable now." Miss Lillian clasped her hands, the picture of serenity.

"You'll need more help—" Alex began.

Sunny took a deep breath, expecting Miss Lillian to explode, but Miss Lillian appeared amused.

"I have enough for my needs, thank you very much. Harris won't leave me. I don't think we need to concern ourselves with that."

"But that's just it, Mother. If you became incapacitated, you might need more—a woman to help you—permanently." He glanced over at Sunny and frowned. "You might have to liquidate capital. Remember what the markets have been doing."

"And leave less money for you? Your father left you a gracious plenty."

"Mother, please," Alex said, with a conciliatory smile. "I'm willing to keep the island, but if we can make it pay its own way, everybody wins!"

"Except Neil, Angus, the wildlife, and the island people."

The smile faded, and deep furrows formed on Alex's brow. "There are plenty of nature refuges already, Mother. We can find a job for Neil . . . and Angus too, in the project I propose."

Miss Lillian took a sip of her coffee. "That's preposterous. For one thing, Angus might have his own plans for the future. Are you going to find jobs for your own children too, in this project? It might do them good to clean houses or grow vegetables."

"Leave the girls out of it," Alex muttered.

Kiki laid her hand gently on her husband's arm and her voice became even silkier. "Have you told Mother Lillian the news about Neil? I believe he has a girlfriend."

Miss Lillian's head whipped her way. "What?"

Sunny's stomach turned a flip, and she dropped her pen. She quickly scooped it up from the terracotta tiles.

Kiki sighed and simpered, sighed again, then put on a sorrowful expression. "I wished we didn't have to tell you this, Mother

Lillian, but I heard from a friend of mine down at St. Simons that her daughter saw Neil out on the sailboat with some woman." Kiki inspected her fingernails, the looked up from under her eyelashes.

Miss Lillian sniffed. "What of it? I don't hold with gossip. Neil told me he was having a photographer this week for a few days. If he wanted to take her out in the boat, that's his business."

"Well, I hear this photographer was quite—mmm—attractive."

"Who is this snoopy friend of yours and why is she so concerned with my business?" Miss Lillian retorted. "And how old is this daughter anyway? And how did she know it was Neil? Did you send her over there?"

"Mother, really!" Alex's expression became perplexed as he looked from his wife to Miss Lillian. "Let's not get into all that." Kiki slid back in her chair and crossed her arms. Alex thumped his charts. "We need to find a way out of this dilemma."

Miss Lillian sat poised and quiet for a moment, letting the silence speak. Then she leaned forward and tapped Alex's pile of papers. "You could sell Angus your share. Then Angus, with Neil and me as trustees, would own the island, and you'd be free of the headache."

And so would Miss Lillian.

Alex sighed audibly. "Angus doesn't have enough money in his trust fund to buy it, and he's a minor, so borrowing is out, unless you want to lend him the money. For many reasons I'd advise against it. Please don't make light of this, Mother. I've taken the liberty of engaging a firm to make a preliminary study of the suitability of the site for an upscale resort and marina."

Miss Lillian leaned forward, eyes blazing. "And who paid for this study, Alex? Did it come out of your funds, or island funds? Talk in plain English, Alex. You want to turn us into Jekyll Millionaire Colony Revisited."

Alex held up his hand. "Please let me finish, Mother. "This is just a study. In the best scenario, the revenue generated will make it possible for a small portion of the island to be reserved for a suitable nature preserve, and the sustainability of the property for the family will be assured."

Miss Lillian thumped her stick on the floor. "Your father wanted it never to be developed."

"It would be a most exclusive project."

"With exclusive people, who need water, electricity, food, drink, a club, saunas, hairdressers, manicurists, masseurs..."

"Little St. Simons—"

"That island, I might remind you, is pricey, but rustic, meant to be a retreat from civilization and a nature preserve. Small scale, no TV, and food at the communal table. That's not the kind of project you're thinking of, is it?"

Kiki hunkered back in her seat like a vintage locomotive gathering steam. Sunny could almost see the smoke coming out of her ears. "But what's the alternative?" Kiki burst out. "Eating away at our capital until it's all gone? Losing this house and your beautiful garden? Just for the sake of a few birds and turtles?"

Harris peeked in the door to check the coffee, then discreetly withdrew. Miss Lillian became still and grasped her stick. Alex sat white-faced, unwilling to look at Kiki.

Finally Miss Lillian laid her stick aside and broke the silence. "Well, if things are that bad, I should have been better informed. But I think you both want something you're not admitting. And you never answered my question about who paid for the study. I think your silence on this point gives me the answer."

She paused for a good long time before she continued. "Thank you, Alex, for all your attention to our beloved island. May I remind you that your father's grave is there, along with your sister's? I want them to rest in peace. So, my dear, I'll come up with my own plan for saving the island."

"You're not thinking of selling to the state or the Park Service?" He looked momentarily hopeful.

She thumped her stick. "No. Developers pocket politicians like small change."

"Property taxes," Alex warned. "They forced the sale of Ossabaw."

She looked at Alex evenly. "Well. We're not out of money, Alex, and Wesley will help me navigate some exemptions."

Alex gazed out the window. "Mr. Wes is getting old, and the political landscape has changed a lot from your day, Mother."

"Not that much," she snapped. "Alex, I'm tired of discussing this."

"The trust is bleeding cash."

Miss Lillian thumped her stick. "Enough. Leave me with the facts and figures. I'm perfectly capable of managing this situation without your help. I can hire an outside consultant, Alex."

Alex and Kiki both gaped at her, stunned for a moment. "You wouldn't do that," Alex spluttered.

Miss Lillian sat back very straight and put both hands on the stick of her cane. "Maybe not." She paused. "This seems as good a time as any to tell you that I'm going to throw a party on Issatee to celebrate my seventy-ninth birthday.

"I want you to see for yourself the wonderful work Neil's doing. I want the whole family together there, including your girls, Alex. And while we're all on the island, we'll have a moment of remembrance for your father and Julie."

Alex gathered up his papers and began stuffing them back in his briefcase. "When is this party going to happen?"

"Mid-June. I will decide on my public birthday, like the Queen."

"I'll have to check my calendar," Alex said.

Kiki carefully stowed her little golden pen and notebook in her Birkin bag. Sunny was proud of herself for recognizing the pricey purse. It had been worth it, studying all those *Town and Country* magazines she'd found.

Miss Lillian told Sunny to wait in the library while she saw her guests out. Sunny gazed at all the photos on the wall again, wondering if one of them could possibly be Weezie. Ten minutes later the older woman pulled her scooter up to the library door, grinning like a raccoon.

"My girl, I've got them running," she said. "And I've given Miss Kiki a good reason to strike again. Now, let's put our heads together and figure out how to catch Kiki red-handed trying to murder me at the party."

"Miss Lillian, I don't think you have dementia, but when you talk like that . . ."

"Sunny Iles, I know what I'm doing. We have to plan carefully and be ready for her. Now, until we go to Issatee again, don't leave me alone with Kiki. Don't even let her in the house if Alex isn't with her. We must close off any opportunity."

"Yes, ma'am," Sunny said, hoping beyond hope that Harris was on their side.

"Don't call me ma'am," Miss Lillian growled. "I'll have my nap now."

With an hour to kill, Sunny arranged Miss Lillian's medications in the weekly pill minder, then went back to the library in search of the mythical Weezie. She flipped through pictures in plastic sleeves in a stack of old photo albums, but very few were labeled. She really hoped her "mother" wasn't there. If Weezie didn't really exist, then all was well.

On the bottom of the pile of albums lay an old scrapbook, where black-and white pictures and faded color photos had been mounted with corners.

One snapshot was labeled *Cousins, Issatee, 1956.*

CHAPTER FIFTEEN

Seven bathing beauties extended legs toward the camera like a line of budding Rockettes, each laughing. Five wore full-cut suits, two wore modest two-piece garments, and one wore a plaid cotton suit with boylegs. Suits not meant for serious swimming. Sea oats, tawny crescents of grain, waved behind the glossy girls, all with the reckless prettiness of youth. Sunny picked out Miss Lillian's features clearly enough; another girl resembled her enough to be her sister, Zoe, the one who was now in the nursing home. The five other girls were of varying ages and heights. Was one of them the elusive Weezie?

She nudged the photo gently. If she could pop it out from its mounting corners, she might find names written on the back. But just as she got a nail under the edge, Harris appeared at the door, glowering. "Miss Iles? Would you take the cleaning delivery to

Miss Lillian's dressing room? She's awake and wants you now. "

Guiltily, Sunny shoved the scrapbook back on the shelf and took the plastic-wrapped garments he held. *Four more weeks.*

"Ah, there you are, Sunny," Miss Lillian said. "With the cleaning. Good. I'd like for you to help me decide what to take to the island next. Let's see if I have enough to wear until I get this wretched cast off."

"Of course." Sunny unwrapped the clean clothes and hung them on matching fuzzy hangers in Miss Lillian's closet and then bundled the plastic and wire hangers for recycling. She'd just taken a breath to ask Miss Lillian to tell her more about Weezie when the phone rang.

They waited in suspended animation for Harris to answer it, as he insisted it was his job. In a moment they heard his footsteps on the stairs, and then he appeared at the door.

"You could have just paged me," Miss Lillian said, glancing at the old-style intercom.

"I wanted to deliver this message in person," Harris replied. "Miss Kiki insists on talking to you. She's planning a charity lunch and wants to discuss it. I told her you were not at home, and she laughed at me and told me not to try that old dodge. She said she'd be right over."

"Charity lunch? Kiki? Phooey." Lillian grabbed Sunny's sleeve. "Come on, Sunny, quick. We're out of here." Harris bowed and left.

"But where are we going?" Sunny asked.

"To Walmart," Lillian said. "I need some slacks."

"Walmart?" Sunny hadn't seen anything in Miss Lillian's closet that looked as if it cost less than $200. At least.

"Of course. I'm not going to be in this cast forever. I want something inexpensive with wide legs. I can't go everywhere in caftans and I don't have enough palazzo pants."

Miss Lillian had wanted to take her old Jaguar for speed, but Sunny balked at the stick shift, and she bundled Miss Lillian into the white Lexus SUV. Then she tore out of the driveway, just like her almost ex-husband, Kyle, would have. Maybe she'd learned a few things from him after all. At the corner of the street, she glanced in the rear view mirror. Kiki's car was turning into their driveway.

At Walmart, Miss Lillian commandeered a motorized shopping buggy, and Sunny barely kept up as her boss buzzed through the enormous store, delighting in blenders and fans and maxi skirts, socks and scarves and salad bowls. She bought three pairs of wide-legged slacks, touted as the latest style—one pair in white, one in blue, and one in navy. By the time they got back to Stonehaven, Kiki had left for a hair appointment and Sunny spent the rest of the afternoon hemming the pants to the exact length Miss Lillian wore.

A tired Sunny was looking forward to a nice supper with her daughter and forgetting about work. On the way home, making a hurried stop for salad mix, she found plump, fragrant strawberries that reminded her of the last dinner she'd shared with Neil. She plopped them in her basket, along with a pint of potato salad and a quart of chocolate ice cream for Avery. That girl burned calories like a steam engine. The checkout line was long, and by the time she pulled into the driveway of the townhouse, her feet protested against standing one more minute.

Surely Avery had taken the chili and cornbread out of the freezer and put it on the stove.

She turned the key and pushed open the door. The house smelled, not of chili and cornbread, but of perfume and dirty sneakers and something indefinable: something that slammed her with the memory of a night at the party in somebody's basement when she was sixteen and first met a friend of somebody's brother, a lanky singer named Kyle Magee who wanted to be a country music star. "Avery?" Sunny called.

Music was going; bass notes thumped from upstairs. "Avery?" she called again. Too many feet scuffled above her head. She set the plastic bags on the table, marched up the stairs, and knocked on Avery's closed door.

"Oh, shit!" The baritone voice wasn't Avery's.

Sunny turned the doorknob. Locked. She rattled it, banging on the door. "Avery, open up! Who's in there?"

Rattling papers, whispers. The lock snapped loose and the door swung open. Sunny faced a tall, muscular young man with bleary eyes and a sun-bleached bedhead. "Uh, sorry. We were just studying."

Sunny set her hands on her hips. "Avery, get out here."

The music switched off and her breathless daughter scrambled into view. Fully dressed, she was, but Sunny figured plenty of mischief could be accomplished in Lycra and low-slung jeans.

"You know the rule. Guys in the living room," Sunny said.

"But we needed to use the computer—"

Sunny gave her a hard look. "It's a laptop." She turned to the hulking boy. "Dev, I'm sure your mother will be expecting you for dinner. Sorry I can't ask you to stay, but—"

"I was just leaving," Dev Wilson said. He picked two books and an iPad off the bed and retrieved a workbook from the floor. He gathered some printouts from the computer desk and tucked them into a book. "See ya, Avery. Thanks. " He nodded in her direction and swiftly scuttled downstairs and out the front door, slamming it shut behind him.

In Avery's bedroom, the rumpled comforter, piled pillows, and open books suggested that the two might have really been lying on the bed studying, but who knew what else had been happening? Black light, Sunny thought. You can spot bodily fluids with an ultraviolet light wand. She made a mental note to buy one.

"We weren't doing anything wrong." Avery insisted.

Maybe there wasn't any hanky-panky this time, but this was gateway behavior. She recalled the sheets he'd gathered from the printer tray. "Did you write a book report for him? An essay? A history paper?"

"I just helped him type it," she said. "His motor skills are off."

"He's an athlete, Avery. Motor skills are what he has. "

Avery tossed her head, with an air of major condescension. "Mom. There is a difference between fine motor skills and gross motor skills, and he's under a lot of pressure."

Sunny folded her arms. "What do you know about motor skills?"

Avery gave her mother a sullen look. "We study this stuff in health class."

Sunny gathered up the books from the bed and straightened the covers, as if tidying the arena could organize her roiling emotions. "Let's deal with the Dev Wilson question later. Get supper started, like you were supposed to, while I change clothes. I've got something else to talk to you about." She turned to leave and took two steps before she turned back. "No, I'll tell you now. I'm going back to the island. This time, you're coming with me. Your presence is requested."

"Noooooo!"

Sunny ducked into her bedroom and closed the door to escape the angry wails. She snuggled gratefully into her comfortable old jeans and NURSES STICK IT TO YOU T-shirt.

The chili was half eaten before Avery came out of her sulk. "Mom . . . I'm sure Dev's mom would let me stay in his sister's room. You remember Margaux, right?'

"I remember Margaux. Only too well. Didn't she run off to Oregon to marry somebody she met on the Internet?

"Oh, that was kind of a fiasco. She's in college now."

"Over my dead body will you stay with Dev."

A definite conversation stopper. Avery wanted the TV on during dinner, Sunny didn't, and Avery was on the Bad List, so she didn't get her way. Nevertheless, she replied in monosyllables to Sunny's questions about school and friends. Sunny didn't want to nag her about Dev, but she wondered just how far he and Avery had gone. One of the other moms had told her that the kids were really into oral, because you couldn't get pregnant that way. Avery asked if she could turn on the radio and Sunny reluctantly said yes, just to drive away that image from her already-revved up mind.

The thought that had been worrying her like a mosquito finally bit. The image of the photographer, or whoever she was, on the island with Neil, sailing with him on the boat. She felt a little sick, and it didn't make sense. She'd had one night under the moon—one kiss—clouds and stars, smoke and mirrors, a mistake in judgment. For one thing, *no way* would she ever get on a sailboat.

But still, it was okay to worry about the crow, Blackjack. Would it be too weird to call Neil and see if the bird had survived? After all, that was *her* fig the crow had swallowed. More ways than one to get killed on that island.

Thinking of calling Neil made her remember to confiscate Avery's phone before she went to bed. Avery retaliated by barricading her door for the rest of the evening. Sunny gazed at her phone longingly, but she didn't know Neil's number, and she didn't know if he always took calls. She sighed as she clicked off the light. Work must surely be better tomorrow.

The morning was brilliant with sunshine and a cloudless blue sky, a fresh breeze coming in from somewhere. The weather made her feel upbeat, not easy considering the chilly looks Avery had given her that morning. She opened the back door at Stonehaven with hope.

Angry words were tumbling down the back stairs like so many ping-pong balls. She could hear them whacking the air as she yanked off her sweater and hung it in the closet of her sitting room. She drew a comb from her bag and untangled her mane, listening.

"I will not go, Madam. I shall not set foot on the bloody island."

"Harris, you always resort to the Queen's speech when you get angry."

"I'm ready to go back to England any day, Madam. I'm sure I could get a position there, maybe with a diplomat. Maybe even an *African* diplomat."

"Why don't you just go to Turtle Point and make peace with your sister?"

There was an ominous silence. Then, "I do not believe in root, but it was not sisterly of her to put a spell on me."

"Harris, how can you possibly think she has put a spell on you in this day and age?"

"That is not something I wish to discuss, Madam," he said. "Sack me if you will."

"Of course I'm not going to sack you," Miss Lillian said.

Sunny decided to go out and come back in again and slam the door. She did so, rattling the dishes in the glass-fronted cabinets.

The voices broke off. In a moment Harris stepped down the back stairs.

"Is our lady all right this morning?" Sunny asked.

Harris looked down his nose at her, and she could almost see ruffled feathers around his shoulders. "She's all right," he said, biting off the words. "She's waiting for you."

Sunny nodded and mounted the stairs two at a time. She found Miss Lillian still in bed. "About time you got here," she sniffed.

"Sorry," said Sunny, crossing her fingers behind her back. She didn't want to let on she'd been eavesdropping. "There was a pile-up on the expressway."

"Well, you can take this tray now, and then you and I will take care of the mail and plan the party details and think about our little scheme. I'm trying to persuade Harris to come along to help out. Neil can hire people on the island, but it would be so nice to have Harris there overseeing the cooking and serving. He's so good at it."

"And he doesn't want to go?" Sunny prompted. She wanted to hear the whole story, as she wanted to make sure of Harris's loyalty.

"Of course not," said Miss Lillian. "And a reunion with Esther is long overdue. But he'll come around, I think. Now go ahead and get this tray out of the way."

"But you've eaten hardly anything," Sunny said, leaning over the tray. "You need protein to heal."

"Oh, don't start getting all nursey on me," Miss Lillian said. "You can bring me another cup of coffee."

Sunny sighed. Would it do any good to lecture Miss Lillian on bones needing calcium to knit, vitamin C to heal, protein to repair torn muscle? Maybe she could ask Harris to sneak more protein into her food somehow. Make a smoothie or something.

She took the tray down and caught Harris just going out the door. "Ah, Miss Iles. I'm just going to the farmer's market for some fresh berries. You'll oversee things while I'm there?"

"Of course," Sunny said. "She's not eating this morning. She needs protein . . ."

"She'll be hungry by tiffin," Harris said. "I'm serving quiche and some fruit." He gave a curt nod and walked out the back door.

Tiffin? What was that? Sunny watched him drive away in the vintage PT Cruiser that Miss Lillian kept for errands. He liked it, Miss Lillian had told her, because it reminded him of the taxis in London where he'd learned to be a proper butler.

She put away the uneaten food and stacked the dishes in the dishwasher. Then she reported back to Miss Lillian, taking the paisley notebook. Miss Lillian waved her to a chair by the bed. "We'll just work here, dear. There's no point in getting up and dressed only to change again when Flip comes at eleven."

Flip! "Another swimming lesson?" Sunny's stomach tightened. "Doesn't it bother you to swim? I mean, Neil told me what happened to Julie—" Dear God, what had she said?

At first, Miss Lillian looked taken aback, then her face softened into thoughtfulness. "I should have told you. Let me just say this. If you fall off a horse, one way to deal with the fear of falling again is to avoid horses. But just think how much you'd be missing! Especially if you loved the freedom and joy of coursing across a beach or a meadow on a horse's back, and if you love the marvelous ability to control such a huge beast. So you get back on, if you're wise.

"But there are some things we can't control, and we can hide in our caves, can't we, to be safe from storms? Then we'd never see the sun shine, never see the flowers grow. Yes, I have reason to fear and hate the water. But the ocean's only salt water, subject to the tides and currents. It's not evil, like that woman who's plotting to kill me so she can have my island. Now sit down and take out your pen."

Sunny sat down abruptly. "But can I ask you something?"

Miss Lillian inclined her head.

"Can't you just take them out of your will or something? So if something happens to you, they get nothing?"

The older woman gave her a mirthless smile. "If only it were that simple. No, the island is in trust. Long explanation, dear. And my son is my son. I think he's redeemable. His father was a hard act to follow, and he died before Alex made his mark on the world. Oh, if that son of mine hadn't . . . ah well. Water over the dam, et cetera. Let's get started on that party."

At the end of forty-five minutes, Sunny had listed food to be served, food to bring, food to buy, and items to check with Neil about. Did he need extra sheets and towels? Flowers? Tableware? She had written down Harlan's phone number and instructions that she should tell him this time they would be driving down, as well as her own phone number so that they could coordinate.

"Very good," Miss Lillian said, beaming. "And now it's time to change for the pool."

"But we haven't checked the mail yet," Sunny said, desperately trying to put the moment off. "There might be an invitation or something to plan for."

"The mail won't arrive until noon," Miss Lillian purred, and glanced toward the window. "Oh, look. I see Flip's car. He's early. Hurry! We need to finish on time because I have three friends coming for lunch."

"You do?"

"Oh, sorry. I forgot to tell you. You won't need to join us." Still, she might have at least warned Sunny. Maybe she *was* having memory loss.

The lesson was ghastly, as usual. Sunny managed to keep her head above water, but she *hated* it, hated it. If a job hadn't been offered her in North Carolina, she'd opt for Arizona. Dusty plains, deserts, that's what she needed.

But he *did* say she was a tiny bit better. "Maybe you're not a sinker after all, Sunny."

No sooner had Flip left than Miss Lillian went to shower off with Ultra Swim to get the chlorine out of her hair, and Sunny, not having time for her own shower, dried her boss's hair. The expert short cut fell into all the right places. Sunny's Pool Hair looked hideous, as usual, turning greenish and crackly. "You can wash it while we're having lunch," Miss Lillian offered.

Instead, Sunny hid away in the kitchen after the guests arrived. She peeked through the door and saw three impeccable ladies in bright colors who swooped down and ate quiche and mixed fruit and small chocolate cakes which Harris called pettyfores. She asked him if he meant pinafores, and then he smiled and wrote it out for her: *petits fours*. It was French, he said.

Oh, she felt so ignorant. She'd never be able to fool Alex and Kiki for much longer. She was supposed to have a French father!

The ladies, before setting off on their afternoon shopping excursion, begged Lillian to come with them, saying they would push her around in her portable wheelchair. Of course they didn't mean it, since they wobbled on their rope-soled, open-toed wedges.

Miss Lillian demurred, and called for Sunny to help her onto the scooter so she could see her guests out. After the door was closed behind them, Sunny said, "I could have taken you shopping with them."

"I've had enough shopping this week," Miss Lillian said. "It doesn't entertain me anymore. What I want money can't buy." She looked pointedly toward the oil portrait of Julie that hung over the parlor fireplace. This one featured Julie in riding togs, holding her helmet, her white-blazed chestnut horse in the background.

Miss Lillian kept her eyes on the portrait. "There's a shelf full of trophies and ribbons downstairs in the game room. That horse almost killed her once, but it didn't stop her riding. Broke her wrist, ended her tennis playing, and she was good at that too. The doctor said if that wrist hadn't broken her fall, she might've landed on her neck and been paralyzed like Christopher Reeve." Lillian paused. "She rode a horse on the island. Neil still has it."

"Well," said Sunny, unsettled by the mention of Neil. "I went to get the mail while you were having lunch. Would you like to see it?"

"I need a nap," Miss Lillian said. "And I'm sure I've given you plenty to do. Talk to Harris about the party."

Sunny made party-related phone calls, putting off calling Neil until last. He didn't answer. It gave her a funny flipping sensation to listen to the phone ring and ring, to hear his recorded voice on the other end in a flat tone, like a robot. She wondered if all the joy of living had been knocked out of him by Julie's death.

She had to quit thinking about him. Not only was he all wrong for her, there was no way on earth she could compete with that perfect, beautiful, talented, accomplished, *dead* horsewoman on the wall, who would never again do anything wrong.

She finished her chores, then she took the pile of mail upstairs and laid it on Miss Lillian's desk, not allowing herself to shuffle through it. If there was a letter from Neil, she couldn't bear waiting. Better not to know.

Miss Lillian was sound asleep, so Sunny tiptoed back downstairs and drew out the album with the pictures of the cousins. She slipped her finger carefully under the photograph and slid it out from the corners. There were no names written on the back.

Harris, who had apparently joined the Library Police, chose to come in with a dust cloth and bottle of lemon oil. "Miss Iles, *what* are you doing with that picture?"

She decided to level with him in hopes of getting information. "I'm trying to find out what Weezie looked like," she said, "since I'm supposed to be her daughter."

"I suggest you replace the photograph. Miss Lillian is very particular about her albums."

"Well, can you tell me anything?" Sunny slid the photo back into its corners.

Harris stood back and looked at her. "I don't approve of this deception," he said, frowning at her clumsy efforts with the photo album, "but it's not my place to disagree. Miss Weezie was a redhead." He walked over to a framed group picture and pointed a finger at a girl who looked about twelve, with pudgy cheeks, squinting at the sun. "This is Miss Louisa Alexander." He stopped to consider. "That person she married might have been fair, but I don't recall what he looked like then. He was balding and bearded by the time he became famous."

Sunny thought about the wonderful paintings she'd seen in the island book on the coffee table. "What did he paint?"

Harris's eyebrows shot toward the ceiling. "You never learned about Roussel?"

Sunny huffed with exasperation. "Of course not. I grew up with Velvet Elvis and Blond Jesus on the wall. With little children like Dick and Jane."

"Hmf. Speaking of Jesus. It was quite scandalous, that painting that gave him his fifteen minutes of fame," Harris said. "You just can't portray Jesus and the Magdalene like that. Roussel was denounced from many pulpits."

"Like what?" Sunny asked. She hadn't been to Sunday School very much as a kid, because her mama was usually sleeping off Saturday night, and she didn't have any good clothes like the other girls, who wore flowered cotton dresses and bows in their hair.

"Use your imagination. I'll return to my dusting." Harris removed a golf trophy, sprayed the side table on which it rested with lemon oil, and wiped the mahogany down.

"Where is Weezie now?" Sunny asked.

"I can't help you there," Harris said.

"But you hear things, right? Do you know whether she's dead or alive?"

"I don't think she'll bother you in either case," Harris said. "Nobody has heard from her in sixteen years."

CHAPTER SIXTEEN

Neil watched Harlan's boat pull away from the dock after Orrie's visit, torn with frustration and guilt. Maybe Orrie would hate him now. She wouldn't come back any time soon. He felt that he'd been a brute, but he'd been cornered. If only yesterday could have ended the way it started out—in a friendly way, as fellow sailors. It felt good to have her with him on the boat, and she'd looked—what was the word Lillian liked to use—*fetching* in her orange bikini top and khaki shorts, the wind whipping her hair. She hadn't lost her touch for sailing. She was almost as good a sailor as Julie had been. And her observations were just as keen.

She'd made the sandwiches for lunch—ham for him, cheese and tomato for her—and then she'd gone out birding with her camera and scopes, while he'd worked at the nature center on a program for the group of Boy Scouts due to arrive the following week. Things started going downhill at suppertime, just about the time he'd poured the second glass of wine.

He was just congratulating himself that she'd liked his shrimp and rice dish when she said, "Neil?" He tensed at the rumble of freight in that question. Orrie smiled and tilted her head. "I'm getting tired of teaching. I'm thinking of free-lancing. I've got a good resume now, lots of editorial contacts, and I think I could make a go of it."

He hoped he was wrong about where she was going with this. "Take a little advice. It's hard on your own." He shied away from her hazel-eyed gaze. "You might need that cushion. And the health insurance."

She shrugged. "I'm in great shape. I don't have expensive shopping habits. And I like good, plain, cooking—just like this." She touched her fork to her plate and smiled. Fetchingly. He noticed the cleavage above her aqua tank top, and the way her face glowed with a little sunburn on her nose, her wide mouth touched with gloss.

But good plain cooking? Ha. "What about the baby portobellos and arugula you used to love?"

She didn't blush or smile, as he might have expected her to. Instead she waved a hand. "Oh, you know, with a little creative gardening and a cookbook? Maybe I'm ready to settle down."

"No kidding," he said. He smiled, but she didn't smile back. Holy hell. She was serious.

She leaned forward. "Did I surprise you? Is it so unusual that I might want the picket fence, the sunflowers, the tomatoes, all that? Maybe even a frog-legged kid?"

"No, not so surprising," he said carefully, spearing his last shrimp, trying to pick a path through the minefield. "Most women do like all that. But they don't like being isolated from so-called civilization."

"You're not isolated if you're with the one you love."

He drained his wine. "You have a point, Orrie. Let's continue this discussion over dessert on the porch. Right now, I need to check on the horses, because I'm beat and might forget if I leave it too long."

He pasted on an insincere grin, feeling guilty as hell. He'd already tended the horses, but he needed to get away, let her simmer down. He said, "How about bringing the wine out and some of those paleo cookies you brought? The date and coconut?"

Her face was a map of mixed emotions: pleasure that he wanted the cookies, anxiety that he was avoiding the issue. Still, he walked away alone.

The breeze, the moon, the cicadas, the frogs, the drifting fragrance of the honeysuckle—all should have made a magical evening if it had been Sunny instead of Orrie as they rocked on the porch in the weathered chairs. With Oriana there was this unspoken Thing between them, and so they drank their wine and ate the cookies and talked about the birds she had photographed, and he told her about Blackjack the crow eating the poisoned figs. She frowned when he mentioned Sunny, so to keep her sweet he segued into telling her that the crow was all right but recuperating down at Esther's cottage on the other end of the island, as she had some special herbs to give the thieving creature. He hadn't even had to take Blackjack to the mainland for the vet. In fact, he wasn't even sure Doc Smithers treated birds.

He realized he was blathering. She rocked, listening, biding her time, and when the glasses were empty and the cookies were gone, he knew he had to say something. He knew what she was offering. He suspected he was going to lose a friend.

A year earlier, to stave off loneliness, he'd asked her to come live here, but she refused. She told him he was too isolated, and that he wasn't ready. Was he ready now? Now that he'd met Sunny? After just one kiss—though to be frank it was really more than a kiss—could Sunny have made that much of a difference? She was all wrong for him. Maybe it was *because* she was all wrong for him that he liked Lillian's cousin, or whoever she was.

He rose abruptly from his chair. "As I said, Orrie, I'm beat. I'm turning in. Would you lock the front door if you're going to sit up a while longer? We don't want any critters coming in."

She didn't move a muscle, but stared out at the stars. "I think I'll stay out a few more minutes. Not long. The mosquitoes are ferocious."

He heard the front door click shut from his room and felt rather than heard her presence in the house. When he finally lay on top of the sheets, the ceiling fan turning lazily, the window open to the night and the breeze, he heard water running in the other bathroom. He took up his Carl Hiassen paperback and read while she stirred in her room, unzipping a case. She was probably undressing—what had she usually worn to bed? A tank top and shorts? He laid the book aside, wishing that it was Sunny across the hall undressing. What he wouldn't give to see Sunny naked.

Thump! A startled Neil looked up and found Rambo perched on the window ledge. The cat waited while Neil got up and unhooked the screen. Outside, the sweetness of flowering tobacco filled the air, while a full moon lit the sky and swamp frogs trilled in top voice. The lion-like cat leaped in and settled in the chair opposite Neil's bed, tucking in his paws, as though to watch and make sure his human didn't get into trouble.

After a time, Rambo was snoring and Neil was trying to erase the image of Sunny from his mind so he could sleep. And then the hinge on his door squealed, ever so softly.

Her scent reached him as she hesitated. She sucked in a breath, took a step forward, and then she was slipping into bed with him, hands traveling over his broad back, along his biceps. Hands stroked his back, smoothed his butt, reached around, and by this time he was stirring and breathing harder and her hands were stroking him, cupping him, and his brain got disconnected from whatever he had been thinking, now unimportant in the grip of this deliciousness. He shifted around to face her.

"Neil," she whispered, "you wanted me to come to you, didn't you—I'm sorry about last year—really I am—I've missed you so—"

His voice was thick. "Maybe we shouldn't be doing this."

"Of course we should," she said, and lowered herself and licked his stomach, making a snail-track on his belly. At that moment he knew the train had left the station. And damn it, Rambo slept on.

Harlan's boat had disappeared, and a blue heron flapped up from the reeds, a shining fish in its mouth. Neil walked back to the cabin carrying the mail Harlan had brought, trying not to remember the rest of the night. Just stop right there, freeze frame. Nope.

Afterwards, he'd been lying there looking up at the ceiling, wondering what to say to her. She was never talky, the way Julie had been. So, he thanked her.

She pulled away. "You *thank me*? You *thank* me?"

He felt a blush rise to his face as it did that night. "Well, I—I don't have anything else to offer."

Her voice was clipped, hurt. "I didn't do it to *get* something, Neil. I wanted you."

He felt stupid, like somebody in a Woody Allen movie.

She crept out of his bed and he heard her footsteps across the hall and the water running in the bathroom, and then she was getting back into bed. He heard the bedstead thump.

And then he had to pee so he got up and did that, noting the moon had gone way up in the sky. He got back into bed and this time he slept. Now, the morning after, his head was bad with too much wine and remembering.

Her last words before she got in the boat were, "Who is she, Neil? Who was I last night?"

He shook his head slowly and kissed Orrie's cheek. She had turned away and stepped into the boat without looking back.

He flopped the mail onto the hall table and shuffled through it, discarding the junk mail and catalogs, setting the bills aside. Here was a letter from Lillian—probably with party details. Maybe one of these days he'd get a computer, because Angus had taken their laptop off to school. The boy always complained about having to write an actual letter instead of sending email. When he could get a phone signal, sometimes they would text, but Neil encouraged writing.

He picked up a letter in an unfamiliar feminine hand, from Asheville, North Carolina, addressed to Julie. Who was in Asheville that didn't know Julie had been dead these five years?

He slit the envelope with a cuttlefish bone and unfolded the two sheets of letter paper. Airy writing, blue ink. He'd have to write the person—maybe an old college friend—and tell her what had happened to Julie. Writing those letters was a task he always dreaded.

> *Dear Julie,* he read,
>
> *Here's a voice from out of the past, I know. I'm writing to you instead of your mother because she'd think I was looking for a handout, and everybody asks Lillian for money. But the truth is that I'm looking for a loan, or maybe an investment, and I'm asking if you'll speak to her before I do, maybe prepare the way a little.*
>
> *I've moved my studio here from California. I'm enjoying a modest success for an old lady, and many of my clients are in the East now. The problem is that I have a wonderful conception that I know will sell to some lucky collector, but I need a huge chunk of marble. Unfortunately I'm tapped out at the bank, and I'm having trouble getting a grant because of my age. They like to give them to bright young things that will surely live to produce the*

work. I don't want to let this concept go to waste, but if I can't buy the marble, that's that. Julie, you always were my favorite niece—or cousin, to be accurate. If you can see fit to help your old auntie, all I need is $5,000, which is chump change for Lil. I'll even carve her name on it somewhere, and of course I'll pay her back when it sells.

I do miss you especially, and Lil, and wish I could see you all once more before I become One with the Universe. How does a black sheep come back home? Of course, my dear Paul—did you know about Paul?—he saved my life after Freddy—but anyhow he's passed on now, and I haven't exactly been easy to reach. How are Lillian and Duncan? And your brother? And Cathy? Or did the last thing I hear about the family was that they were getting a divorce? So sad with those girls so little.

Enough about that. Hoping to hear from you soon. I can send you or Lillian photos of my sold pieces.

Love to all,

Weezie

Weezie? Who the hell was Weezie? Wait a minute, wasn't she the one who was supposed to be Sunny's mother? Lillian's first cousin who'd run off with the artist to California and gotten disinherited? When had he ever seen her? Now it came back to him. Years ago, when he'd married Julie, she had come to the wedding. Yep. She was fifty-something then, he thought. She was the one who wore the flowing thing and a big straw hat. She didn't bring any daughter that he recalled. But then he didn't remember much about that day. It had been one big blur.

Neil dove into the pile of photo albums on the bottom shelf of the bookcase and pulled out the white one, the one with the wedding pictures. He flipped through them rapidly—funny how it didn't sting as much to see them now as it had two years earlier. He stopped flipping when he saw her standing with Julie.

Weezie. Suntanned and wrinkly, with long, curly red hair turning gray, wearing a long print skirt of Indian cotton and some sort of folk top and beads, red lipstick, and that straw hat. She had smelled of tobacco smoke. She'd given the impression of being an old soul, a wise woman, and he could tell she'd been a real looker when she was younger. She had good bones.

He found it hard to believe that Sunny was her daughter. Sunny didn't seem artsy in the least; in fact, just the opposite. Of course, that could be rebellion, not wanting to be like her mother.

Perhaps he ought to mention Sunny in his letter to Weezie, and see what she said in reply.

He hoped Sunny was telling the truth. He hoped that she really *was* Weezie's daughter, because he hated the thought that she was some kind of imposter. But really, she'd never get anything past Lil, unless—unless Lil really was demented, like Alex and Kiki were saying.

And Lillian wasn't demented. Not by a long shot. This was getting interesting.

He laid the letter on his desk, then opened the letter from Angus. The kid was asking for money, too, saying how hard he was studying for final exams, and he just needed a little more to last him till the end of term and to get home. Neil laughed. He'd send him a little, not too much. Did Angus expect his dad to forget that the airplane ticket home was already bought and paid for? All the boy needed to do was get his clothes packed, and Neil had paid the school for the shipping charge.

He took up the letter from Lillian. Well, she wasn't asking for money, just sending him a list of the people she was inviting to her birthday party: Wesley Blackshear, his daughter India, Alex and Kiki and the girls, Sunny, and Harris if she could persuade him to drive them down and stay. And, she asked, Angus would be home, wouldn't he? She wanted Sunny to bring her teenage daughter, and the more teenagers, the merrier. Alex's two daughters had howled that they "had other plans" but she was going to work on them. She wanted *all* her family there to celebrate. Not every day you had your Diamond Jubilee plus Four. And then, she asked of him a rather peculiar favor.

He read the request carefully. He'd do it, but first, he needed to open up the Big House. Sinclair Walker, Esther's son, and his wife Naomi were the caretakers, and he'd ask them to air and freshen it. The dorm had already been cleaned for the Boy Scouts, and would need just a tidying and change of sheets after Lillian's party left. The main thing now was to see if he could do what Lillian had asked him, which was to convince Esther to take back her spell, or whatever she had said to Harris. Then, maybe, Harris would forgive her.

He walked out to the Jeep and then changed his mind about driving. He'd ride Shalimar over to Turtle Point. Esther liked the little mare, and the horse needed exercise. He changed direction and walked to the stable, and found Rambo snoozing with Archie.

At that moment Reggie appeared at the stable door. "Can I let Blackjack out of his cage today? He seems powerful ready."

"I guess it's time. Hope he's learned his lesson about stealing food."

Reggie shook his head and scampered off. Neil lifted Shal's bridle off its peg in the tack room, thinking about Weezie. It was going to be a blow to the poor woman to find out Julie was dead and Doctor Duncan, too. He'd gladly loan her the five thou if he had it, but the only money he could call his own was his salary as island keeper. The trust doled out money for the upkeep of the island, and the money Julie had left him was almost gone, spent on things for the island he didn't like to requisition from the trust. Asking the trust meant going through Alex, and then there would be questions he didn't like. Angus had inherited Julie's share of her father's estate, but it was in trust until he turned thirty, with allowances made for his education.

Neil had an interesting dilemma. Should he approach Lillian for Weezie's benefit or not? Weezie hadn't asked him to, but he felt Julie would have done it. Yes, he'd do it for Julie, and for another reason. When he wrote Weezie to tell her about Julie's death, and to assure her he'd pass on her request to Lillian for money, he'd tell Weezie that he'd met her daughter.

CHAPTER SEVENTEEN

M iss Lillian's victory was temporary. She'd managed to avoid
Kiki with the shopping trip, but she couldn't avoid the
luncheon to which Harris was driving her, the luncheon in Kiki's
own Buckhead spider web, the mansion in which she presided.

Sunny rode along with them at Miss Lillian's request, thinking
about Miss Lillian's remark about Kiki's not being able to poison
her with so many guests. When Harris pulled the Lexus up to the
spanking new pile of honey-colored stone and stucco, complete
with state-of-the-art landscaping, Sunny leaped out and opened
Miss Lillian's door. "Are you sure you don't need me to come with
you?"

"Certainly not," Miss Lillian replied. "I can negotiate a luncheon
by myself, as you well know." Harris came around with the folding

wheelchair, gave it to Sunny, and then helped Miss Lillian out of the car.

Miss Lillian, in full dignified-lady mode, allowed Harris to walk shotgun beside her as she made her way up the paving stones on her crutches. Sunny bumped the chair behind them, stopping at the imposing front door with its flanking corkscrew topiaries.

The flower beds in front were lush with blooms, and Sunny marveled at the display of irises and a white starry plant that might be the Star of Bethlehem Kiki had talked about. Yes, Kiki did like her gardens. She probably couldn't wait to get her hands on Miss Lillian's. Unfolding the chair and securing it, Sunny itched to go inside with Miss Lillian, not only to protect her, but to see how the Dragon Lady lived. When she had settled Miss Lillian in the chair, Sunny murmured, "Couldn't I just stand at the back and watch? What if—"

"Nonsense," Miss Lillian interrupted. "Kiki would have a fit. Anyhow, she wouldn't dare do anything to me in her own home, with all those witnesses present. You'd be bored out of your skull. Kiki with a cause? She belongs to the Ebenezer Scrooge school of philanthropy."

"Miss Lillian, then why are you going to this luncheon?"

"I didn't want to. But Alex asked, almost begged me to come. Said it was important to him that I show my support for her. I like to fan any little ember I see for good works, anyhow. Just for my son, however wrong he might be at times, I decided to say yes. Anyhow, some of my friends are coming. "

Sunny shook her head. "I hope everything turns out all right."

"Poof. Don't worry about me. Both of you. The worst thing she could do to me is serve frozen fruit salad. I'm glad it's out of style, because I detest the stuff. It looks and tastes like Pepto-Bismol."

They rang the bell. Kiki, trim and businesslike in a dark suit accented by a silky red blouse and artistic gold pin, opened the door, her bright red mouth in a smile as wide as a spokesmodel's.

"Mother Lillian, you're here at last!" Kiki air-kissed her cheek and wrested the handles of the chair away from a startled Sunny. Kiki then rolled Miss Lillian away without giving Sunny and Harris a second look. The ponderous door swung shut. Sunny looked at Harris. "Why don't you ride in the front seat, Miss Iles," he said, not returning her questioning glance. He sounded almost friendly. She hesitated, and then got in. To refuse would have been unthinkable.

As he drove away, not turning his head, he said, "Miss Lillian is up to something. Please tell me what it is."

Sunny froze. "Mr. Harris," she said, "I need to be sure you're loyal."

"I've been with this family since I was just a lad." His voice quivered, indignant. "You're the one I ought to question, coming out of nowhere with a chip on your shoulder."

How could he tell? "Touché," she said. "All right. I think I'd better tell you what Miss Lillian is planning."

Harris drove steadily toward home while she outlined Miss Lillian's idea to somehow catch Kiki in the act of attempted murder while they were all at her birthday party. "She wants to get out in a boat with Kiki," she said. "She thinks Kiki will manage to somehow push her overboard, thinking Miss Lillian will be slowed down by her cast. We'll have Neil lurking out of sight somewhere, ready to go out and get her on a raft, or his fishing boat if he can hide it somewhere. I hate the idea, but Miss Lillian wants me to video the whole thing with a phone. She's already ordered a new one just for me to use."

"Surely she doesn't really intend to carry out such a plan. It's insane," Harris spluttered. He rounded the next two corners and turned into the steep driveway of Stonehaven, mounting the hill and pulling around to the back. When he killed the engine, he sat silent for a moment. Then he said, "First she needs to come home from this luncheon."

Sunny stared at him. "Why, Harris, do you really think Kiki would try anything in her own house, with all those people there?" Then she clapped her hand to her mouth. "Oh, my gosh. Now I'm believing it, too."

Harris looked at her with a tiny, amused smile. "You doubted Miss Lillian, did you? Well, I have seen a lot, and I would believe anything of Miss Kiki. I noticed her scheming to attract Mr. Alex before the divorce." Sunny started to speak, but he raised his eyebrows. "The help are invisible, you know?" He harrumphed. "I think the Victorians were so proper because they had to put on a good front for the servants. But they didn't fool anybody."

Harris collected the day's mail from the box, informed Sunny her lunch was in the kitchen under a tea towel, and then retired to his private quarters above the garage to have his own tiffin.

Sunny eyed the mail in the basket by the telephone while she washed her hands and dried them. Then she quickly pulled out the letters and shuffled through them.

Junk mail, bills, and charity appeals. A creamy oversized envelope addressed in calligraphy, which must certainly be an invitation. A small handwritten envelope with faint violets scattered across the paper, perhaps a thank-you note. Finally, the one she'd been hoping for—an envelope with the logo of Issatee Island in the corner, addressed to Miss Lillian in Neil's rough scrawl. She couldn't suppress her quickened heartbeat and tingling belly. Had one kiss done all that?

She shook her head. She was hopeless when it came to men. Why should now be any different?

She laid the mail back in the basket. Under the tea towel, she found a turkey and cheese sandwich, a portion of chips, and a quarter of a kosher pickle. She poured herself a glass of sweet tea and took the food to the garden. She sat on a white wrought-iron bench and enjoyed the breeze and the scent of the heavenly pink roses. Still, she'd be counting the minutes until Miss Lillian came home safe and sound.

No, she sighed, she'd be sorting the clothes.

Sunny hadn't wanted to enter the childhood room of Neil's late wife. Dim light leaked through closed venetian blinds, bathing the room in a soft gray calm and a still hush, as if no one had entered the room for years. A faint flowery scent lingered in the air, a scent of furniture wax and long-gone perfume.

She walked over to the tall windows, draped in blue and yellow flowered chintz, and opened the blinds. Sunlight flooded the room, turning motes into fairy dust. On the bedside table, in a silver frame, stood a snapshot of Julie and Neil on their wedding day, Julie laughing with her bouquet by her side, and Neil untangling her wedding veil where it had been caught by a live oak limb, a spark of sunlight dancing in the leaves.

Sunny's face burned. She turned abruptly away and strode over to the big walk-in closet. She slid open the pocket door.

There they were, the rest of Julie's clothes, taken from the island five years ago so Neil wouldn't have to deal with them. The closet was also filled with garments Julie had left behind when she moved to the island, some which went all the way back to her high school years.

Rods were jammed with tops and dresses, suits and skirts and pants. Cedar drawers held cashmere and woolen sweaters. In plastic and cardboard boxes Sunny uncovered cotton shorts and T-shirts.

Miss Lillian had instructed her to sort them into three piles: one for Sunny and Avery, one for the ragbag, and one for the Salvation Army. How envious Avery would be to see all these beautiful things, not that she'd want any. No, they'd be too much out of date for her, too preppy, too *old*. She could always use T-shirts, though. Sunny stacked several of the freshest and most stylish ones for her picky daughter.

How long would this task take? Sunny picked up a pretty crystal bedside clock and watched the second hand tick around. She still had more than an hour before Miss Lillian would call for her and Harris. She threw herself into the work, trying to forget that Miss Lillian might be in danger, and the piles of clothing steadily grew. When she found three prom dresses in a hanging bag, she immediately thought of Avery, upcoming proms at a new school, and their meager budget.

She was wrestling the dresses out of the bag when she heard the scream of an ambulance somewhere to the west, in the direction of Alex's house. Her heart gave a leap and her pulse pounded. Miss Lillian! Oh, it had to be Miss Lillian, something had happened after all! No, she told herself, this was the old-money section of town, and where you had old money, you had old people. Anything could happen—heart attack, stroke. She was fine.

She laid out three dresses: a golden satin, a maroon silk, and an innocent pale peach chiffon. They all would look gorgeous on Avery, and her daughter would say they were bor-ing. She'd just laid the peach chiffon on the bed when the phone in Miss Lillian's room shrilled. The dress slipped off the bed as she bolted for the door, but after another ring, the phone stopped. Harris has it, she told herself, heart hammering. He has everything under control. She picked up the dress, smoothed it, and laid it back on the bed.

She was deep in the closet, reaching for another hanging bag, when she thought she heard a car door slam. She hurried to the window. Harris was screeching out of the driveway, rounding the corner like . . . like her ex, Kyle. She clutched her throat. Why hadn't Harris called her to go with him? He knew she was a nurse, for heaven's sake!

She clattered down the stairs to the kitchen and stared at Harris's posted list of frequently-called numbers. His own cell phone wasn't listed, of course, and Miss Lillian didn't want one—she thought it was "inconvenient" to be always reachable.

Sunny found the number for Alex and Kiki, punched in the digits, and found the line going to voicemail. She tried again and again. She was fumbling with the telephone keypad to call the number listed for Blake and Ellery when Harris pulled up at the back door. Sunny saw Miss Lillian in the front seat, grim-faced.

Sunny plunged outside, raced to Miss Lillian's car door, and yanked it open. "Thank God you're all right! What happened?"

Miss Lillian looked directly at her. "She's tried it again."

"She what?" Dear Lord, please let this be dementia. Pretty please?

"Just get me a cup of tea. No, a cup of bourbon. I know I'm not supposed to have it, but it isn't every day someone tries to kill you for the third time."

Sitting ramrod-straight in a kitchen chair, Miss Lillian sipped her bourbon. "I had a narrow escape."

Sunny and Harris, hovering, waited for her to take another sip.

Kiki, she told them, had thought it would be "adorable" to have a traditional Southern ladies' luncheon menu: creamed chicken in patty shells, frozen fruit salad, petite yeast rolls, and lemon meringue pie. She'd arranged for individual portions of the frozen fruit salad to be served in fancy polka-dotted baking cups.

"My dears, that salad!" Miss Lillian said. "It was the last thing I'd expected from Kiki. She usually serves things like arugula and goat cheese and roasted beets. I was prepared for some sort of exotic poisonous mushroom on my plate."

The mistake Kiki made was in seating Miss Lillian beside her friend Bitsy. After all, Bitsy had tried every diet known to Dr. Oz or Dr. Phil and failed. Her love affairs were all with forms of sugar. And when Bitsy saw that Miss Lillian had pushed her dotty pink, sweet salad aside, she volunteered to keep it out of the Chattahoochee River. Miss Lillian was glad to pass it over.

After the luncheon plates were empty or nearly so, Kiki appeared at their table. "Did you ladies enjoy your lunch?" their hostess asked sweetly, then winked at Miss Lillian. "I hope you liked my frozen fruit salad. Alex said it was a favorite of yours."

"Did he now," murmured Miss Lillian. "How thoughtful." The boy had gotten it backwards, Miss Lillian surmised. He never listened.

Kiki made her way to another table while the pie and coffee were being served. Miss Lillian had taken only a few bites of the tasty lemon meringue when Bitsy shrieked with alarm, clapped her hand to her mouth, and raced for the bathroom. Another guest, who'd once been a Navy nurse, leaped up and followed her.

The EMTs were just loading Bitsy into the ambulance when Miss Lillian left with Harris, noting carefully the greenish shade Kiki had turned, clashing dreadfully with her outfit.

"I hope the police get into this," Miss Lillian said, draining the last of the bourbon from her glass. "My knees are still weak."

"But how can you be sure it was poison?" Sunny said.

"I can't. But don't you think Miss Kiki's quick-cycle dishwasher is chugging away by now? And that cupcake paper is probably flushed down the commode." Miss Lillian held out her glass for more, but Sunny shook her head.

"No more alcohol with your pain meds. Why don't you talk to your friend and tell her to get a blood or urine test? She could have been killed!"

Miss Lillian accepted Harris's offer of some sweet tea. "I know Bitsy. She'll tell me that it was a touch of stomach flu. You know what? She's a big woman, and she'd eaten a lot of food. Maybe that dose of poison, whatever it was, wouldn't kill her. It might have killed a little old lady like me."

"But maybe she really did have stomach flu," Sunny insisted. "Or something else. Does she have a heart condition? Allergies?"

"Whose side are you on, anyway?" Miss Lillian shook her head. "Bitsy takes three or four medications that I know of—Lipitor, all that—but the coincidence is just too great. She eats something meant for me and whap!" She clapped her hands together. "In any case, after that, nobody felt like discussing charity work and the party broke up. So Kiki didn't get to present her baby—the Foundation for Issatee Education." Miss Lillian waited to let this idea sink in.

Harris turned from the sink slowly. "She wants to start a school on the island? The county says there aren't enough kids. They send a ferry for them."

Miss Lillian shook her head. "A school wouldn't help her scheme. No, she wants a fund to send the island young people away to college. She says profits from the resort complex would finance that project long-term, but she wants to start sooner. "

Harris snorted, but Sunny raised a finger. "What's wrong with that? I've got a kid who'd love to have a college scholarship."

Miss Lillian sniffed. "It's not out of the goodness of her heart, dear. She obviously wants the population to become too educated to stay on Issatee, so it would be easier to buy up all their land."

"Yes, that makes sense," said Harris. "I left to see the world. I can't blame the young folks. But I hate to see a way of life disappearing. A culture, so to say. Sometimes I miss it. It's my heritage, after all."

"Let's get back to your friend Bitsy, Miss Lillian," Sunny broke in. "Please, won't you just talk to her?"

Miss Lillian made a sour face. "She's a chatterbox, and I don't want her to know what's going on here. I want to take care of this without a scandal." She sighed and asked for a phone. Sunny took the kitchen phone off the charger and handed it to her, then Miss Lillian punched in a number.

Sunny eyed the basket of mail longingly while Miss Lillian talked. The conversation went on, and on, and on. When Miss Lillian hung up, she turned and said, "Her husband says she's still at the hospital. They're going to run some tests to see if her heart has anything to do with this, and I can't see her today. Tomorrow morning I can visit. Burt is such a dear. He dotes on her, just like my Duncan did."

For a moment, Sunny thought that the departed Duncan had doted on Bitsy, and then realized what Miss Lillian meant. She picked up the mail before Miss Lillian began to reminisce about Duncan. "There are a few letters," Sunny offered.

Miss Lillian banged down her cane. "The mail? What is this obsession with the mail? Oh, if only Duncan were alive, I'd be at that hospital." She sighed. "Maybe I'd better wait and see what they come up with. I'm tired and my ankle is starting to throb. I'm going to lie down a bit. A pill, if you please, Sunny."

She planted her cane, tried to rise, and sank back down. Sunny scurried over to help her. "When we get you settled," she said, "I'll bring you the pain meds."

"If you're going to rest, Miss Lillian, I'll go for provisions," Harris said.

Miss Lillian waved her hands. "Yes, by all means, go. Sunny will look after me."

After Harris had driven away, Miss Lillian gave Sunny a contemplative eye. "Settle me on the chaise and bring me that mail, since you're so interested," she said. "And then go back to work on those clothes."

Sunny opened her mouth, and then closed it again. "Yes, ma'am."

Once again in Julie's old room with the dust motes and the wedding picture, Sunny threw herself into her task, trying to forget about the letter waiting from Neil.

In the last bag she pulled out the dress of her dreams. It must have been a vintage gown, an old one of Miss Lillian's—heavy silk satin, creamy, with a satin rose at the shoulder. The gown was so unbelievably gorgeous she ached to try it on. She shucked her polo shirt and chinos and slipped the beautiful thing over her head. It slithered down her body, hitting in all the right places. Maybe the diet had been working!

She carefully eased out of the satin creation, draped it on the bed, and sighed. It wasn't fair that it fit her so perfectly. She had no place to wear such splendor. Nobody would be taking her to any more balls.

At the end of an hour she'd finished sorting, winding up with a good suit and some skirts and sweaters for herself, a couple of prom dresses for Avery's inspection, and five bags for charity. Only a few things were worn-out enough for the ragbag or trash, mostly work and exercise clothes. And swimsuits.

She hauled the charity bags downstairs and stashed them in the mudroom, and then she found the Salvation Army number. She and a nice woman were working out a pickup date when Harris appeared at the back door laden with brown paper tote bags.

Sunny finished her phone call and then helped him put away corn, beans, okra, tomatoes, and squash. He seemed friendlier toward her now.

"I'm glad you came, Miss Iles," he said, nodding toward the bags in the mudroom. "She hasn't wanted to deal with that task until now."

"It makes me feel funny," Sunny confessed, "wearing Julie's clothes, even though I appreciate them. And it's odd trying to be a member of the family. I don't suppose you have anything else to tell me about Weezie, who's supposed to be my mother?"

Harris just looked at her. "You're very curious."

"I have a reason for asking, Mr. Harris. I think Neil is a little suspicious that I'm an imposter. Not to mention the senator."

Harris smiled and shook his head. "Ah, that Miss Weezie. It's not my place to talk about her. You'd best ask Miss Lillian."

"She always changes the subject," Sunny moaned.

"Well," Harris began, but was interrupted by the bell from upstairs. He nodded. "She wants you, and I'll bet she wants a glass of bourbon," he said, grinning his Uncle Ben's-evil-twin grin. "Take her some tea, ask her about Weezie, and good luck."

Miss Lillian's room, located on the shady side of the house, was comfortably cool, and she was still lying on her chaise with an afghan over her knees, unopened mail piled on the side table. She smiled at Sunny and gestured behind her, toward the window. "I've just had a delicious nap, and now I think I'd like a swim. Help me into my suit, please."

Sunny froze in her tracks, thinking about the gruesome workout Flip had put her through the day before. Would she ever get good at swimming?

She picked the letters off the side table, set the tea on a coaster, and then looked longingly at the mail before she placed it neatly on the desk. When she turned back, Miss Lillian had one eyebrow raised.

"All, right, Sunny, is there a letter I need to see?"

Sunny felt her cheeks burn, then pretended to find a bit of lint on the floor, bending down to hide the red flush. "Well, I happened to notice there was a letter from Issatee, and since the visit's coming up . . ."

"Oh, ho," Miss Lillian said. "Hand it here, along with any personal letters. Toss the brochures for retirement homes that Alex keeps sending me. And let me have that silver thing, if you will."

Sunny passed Miss Lillian the creamy invitation, the violet–strewn note card, and the antique letter opener, and then, finally, the letter from Neil. Laying aside the last, Miss Lillian gleefully slit the invitation and drew out the card. She stared at it thoughtfully. "Well, well. It's an invitation to be a benefactor for the Hospital Ball. That brings back memories. I've never missed one yet. Last year I went with Wesley, since Mary Lynn insisted. She's a dear friend, and I hate it that she's confined to the house. She'd enjoy it this year, because Sydney Fairfield is quite the organizer. Too bad she's a friend of Kiki's. In fact, I saw her at the luncheon."

Sunny felt her stomach drop. Sydney, the woman who'd stolen Troy Bentley from her! At that luncheon! Why, oh why, did she still care? Just thinking of that man still made her blood boil. She couldn't wait to be hundreds of miles from him.

Miss Lillian tapped the thick ivory card on her knuckles. "I'll be able to dance by then, won't I? It's in September. But I'd better take a bodyguard. Kiki might arrange to have me pitched me off the balcony of the Driving Club."

Sunny opened her mouth to speak, but the words stuck in her throat.

Thank God she'd be long gone by then.

Miss Lillian reached for the smaller envelope, slit it, and read it without comment, then put it aside. At last she picked up the letter from Neil.

CHAPTER EIGHTEEN

Neil figured Lillian had gotten his last letter by now. He'd follow that one up with a letter telling her that he'd heard from Weezie and make the case for her cousin's plea for enough money for a chunk of marble. But he had another letter to write first.

> *Dear Weezie,* Neil wrote on his ancient Smith-Corona,
>
> *It's hard for me to say this. Duncan died three years ago. I was pallbearer at the funeral. It's stupid that no one let you know. Maybe Lillian was too distraught to think about it, and Julie—well, she wasn't here to write to you. She drowned here on the island five years ago. Every time I see the light at the end of the tunnel—or is it my cave—*

depression drags me back in. Losing Julie here in Paradise seems like a bad joke on God's part. So I keep to myself.

What puzzles me is that you and your daughter aren't communicating. That is, if Sunny Iles, Lillian's assistant, really is your daughter. Lillian's still as feisty as ever, but her memory might be slipping and she broke her ankle in a fall.

If there's some kind of family issue and you're not speaking to Sunny, let me know. I'm worried that she's not who she says she is. She says she was christened Sunshine and her father was Freddy Roussel. I'd hate to think she's out to scam Lillian into giving her money. I'd thought Lillian had more sense than that, but you never know.

They're all coming down for Lillian's birthday, Alex and Kiki as well. His girls are out of control, I'm afraid. Cathy couldn't fight for them in the divorce because she had PTSD. She was all happy in her tidy little world, thinking she had the perfect life, and when Alex told her he wanted to marry someone else, it knocked her down like a Texas tornado. Therapy worked for a while, and then she turned to religion, and she's now studying for the ministry. The girls have gone to drug rehab once, and may have to go back. I don't see much of them.

I'd like to see some of your sculpture. I want to help you, if I can. Send me some photos through the mail. I'm not exactly a Luddite, but this island is somewhat off the grid. I'll speak to Lillian for you, and maybe I'll trek off the island to come visit you. Heck, why not come to the party? It'll be on June 15. There's room for you in the Big House, of course, but you'll have to share the old place with Alex and Kiki.

> *Best of luck,*
> *Neil*

When he finished, he stamped the letter and got in his Jeep to go down to Turtle Point and see if he could find somebody who was going to the mainland today. He'd see Esther, too. He hoped Esther was in a better mood than the day before. When he'd told her that Lillian hoped Esther and her brother would bury their differences, she just muttered something. Well, at least she didn't say flat-out "no."

Bouncing along the rutty track, flanked by dark-green, swaying palms against bold whitewashes of sunlit sky, Neil was glad of the hushed quiet of the forest. He listened for the bellow of gators, but heard only the chirr and hum of insects. The turtles were now on their way to South America after laying their eggs, eggs that resembled ping-pong balls. Next month, the babies would hatch, and Neil would see to it that as many as possible escaped the raccoons, wild hogs, and gators to make it back into the ocean.

At Turtle Point, people were going about their daily chores—sweeping a porch, weeding a garden, pegging out washing. The island mechanic's house was surrounded by old cars, and the little general store was open today, selling tobacco and flour and salt, notions and oil and beer. Two fishing boats prowled out on the metallic sea, searching for the haul that had been their main livelihood for over a hundred years.

Neil noted with pride the solar panels on the roofs, obtained with a grant they'd applied for. He and Esther had worked hard, and Senator Blackshear had helped.

At Esther's house, people were sitting on her steps and in her porch swing and chair, waiting to see her and get herbs. They greeted Neil, asked how he was doing, and watched with interest when he stuck his head in Esther's door. "Hey, Esther, got a minute? I want to ask you something."

"Here you back again?" Esther grumbled from within. "You got nothing better to do than worry me?"

Neil waited on the porch, knowing that was Esther's way of greeting him. After a time, the door opened and one of Esther's visitors came out. Esther, right behind her, dusted her hands and said to the thin young woman, "You be sure and do what I tell you, and this time next year, you'll be asking me for something to bring on the birth." She turned to Neil, lilting, "I am at your service. Provided you come in and sit a spell."

He followed her inside. Esther's front room was painted blue, a background for colorful quilts on the walls and crocheted doilies atop the sturdy wooden furniture. Wonderful smells drifted from the pots of dried herbs on the shelves of a painted yellow hutch.

Esther motioned him to a rocker and sat back in her faded red easy chair. He relaxed, looking forward to a companionable chat.

Esther fixed him with her canny gaze. "That woman is not good for you," she said.

Neil sat up abruptly. "What woman?" Did she somehow know how he felt about Sunny? A guilty warmth crept up his neck.

Esther leaned back, a slow, satisfied smile on her face. "The tall one. The one who sailed with you. Look at me, Cornelius. Give me your hand." She leaned forward, took his calloused hand in her beringed brown one, and studied it. She looked deeply into his eyes, and then ran her fingers lightly over his face. "But there is someone. I feel it. It cannot be her, the one in your boat."

Was she practicing the root on him? "No. It's not Oriana. But—"

Esther shook her head. "But, you say? But what?"

"The woman you think. It's impossible." Neil felt sweat running down his sides, though a cool breeze was rippling through the house, stirring the curtains.

A knock came at the door, and Esther called out, "Wait a bit, sister. I'm still talking to this fool." She turned back to Neil. "Didn't you read your Bible? All things are possible to them who love the Lord."

"I knew there was a catch," Neil said, shifting in his seat. Esther had been trying to drag him to church for years. He hadn't been inside one since Julie's funeral. He looked at her squarely. Fool, was he? "Esther. I promise I'll think about church, but I need help now. Lillian's coming for her birthday celebration. If Keziah's around, or

Barnabas, I'd like to hire them to help me get ready. I've already talked to Sinclair and Naomi about sprucing up the Big House."

Esther gave him a half-smile. "The young folks gone on the school ferry today."

"I thought those two graduated." Neil raised his eyebrows and glanced out the front window as if they might be in the yard.

"They started in the community college," she said. "You don't 'spect they're going to be fisher folk, do you? Kizzy want to go to pharmacy school. Break my heart. Old remedies not good enough for her. Barney, he say he gone stay here, but want to study fish and stuff like you." She paused and looked at him sideways. *If you'd come to see us more*, Esther meant, *you'd know all that.*

Neil caught the meaning and scratched his head. "Sorry I haven't been around more." It was amazing how much you missed by going inside yourself. Julie had been the one who'd come to visit, listened to the islanders' tales, shared their joys and sorrows, their ambitions and disappointments. And since she'd died—

"You ha'n't been listening to me," Esther said indignantly. "Want me to just leave you to your misery?"

Neil felt his face warming. "I'm sorry, Esther," he said. "I was just thinking about—"

"I know," Esther said. She got up, reached up to a tall shelf, and pulled down a jar. She measured some of the powder out onto a square of waxed paper and twisted it up. She settled it into his hand. "You take some of this once a day," she said. "Twice if you need it. Now git going." She paused and knitted her brows. "That uppity brother of mine coming?"

"I honestly don't know, Esther."

"Humph." She took his arm and walked him to the door, where Corinne Laplante was waiting in a wooden chair. She beckoned to Corinne. "Come on in, sister."

Neil knew he was dismissed, but here was an opportunity. "Corinne, could I order one of your banana cakes? There's a party in two weeks."

"Sure 'nough," she said. "How about a lemon cheese too?"

"Sold," Neil said. "I'll send Angus over to pick them up. I'll be in touch."

He asked around the village until he found that someone would be going over to the mainland the next day, entrusted his letter, and took his leave.

He walked over to where he'd tied his horse on the old hitching rail, wondering who else might be able to help him. Maybe Corinne's niece? He had just mounted Shalimar when Esther opened her screen. "I'll send them kids over this evening."

He grinned. At least he'd gotten a few things done. On the way back he spotted a fat alligator waddling toward the ditch. He smelled something dead in the grass. He hoped it was a pig.

Miss Lillian was resting after her swim. Sunny wrinkled her nose at the chlorine smell that wouldn't go away from her own skin and quietly walked downstairs to see if a cut lemon from the refrigerator would help. She found the lemon quarter, applied it, and dried herself with a paper towel. Then she made her way to the library.

She took out the scrapbook with the beach picture and flipped more pages. She found a later beach photo, a faded color picture.

She winkled it gently out of the corners, and her heart leapt at the handwriting on the back. She studied it carefully. Lillian, Zoe, Geneva, Jean, Louisa: 1958, Issatee.

Louisa. Was that Weezie?

On the late Doctor Duncan's desk she found a magnificent horn-handled magnifying glass, and used it to inspect the picture. Despite the muted colors, she could tell Weezie had red hair. She, Sunny was blond, more or less. And Freddy Roussel was probably black-haired, with her luck. Ha ha. Back at the trailer park there had been a redhead named Clarice who bleached her hair, and Sunny never could figure out why, unless the name Clarice didn't to go with red hair. Maybe it would have been less trouble to change her name. Ginger, maybe, or even Norma.

She put the picture back and scanned the scrapbook carefully, but didn't find any more pictures of Weezie among the movie tickets and matchbook covers and sales tickets for souvenirs. Until the next-to-last page, where the image of Miss Lillian and her cousin had been captured in a new Buick convertible: Weezie looking straight at the camera, grinning with a wide lipsticked mouth, curly hair tied with a polka-dotted scarf, gesturing with a long cigarette holder. She looked like trouble with a capital T. This was supposed to be Sunny's mother? Well. At least the Trouble part was familiar.

She heard footsteps in the hall and turned to see Harris, trundling a canister Electrolux behind him. He leaned in the door and gave her an arch grin. "Snooping again, Miss Iles? Don't you have anything to keep you busy?"

She cleared her throat and closed the album. "I was just looking for more pictures of Weezie. I found them. Now all I need is a book that will teach me what I need to know to pass as Weezie's daughter. Emily Post or something."

"I don't think Miss Weezie cared about etiquette," Harris sniffed. "A free spirit, she was. But if you'd like to know what they used to call 'genteel ways,' I'll help you. Come along to the dining room after I finish this hall carpet. I'll show you the correct way to set a table."

"But I won't have to set a table, will I?"

Harris raised one careful eyebrow. "All well brought up young ladies know their table settings so they can instruct their servants. Most people nowadays do not have an education in the domestic profession. You must know how to use silver correctly. I noticed you mixing your forks at the luncheon with the senator. "

Sunny flushed. If Harris had noticed, had the others? She felt defensive. "But Harris, no sane person needs more than one fork to eat a meal."

Harris shrugged. "With that attitude, you might as well be carrying a sign that says I AM A FRAUD."

"Fraud, am I, Mr. Harris?"

"If the nurse shoe fits, Miss Iles."

"It wasn't my idea to pose as her cousin!" Sunny protested.

"Do you want to learn to be a lady or don't you?" Harris lifted his eyebrows, daring her to say no.

She met Harris in the dining room after he'd vacuumed. Wearing a pair of cotton gloves, he took a linen place mat from a drawer and laid it on the polished mahogany table, and then opened the china cabinet. She couldn't believe people actually ate on that fancy china, with all those birds and flowers under the food, but apparently that was the norm at this house. He unlocked a drawer with a key from his big ring and began to lay out spoons, forks, and knives. Sunny counted nine pieces, and gave a yelp. "Why so many?"

Harris shrugged. "We don't have many formal dinners now," he said. "Not as we did when the Doctor was with us. Times are changing. Standards are not as they were in the day." He pointed to the outside fork. "When you are confronted with this array, you work your way in. Start with the fork farthest from the plate for the first course. "

Sunny remained quiet and listened while Harris explained, then, when he went to another cabinet for crystal glassware, she saw her chance to probe for more information. "You've been with the family a long time, haven't you, Mr. Harris?" she began.

He gave her a half-smile, setting fragile-looking crystal stemware in the one o'clock position. "Water, red wine, white wine. Later, I'd place the dessert wine."

Then he gave her a sideways glance. "Yes, I've worked for the family since I was just a lad. My mother cooked and I used to do odd jobs for them, and the doctor saw that I was very able. He offered to send me away to school if I'd come back to work for him." He smiled broadly. "After a while he had a fancy that he'd like a proper English butler, so off I went to England for training."

He tossed it off casually. Sunny had a feeling that he'd first worked on the island at the Big House, but she didn't want to ask him and risk his clamming up. Harris flipped napkins around as if he was performing magic tricks. Sunny was impressed at the fan and the rabbit.

"Can you teach me napkin folding? Wow!" She grinned and meant it. That would be so cool!

"Another time."

Harris was almost friendly. Maybe she could risk a personal question. "Did you ever mind this kind of work?"

"No." Harris gave her the evil eye and retreated like a turtle back into its shell.

Sunny tried another tack. "Let me ask you one more question and then I'll stop. You say to ask Miss Lillian about Weezie. Mostly, she just brushes me off. All I know is that Weezie is a real person with red hair and is kind of a character. What if she shows up one day?"

Harris smiled gently. "We'll welcome her. But since no one has seen her since Miss Julie's wedding, I find that unlikely." He slid open a concealed door in the paneling, and Sunny blinked. This place was full of surprises. Harris was saying, "Here's where we keep the Christmas dishes—service for twenty-four. There's always a big dinner on Christmas day. Miss Lillian makes it a point to ask those of her friends who have nowhere else to go. It's a delightful day, heartwarming. I hope she does it again this year."

"You're evading my question, Harris." Sunny regarded the stacks of dishes, their gold rims winking in the sunlight streaming past the dining room draperies. Those dishes would all have to be washed by hand. Would she be expected to help wash? But then it occurred to her that she wouldn't be here for the Christmas festivities, and she felt oddly hollow.

Harris gazed at her speculatively. "I don't like to carry family tales. It isn't proper. But since you're after me like a hound, I'll tell you this much. Miss Weezie was popular, she dressed in unconventional ways, she did outrageous things, and she ran with a crowd of which her father disapproved. When she announced she was marrying an artist, her father disinherited her. And that's really all I know."

Sunny nodded. Harris knew more, of course, but she didn't want to risk shutting off the supply line. "Thanks, Harris. I wish you weren't so proper."

He stood tall. "Somebody has to have standards. There are so few these days." He closed the Christmas cabinet and began to put away the china and silver he'd used for her lesson. He locked the silver drawers and slipped the key ring into his pocket. "Any questions about settings? I'll give you a lesson on how to eat difficult foods tomorrow. Asparagus, mussels, and such."

"Sounds—um—interesting." She had never eaten those things. She didn't even know there was a right and a wrong way to eat them. "I think I have the table setting," Sunny said. Just then something Harris had said struck her. "You said you hoped Miss Lillian would do her Christmas dinner again this year. Why would she not?"

His face grew hard. "Suppose we fail in our job of protecting her?"

CHAPTER NINETEEN

On the way home from work, Sunny mulled over what Harris had said and almost missed her exit on the expressway. She had to swerve across two lanes of traffic to reach the right lane. Horns blared in her wake, but she hardly heard them. What if she and Harris failed to protect Miss Lillian? First, she'd tumbled down the stairs. That could have been an accident. She'd said it wasn't. Then there had been the figs, the poisoned fig Sunny almost ate, and then the frozen fruit salad containing God knew what. Before that, the fake electricians—what on earth were those guys planning to do? Rig the wiring to electrocute them all?

Miss Lillian had given Harris firm orders to admit no service personnel he hadn't previously called, and he assured her he never did so, especially if they said they'd been sent by Alex or Kiki.

Sunny shook her head. She wished she could have been at the luncheon party to see Kiki in action; was that woman really the kind of person who'd murder her mother-in-law? And could Alex have been involved? On reflection, she thought not. He might be under Kiki's spell, but he appeared to be a man who loved his mother, despite their differences. Miss Lillian was probably right. He was struggling to become his own man, still coping with the shadow of his father.

And now, she felt that Miss Lillian was just tired of all the drama. Not afraid, but annoyed, the way Sunny's mother had been annoyed when she slapped at the marsh mosquitoes near their trailer park, the mosquitoes that would descend on them whenever they tried to sit outside and catch a cooling breeze. Her mother's cigarettes drove them away, but the booze in her hand attracted them.

Miss Lillian couldn't just slap away attempts on her life! She refused to call the police due to the old-money horror of hanging out the dirty linen in public. They wouldn't believe her anyhow. She was sure Alex and Kiki would convince any policemen that the old lady was ready for a memory care center.

Was Miss Lillian still in control of her faculties? Did she have enough wits to catch Kiki at her own game? The plan she had outlined to Sunny was ludicrous, and frightening, and it would mean that Sunny would have to get very, very good at swimming. She was to have another lesson with Flip the Fish tomorrow.

Maybe, just maybe she could forestall the plan. Maybe, if she could find out anything to implicate Kiki, Miss Lillian would go ahead and call in the police, or at least confront her son.

Now what kind of poison could Kiki have put in that salad that would mimic natural symptoms? Miss Lillian had said that her friend had rushed for the bathroom about the time dessert was served. So—Sunny needed to look for a toxin that would take effect in about ten minutes. She'd never nursed a patient who'd taken an overdose of anything but drugs, and she'd known of a few kids who got into something they shouldn't and had to take ipecac. No help there. She remembered a book on toxicology she'd used in nursing school. Maybe she hadn't sold it.

First, she had to let Avery know about the possible prom dresses. Sunny let herself into the townhouse, turquoise tulle and golden satin over one arm. Upstairs, a boy band's muffled rhythms thumped from Avery's room, but Sunny was relieved to find a tossed salad waiting in the fridge along with some beef patties. The George Foreman grill hunkered on the counter next to an 8-pack of buns.

Sunny went to the stairs and shouted, "I'm home, sweetie. I've brought something for you. Something gorgeous. And some really cool T-shirts."

Silence.

"Avery?"

"I'm studying, Mom," came the faint reply.

"Don't you want to see what I have for you?"

Silence.

Sunny stalked upstairs and called outside the bedroom door. "When you get ready, the gorgeous, beautiful *prom gowns* will be in my room."

She laid the dresses and the plastic bag of other hand-me-downs on the queen-size bed she'd bought in better times, then walked downstairs for a glass of wine and the TV news.

It had been a long day.

During a commercial, she checked her email and found one from Roger Humbolt, her future boss, asking her if she'd received the forms he'd sent a week ago. He apologized for not having e-forms just yet, but he was still organizing his office.

She picked up the snail mail from the table, separated out all the junk. No envelope. She took the junk mail straight to the trash. Wait . . . what if she'd tossed Dr. Humbolt's envelope by accident? What if it had been stuck inside one of those catalogs she always pitched, not wanting to be tempted into spending money? She began to dig in the bin, and sure enough, she found the unopened letter near the bottom of the trash bag, creased and crinkled and stained. Not stuck in anything. She was quite sure she'd never seen it before.

She ripped it open and found a form and a letter from her future boss.

He began the letter with the usual formalities, and followed with *looking forward to seeing you and your daughter—there'll be a good school for her here. Almost sixteen, I understand, and probably as pretty as her mother. I'll be happy to help her in any way I can. She'll love it once she gets here.*

Avery! Sunny fumed. Avery had tossed this letter, something Sunny needed for this job. And Roger Humbolt had been good to offer her this job. So she had been quick to take it, and she hoped she wasn't making a mistake. She'd asked around about his divorce, and found it was going to be nasty. Drama everywhere she turned. Her friend Lori-Lee, another single mom, said that Roger Humbolt had asked her to consider the job, and she'd turned him down. She had a daughter who was into beauty pageants, and they didn't want to move from the city and all the connections they had in that world.

Sunny went into the kitchen, whipped on an apron, and started to grill the burgers. The wheezy hood above the stove did a rotten job and greasy smoke filled the room. She opened the back door to let the choking fumes out.

Avery came slinking into the room at the smell of burgers. Teenagers, she'd found, were like cats or dogs—no matter how they sulked, they'd always come at the smell of food. The girl grabbed the forks and knives and set the table, saying as little as possible.

When they were seated at the table with hands wrapped around a piled-high burger, Sunny gazed wistfully at Avery's baked potato glistening with butter and sour cream. And then Avery finally spoke. "Are those dresses really for me?"

Sunny lowered her burger. "Compliments of Miss Lillian. Her daughter wore them. The cream satin one was Miss Lil's, and I have dibs on it."

"I like the others better. That one looks ancient."

Ouch.

Avery tossed her hair and tried to look nonchalant. "The two I like aren't in style, but the fabrics are to die for. Maybe I can do something for them with that ancient clunker of a sewing machine you have. When are you going to get something decent?"

"When I have two nickels to rub together," Sunny said, and took a bite of hamburger. Avery waited, poker-faced. Sunny swallowed, took a drink of Coke, and stared at Avery pointedly. "When I start this new job, we can afford a good machine, and if you try to sabotage me again, there won't be much of anything." She whipped the envelope out of her pocket and waved it under Avery's nose.

The girl shrugged, eyes still fierce. "Well, if going back to that hospital is out, can't you keep the job with the old lady?"

"Staying with Miss Lillian is out of the question!" Sunny's heart began to hammer and her face grew hot. "For one thing, it's way below my training. As is the pay. And her name is Miss Lillian, not the Old Lady."

Avery shrugged and licked ketchup off her finger. "It seems like a pretty good set-up. Free clothes and all. And didn't you say something about living in a guest house? That would be really cool. I wouldn't have these stairs. Why did you get this place anyhow?"

"It was what I could afford, Avery, and near the hospital. If we moved to Miss Lillian's, you'd have to change schools," Sunny said. How could she tell her daughter that something dangerous was going on? Was her employer in danger, with only a butler and a nurse to guard her?

Could she explain to Avery that the "Old Lady's" daughter-in-law and the woman who had stolen Troy Bentley were BFF's and that it was conceivable she might run into her, just as Avery had predicted! She'd just narrowly missed doing so at that luncheon.

That would never do.

If she ever did run into Lady Sydney Fairfield, she hoped it would be in a Sherman tank.

"Where did you go, Mom? Earth to Mom."

"I'm right here, daughter of mine, waiting for you to apologize for tossing my letter in the trash. It won't do you any good, because I've already made arrangements. With Dr. Humbolt's advice, I've made a deposit on an apartment, paid an electricity deposit, talked to the school nearby, and lined up some guys to help us load a U-Haul truck. I've asked Manny and Maria to go with us and drive the truck. I've started the process to get my license in North Carolina, and I'm expecting some important papers to arrive in the mail soon. So, please don't try to screw things up."

Avery leaned forward. "Look, Mom. You could have at least come to me and talked this North Carolina plan over, asked me how I felt about it before you agreed to go. No, you go ahead and plan things by yourself. And you've asked my friend's parents to help without telling me! If I had a father I could go live with, I would."

"That is not my fault, Avery."

"Maybe if you hadn't left him . . ."

"Maybe we would all be dead."

A lot of Kleenex got ripped from the box before Sunny and Avery finished all they had to say, settled into silence, and did the dishes together. This was not the end of it, not by a long shot.

Three more weeks. She had just three weeks to convince her daughter that there was life beyond the borders of this city, and to find out whether Kiki was indeed trying to kill Miss Lillian and, if she could, figure out how to put a stop to it. And Neil? He was just another Mr. Wrong. She was sure that when she got to the new job, with new people and new challenges, thoughts of him would float away like vapor.

Why go chasing rainbows?

After the dishes were done and put away, and after Avery had left for her room, Sunny sat down at the kitchen table, forms spread out before her. She picked up a pink ballpoint pen that read *Westbury Hospital*, tossed it away, and found a plain black Bic.

After she filled out the forms, stuffed the return envelope, and stamped it, she went into the old suitcase under the bed, where she kept all her papers and books from nursing school, and found her poisoning and toxicology handbook. After half an hour of searching the pages, she knew she'd need more information. Information she'd have to get from Miss Lillian.

On the way to work the next day, she drove by the post office and mailed the forms. She hoped Miss Lillian would have news about her friend who'd collapsed at Kiki's disastrous party, and then she could ask her questions.

When Sunny brought Miss Lillian's breakfast, she didn't need to ask; Miss Lillian wanted to rant about Bitsy's trouble.

"I need coffee, quick. Did you know those doctors didn't test for poison? Her doctor said she must have taken too many of her hypertension pills, but Bitsy said she hadn't, and they wouldn't take her word for it. Said she was confused. Ooohh!"

At that moment Harris entered with a vase of creamy pink roses. "The senator sent these, Miss Lillian," he said. "I thought you'd like them here."

"Yes, thank you," Miss Lillian replied. "Just set them on the dresser so I can see them, and don't go. I want you to hear this."

Miss Lillian went on to tell them that Bitsy hadn't wanted to make trouble for her hostess, so she didn't insist on further testing. Sometimes, Bitsy had admitted, she did get confused as to whether she'd taken her pill or not and took another one. Or two. Her internist seemed okay with that. Bitsy just adored him, he was so good-looking and so charming, so she accepted whatever he told her.

"What were her symptoms exactly, Miss Lillian?" Sunny asked. "Remember as much as you can. I might have seen a case like it."

"Let me think," Miss Lillian said. She closed her eyes. "She finished the salad and remarked that it tasted even sweeter than the first one. Had more maraschino cherries in it. She was going to tell me something she heard at the beauty salon when her face got red and blotched. She clapped her hand to her mouth and raced for the powder room. That's all that happened at first."

"But later?" prompted Sunny.

"By the time the EMTs got there she was confused, dizzy, and lying down. They thought she might be having a heart attack since she's so heavy. They asked her if she was on heart medication. That's all I remember."

It could be poison, and the book had hundreds of poisons. Sunny would try to narrow it down by how fast it acted and how easily Kiki could obtain it.

"I have something to add," said Harris.

Doing a little undercover work of his own, Harris had found that less than an hour after the party, the bathroom at Kiki's had been scoured, the luncheon plates washed, and the frilly cupcake papers that had held the heart-shapes of frozen fruit salad were taken personally by Kiki and placed in the garbage bag that would be picked up the following morning.

There was nothing to report to the police, except the ravings of an elderly lady named Miss Lillian. They would be unlikely to go digging through the heaps of garbage bags in the landfill for traces of poison.

Sunny had been getting a sinking feeling ever since Miss Lillian mentioned Bitsy's internist. "Who . . . who was your friend's doctor, Miss Lillian?"

"Oh, a very reputable man, I hear. A Dr. Troy Bentley."

Sunny's stomach churned, and bile rose in her gullet. "Excuse me, Miss Lillian."

She ran down the stairs and lost her breakfast on the grass.

She hurried over to the pool house, still shaky, and cleaned up and got a drink of water. On the way out, she noticed a shady corner that Miss Lillian had planted with caladiums and coleus, two plants that Sunny remembered from childhood. Lots of people had grown those in the mobile home park where she'd lived. She walked over and saw a charming background of pointed green leaves. Leaves of lily-of-the valley, flowers that her mother had planted for their scent, and had forbidden her to pick, because they were poisonous.

CHAPTER TWENTY

The toxicology handbook confirmed that the symptoms Miss Lillian remembered her friend having could have come from ingestion of either lily-of-the-valley or Star of Bethlehem. But as the actions of these plants' poisons ultimately affected the heart, and as Bitsy was already taking heart medication, that fact might be what had saved her. Still, without a test for poison, there was no proof.

Sunny reported these facts to Miss Lillian, and Miss Lillian became more determined than ever to trap Kiki.

As the days for departure for the birthday party flew by, there was an ominous silence from Alex and Kiki. Laying low, Miss Lillian proclaimed. She wasn't worried they'd bolt. They knew better than to back out of one of her parties.

And now, Sunny thought with mixed emotions, it was her last week of employment at Stonehaven. The next day, they'd leave for the island. Fighting back regret at leaving, she resolutely kept her mind on the new job, the new surroundings ahead, and packed Miss Lillian's island party wardrobe. She folded a striped linen top to go along with the palazzo pants and long skirts and the big cartwheel hat. She tucked one white sandal and one espadrille and one pristine white tennis shoe into shoe bags.

As she folded a slithery azalea-pink nightgown, she thought of Neil as he stood on the dock that first day, and the way their eyes had met. And oh, the kiss. It was enough to start the butterflies again. She wanted to look good for him, but not sexy, which would alarm Miss Lillian. She'd already packed her best hand-me-downs. She wanted to leave happy memories behind with both Miss Lillian and Neil. Oh, Neil. She'd had enough complications in her life, and she didn't want to grieve over something that could never work out.

She wasn't Julie. She couldn't live on that island, and he would never leave. Not to mention that it appeared Miss Lillian was hatching other plans for him with the senator's daughter. She might not take kindly to the hired help snatching away her beloved son-in-law.

Sunny ducked into the closet to fetch a pair of wide-legged capris she thought would be perfect for the beach picnic.

"Sunny . . ." Miss Lillian called out from her chaise.

"Yes, ma'am?" Sunny emerged from the closet with the white linen pants. If only she could talk Miss Lillian into wearing them.

Miss Lillian sighed. "Not *ma'am*, but I guess you can't rid yourself of that habit. I want to talk to you. You're learning very well how to be my cousin, and I must congratulate you."

Sunny beamed with pleasure. "Thank you, Miss Lillian. I enjoy this job." Except for the attempted murders. The thought sobered her and wiped the smile away.

"Yes." Miss Lillian didn't notice her change of expression, and settled back with a cat-licking-cream-off-her-whiskers face. "And I appreciate you, dear. I have a proposal for you."

Sunny folded the capris and put them in the suitcase. "I'm listening," she said, hoping it didn't have anything to do with the plan to trap Kiki. That little venture was already too risky.

"Well," Miss Lillian said. "I've become used to having you around. In fact, as the song goes, I've become accustomed to your face. How would you like to have a permanent job as my assistant? My ankle's almost healed, but I'm not as young as I used to be, and an extra pair of hands would be so welcome. There are things Harris can't or won't do, and you'd be perfect! You'd be so helpful when I have to deal with Kiki. Of course," here she gave Sunny a mischievous smile, "if my plan works, I hope she'll be exposed for the evil schemer she is. Then Alex will leave her and go back to Catherine. If she'll have him."

Sunny took a deep breath. "But Miss Lillian," she blurted, "if your plan doesn't work, we could all be dead."

Miss Lillian gave her such a look that Sunny took a step back to dodge the death rays shooting from her eyes. "Sunny. I have thought about this in detail. I am not demented. The only thing that can spoil the plan is negativity. If you're going to be like that, I may not want you after all."

"I'm very sorry," Sunny said, deflated. Why did she say that? Did she want the job, on some level? If the plans worked, could she stay? It's just what Avery wanted. And she could see Neil. But damn it, Neil was *not* in her plan.

A modern woman wasn't *supposed* to want rescuing anymore; she was supposed to be strong and independent. All very well and good, but oh, how Sunny yearned to be Cinderella. Not sweeping the hearth forever, on the outside looking in. She wanted to be inside the castle. Being with Neil would mean she'd still be on the outskirts. And anyway, what if she stayed and he married that senator's daughter? Heartbreak on toast for breakfast.

Miss Lillian broke into her thoughts. "You know I'd make it worth your while."

Sunny took a deep breath and quickly shifted gears. "Miss Lillian. I'm grateful for the offer, I truly am. But I'm already committed to a doctor who's offered me a good job in his office. I'll have regular hours and less stress, and have more time to spend with my daughter."

Miss Lillian dove right in. "But if you stayed, she'd be right here in the guest house, wouldn't she? How ideal! I'm eager to meet her. Didn't you say she has special needs?"

"Yes." Sunny explained about the prosthesis without going into detail about the accident. Then she said, "She doesn't want her disability to define her, you know. She's a talented seamstress and wants to be a clothes designer. She wants to attend the Parsons School of Design in New York."

Miss Lillian beamed. "With that much desire, she's sure to be a great success. You know what? I'm really interested in having your daughter meet my granddaughters, Blake and Ellery. I want them to know a young woman with pluck."

By this time Sunny had learned more than she wanted to know about Blake and Ellery and their spending habits and trips to rehab. "Avery doesn't want to go to the island," Sunny said. "She doesn't like beaches. Swimming suits are awkward. I thought the North Carolina mountains would be a good place for her—the weather is generally cool, and jeans are practical year-round."

Miss Lillian was looking at her curiously. "Oh, rubbish. Let's think of something that will lure her. Does she like boys yet?"

Sunny shrugged her shoulders and folded one last caftan to put in the suitcase. "I wish she didn't. She's hung up on a football player who's just using her to help with his term papers."

Miss Lillian put her finger to her chin. "Well, then. Let's give her a way to make the term-paper boy jealous. Perhaps by meeting a good-looking young man in a smashing uniform? I'll give you one of Angus's military school pictures. He's handsome, even if he is my own grandson."

Sunny thought she knew what Avery's reaction would be and snapped the suitcase shut. "Miss Lillian. She'd either ignore him or, worse, really fall for him."

Miss Lillian shrugged. "So what? At that age it never lasts."

Sunny laughed. "If I had believed that when I was sixteen, Miss Lillian, it would have saved me a lot of trouble."

"You'll have to tell me about it sometime." Miss Lillian was already rummaging through a box of photos in her desk. Sunny was amazed to see that Miss Lillian kept pictures in boxes instead of having them in albums or digitized, and now she was holding out a print for Sunny.

The boy in uniform was grinning at the camera, his hair shorter and darker than in the photograph Sunny had seen beside the bunk bed on the island. He still sported his island tan and perfect teeth. Miss Lillian wasn't wrong about his looks. If any boy could impress Avery, this one just might.

Miss Lillian slipped the picture into an envelope and handed it to Sunny. "Good luck. I do hope your daughter will be a good example to my granddaughters."

More likely, the girls would be mean to Avery—shunning her, ignoring her, making snide remarks, giggling behind their hands. Sunny slipped the picture into her pocket. Avery knew to ignore teasing—she'd developed a pretty thick skin—but just the thought of these overindulged girls might make her bristle and behave badly.

Sunny's shoulders sagged. Her job was to keep Miss Lillian from getting killed. If there really was a killer. And now, enter Avery, complicating matters. Not to mention this thing with Neil further complicating matters, and Kiki and Alex and the teenagers from hell.

"Go ahead and talk it over with your daughter," Miss Lillian was saying. "Then let's go over our scheme and how we can fit her into it."

Fit her into it? Sunny grabbed the back of a chair and squeezed hard. She was back in Wonderland again.

And now there was one more problem she needed to solve before she left for North Carolina. "I have a question, Miss Lillian," she said. "Does your daughter-in-law always wear those diamond earrings?"

Miss Lillian snorted. "Of course. She hardly ever takes them off. Managed to sweet-talk Alex into giving her a pair for a wedding present."

"Did she ever lose one and maybe have it replaced?"

Sunny wasn't prepared for Miss Lillian's reaction. The older woman gripped the chair and turned positively pale. "Why do you say that?"

Sunny made her confession. "When we were at Issatee, I found one near the path at . . ."

"Yes," Miss Lillian interrupted. "Why don't you just keep it? Let's hear no more about it."

Maybe she didn't want Kiki to have it. Maybe Kiki had already collected the insurance or something. Sunny didn't feel right keeping it. Maybe she'd give it to Neil. And let him sell it for the island.

That same day, Neil stared at the envelope from Orrie. He was sure it would be apologetic, standoffish, and full of suggestive comments. He laid it aside for later, because he still had to go up to the Big House and see how the cleaning was coming.

He pushed away a thought of Sunny, the way he'd seen her backlit on the dune, hair in the wind tickling his soul like pale champagne. He thought of their kiss, sticky as fudge, hot in the moonlight, dark and sweet.

He tossed ads and special offers in the trash, and set aside a newsletter and an envelope from the turtle watch people to read later. What was this? A reply to his letter from Weezie? He tore it open. Now he would find out the truth about Sunny. He scanned the letter quickly. What? Nothing? Maybe he'd missed something. He read the letter again, this time carefully.

> *Dear Neil,*
>
> *Thank you so much for your letter. It grieves me so to hear about Julie. You and she made a good team and you were both doing such wonderful work. Of course, I'm devastated to find Duncan gone. How Lillian must miss him and Julie! I need to end my self-imposed exile and come to her, the sooner the better. We were great friends once, but time and tide have floated us far from one another. I'm rather ashamed that it took a selfish desire on my part to try to contact Lillian through Julie. The bad thing about being any kind of artist is that you must be a bit selfish to get anything accomplished.*
>
> *I was angry at Lillian in years past for not taking my part about marrying Freddy. She told me I was only marrying him to reject my parents' way of life, and that it would never turn out well.*

And you know what? It didn't. I couldn't forgive her for being right, but as you see, everything came out well in the end.

I found my Paul after I found myself, and I hoped it would last forever. It did last until he died, just a year ago. I left California and moved to Asheville, some instinct tugging me closer to my native soil. And would you believe, last week I met Alex's Catherine in Earth Fare! She told me she dropped out of theology school and is now teaching yoga. She's stronger now, and she yearns for her daughters. She's thinking about petitioning for custody. After all, they're fourteen now, and can choose to live with her.

I won't tell Lillian I'm coming. I'll just turn up and surprise her, so she won't have a chance to turn me away. She was never the one to suffer fools gladly, and she thought I was an enormous fool to "throw my life away," as she put it. Lillian was always one to color within the lines. Boldly, to be sure, but I was the one who never admitted there were any lines to start with.

Thank you so much for writing to me. I'll be sure and come to see you when I come to see Lillian. It will be wonderful to set foot on the island again.

Bless you and keep you,
Louisa Beringer

Why hadn't she answered his question about Sunny? Maybe she just wasn't ready to talk about her family problems. Or she didn't want to put them in writing. Maybe he should have given her his phone number.

Neil looked up at the top shelf of the kitchen hutch and gazed at the two hand-carved wooden bowls Weezie had given them for a wedding present. Julie had cherished those bowls, while the china and silver wedding gifts, meant for a life they'd never live, stayed in storage at Stonehaven. Still, Julie hadn't wanted to sell her tableware, even though Neil had pointed out that they could use the money for helping the wildlife.

"Someday we might want it . . ." That was Julie's refrain. Not quite willing to turn her back on her past.

If Julie had lived, would she have grown tired of the isolation? Would she have yearned once again for the life she'd left to marry him? After Angus was grown and perhaps gone to pursue his own dreams, would this island and his love have been enough to keep her happy?

Harlan had told him to stop dwelling on the past. Right now he needed to focus on saving the island. He didn't like Lillian's harebrained scheme, but it just might work. And Sunny would be here. Impossible Sunny. What was he going to do about her?

CHAPTER TWENTY-ONE

As Harlan's ferry picked up speed in the open water, Sunny longed to stand up in the boat and watch the approach to Issatee. But all around her was the vast blue-gray expanse of rippling, sun-sequined water, and this time she knew it was chock full of alligators. By now she could swim, sort of, compliments of Flip the Fish, but she couldn't outswim one of *those*.

She gripped the faded orange seat cushion. Even as the salty wind battered her hair, she wanted to get up and pace, but all she could do was hold on. If the boat wasn't bad enough, her stomach clenched at the thought of their plan to stop Kiki, which would involve Miss Lillian getting out in a boat with the Dragon Lady. Miss Lillian was going to use herself as bait, and they would all be waiting to save her. The whole thing gave Sunny the shivers. She hoped beyond hope that the mysterious attacks would go away after this caper, and that Miss Lillian would be secure. Then Sunny could go off to North Carolina in peace.

The sputter and tick of the motor slowed, and then they were slicing down the creek through the reeds, twisting and turning, while great white birds rose and flapped across the water, a breathtaking sight. She thought of Blackjack the crow. Neil had said in his last letter that Blackjack had recovered, but the bird had definitely stopped stealing food off people's plates. He'd also said that the lab test had been positive for botulism. Which proved exactly nothing.

Avery, with her lime green second-hand Michael Kors anorak fluttering, tried to act cool, but her wide eyes betrayed her. In the end, it was not the picture of Angus that had convinced her to come, but surprisingly, the information that the other girls would be there. Avery was curious to see what they would be wearing.

And then the boat was docking. Here was Neil to welcome them, wearing khakis and a fairly clean shirt with sleeves rolled up, accompanied by that big orange cat waving his tail. Sunny tried to quell the quivering in her belly.

Their eyes met when Neil reached for her hand to help her out of the boat, and for a moment that *thing* shimmered between them, fragile and tentative, each having an acute awareness of the other. She turned away in order to keep her voice matter-of fact and efficient, to keep Avery's fine-tuned emotional radar from picking up any signals. Miss Lillian wouldn't notice, because Miss Lillian never noticed anything that would conflict with her well-made plans.

To Sunny's surprise, Miss Lillian had warmed to Avery already. On the trip down, they discussed fashion and designers together; both enjoyed style, and Miss Lillian was able to give Avery some tales about shopping in Paris and meeting Yves St. Laurent. Avery was entranced.

Sunny felt impatient and jealous. Every time she tried to look fashionable she felt she looked just plain silly, so she loved her uniforms. They were sturdy, simple, and cheap. On the other hand, the hand-me-down clothes she'd been wearing brought out an appreciation for quality. The polo shirts didn't lose their shape and soft feel after three washings like those from discount stores. She was beginning to see the difference between glitz and value.

And now she watched Avery meet Neil with narrowed eyes, sizing him up as friend or foe. Neil extended a hand to her daughter as he would any other girl when he helped her out of the boat, not assuming she might be made of glass. In return, Avery seemed to relax.

Miss Lillian, not wanting another wagon ride, had arranged to have an antique wicker wheelchair, cleaned and fitted with fat tires, brought down from the Big House. Harris insisted on pushing her up to the house in it.

Avery made her way alongside Sunny and Neil. She looked over at Sunny and smirked, and Sunny knew Avery had caught on to the thing between her and Neil. Was it that obvious? One of her patients had told her a Middle Eastern proverb: There are three things that cannot be hidden: love, a mountain, and a man riding on a camel. But it wasn't love. It was just attraction.

"Where are the others?" Avery wanted to know, as the lodge appeared ahead. "Where are we staying?"

"They'll be here a little later," Neil said. "Alex said something about Kiki wanting to stop off at St. Simons to see some friend of hers who has a house there. Your mom and Miss Lillian will stay in the Lodge. The other grownups will stay in the renovated wing of the Big House, and you kids will stay in the dormitory—boys on one side, girls on the other."

Avery started to say something, but Neil kept on. "Angus is down at the other end of the island visiting some of the folks there. We probably won't see him till around suppertime. I'll put you in the room with your mother, if you like. There are bunk beds."

"Bunk with Mom? No, thanks. I'd rather stay in the dorm," Avery said.

Neil studied the set look on her face. "All right. And Harris, you'll stay in the butler's suite in the Big House, as usual, if you don't want to stay with your relatives."

Harris nodded. "The suite will be most suitable."

"All right, then," Neil said. "Let's go."

Avery stared at Sunny, daring her to try to baby her, and Sunny knew better than to intervene.

Miss Lillian had decided that Angus and Avery would have to occupy themselves after supper so that the adults could talk about strategy. Avery said she didn't care what they did, as long as it wasn't boring, and by the way, where was the TV, and why didn't her smartphone work?

"Phone service is iffy here. My suggestion is to read a book," Neil said. "My old tube TV set quit working two years ago and I haven't replaced it. I have a few DVDs I show the kids on the A/V equipment down at the nature center. You could go there."

"By myself?" She looked delighted.

"The stuffed alligator doesn't bite," Neil said, glancing toward Sunny. "We'll start fixing supper as soon as Angus gets back. If he doesn't come soon, we'll just go on without him."

He'd planned a low country boil and already had an iron pot heating out back, shrimp and corn and sausage waiting in the porch fridge along with peeled potatoes. He'd also provided a plastic-covered bowl of coleslaw.

Miss Lillian, gin and tonic in hand, relaxed in a cedar lounge chair in the grassy area back of the house while Sunny and Avery arrayed the picnic table with a red-checkered vinyl cloth, plates, cutlery, and good cloth napkins, as well as a tall pile of paper ones. Jugs of lemonade and tea stood ready on a side table. When Sunny brought out a tray of glasses, the sun was lowering in the sky, splashing pink and orange across the horizon. Angus still had not appeared.

"You don't think something's happened to him?" asked Sunny, thinking of sharp teeth and long snouts, not to mention that she was starving.

Neil shook his head. "That boy. He just loses track of time out there. He loves this place."

"Then why on earth does he want to join the military?" asked Miss Lillian sharply. She lifted a cheese straw from the dish at hand and munched it.

"He's exploring what he wants to do. Young men have to test themselves," Neil said. "Anybody want a beer?" He walked over to the cooler.

"Did you?" Miss Lillian asked, reaching for another cheese straw. "Want to test yourself?"

"Yes," Neil said abruptly, and popped the top of a Jekyll Big Creek brew. He handed one to Harris, who was standing by the kettle.

Harris took it reluctantly. "Mr. Neil, the food's ready," he said.

"And where are the others?" Miss Lillian demanded. "I know that Wesley and India aren't coming until tomorrow, but I'd thought my son and heir would have the decency to be on time."

"Wait," Neil said. "I forgot to check my messages." He punched a few keys, listened, then he nodded grimly.

They'd all heaped their plates and taken their places at the picnic table when Angus showed up. "Hi, Gran," he said, moseying over to kiss her on the cheek. Sunny thought she detected the odor of horse.

"Hi, guys." He waved to the rest of the table, then walked over to the pile of corn and shrimp and potatoes fished from the pot, grabbed a heavy china plate, and filled it. Then, blushing, he passed the newcomers in the group and awkwardly edged himself in at the end of the table across from Avery. Miss Lillian made the introductions.

Angus mumbled a greeting and began to gnaw on an ear of corn, elbows searching for space. Avery regarded him skeptically, but no one could deny he was a good-looking kid, even if a little grubby, with bronze hair and a light tan and a good build.

You could almost see the mutual attraction start: the wariness, the slight flush, the widened eyes, the gaze shifting from the new, delicious person down to the plate of suddenly less interesting food. Sunny ached for her daughter. Here came letdown on a silver platter. As soon as he found out about her leg, he'd act all funny and beat a hasty retreat.

She'd been a fool to let herself be talked into bringing Avery. She cast a despairing glance at Neil, to see if he had any inkling what was going on. But his happy expression and infectious grin telegraphed that everything was all right in his world. "Eat up, guys, there's plenty!"

Perhaps he was happy because he'd received a message that Alex, Kiki, and the girls were staying overnight on St. Simons with their friend and the friend's sixteen-year-old daughter. Miss Lillian wasn't happy, for sure. Sunny bit her knuckles. She couldn't let Avery stay in the dorm with just that boy.

Right in the middle of washing up, Angus volunteered to take Avery to the beach to watch the sunset. Sunny protested that they shouldn't stay long, and that Avery would have trouble walking on the sand.

"I will not!" she exclaimed. "Mother, I'm not four years old." She turned to Angus. "She babies me because I'm missing part of my leg." She pulled up her capris and stuck out her leg. "See? Feel?"

Angus didn't feel. He glanced briefly and shrugged. "Bummer," he said. "Now it wouldn't be fair for me to chase you."

"Ha!" Avery said. "Just try."

"Stop it, Angus," Neil said.

Miss Lillian sniffed. "My dear, she's really quite safe with Angus."

"Sunny, you're overruled." Neil was still smiling.

They don't see it, they don't see it, Sunny thought, but there was nothing she could do.

"Come on," Miss Lillian said. We'll make our plans here at the kitchen table. Neil, get us some graph paper so we can make notes and sketch out just where everybody has to be when."

The graph paper was brought, and they all sat down. This plan was crazy, this plan was foolish, but Sunny couldn't say so. She was just the hired hand and things were all complicated by the fact she was in love with this—

No, no, she wasn't.

"Lillian. I know what you're trying to do, but I still say it's too risky," Neil said. "We don't have to do this."

"Yes, we do. I'm tired of all this foolishness."

"Foolishness? Why don't you hire a private eye to follow her?"

"She's not stupid. She would figure it out and say I was demented again. I say this is the best way."

"Okay, let's see what you have in mind. Let's see your plan."

"What about the children?" Sunny drummed her fingers on the table. "I'm not sure they need to be included."

"They will have to be told, but only at the last minute, and yes, they need to play a part."

"But—"

"Angus can do what I tell him and not ask too many questions. But your daughter is the wild card, Sunny. Can she do what she's told?"

"Sometimes," Sunny admitted.

"Well, we'll just have to deal with it," Neil said. "Our other guests, so I'm informed, will arrive tomorrow afternoon. I've arranged for Harlan to bring Kiki and Alex and the kids along with Wesley and India all at the same time."

"I still haven't decided whether to tell Wesley what we're up to," Miss Lillian said.

"Don't," Neil said. "He'll try to talk us out of it. He's a lawyer at heart. He'll be great for a witness, though."

And so they set down to plan just how to get Miss Lillian and Kiki together out to sea in Angus's inflatable sailboat. Miss Lillian was sure if they got out far enough, Kiki wouldn't be able to resist finding a way to overturn it or to push Miss Lillian overboard. Neil would drive back to the boat house as soon as the sailboat set out, and would motor back over in the little fishing boat to lurk nearby. Sunny was given a phone with zoom capabilities and instructed to take a video. At least she knew how to do that. Troy Bentley had had one like it.

Sunny recalled that the Red Cross booklet said that it could take less than a minute for someone to drown.

"What if I can't get there in time?" Neil said. "Lillian, I don't want you in danger."

"Look, I'm a champion swimmer," Miss Lillian said. "Cast and all. Isn't that right, Sunny?"

Sunny shrugged. "I've seen Miss Lillian eat up laps in the pool. But wow. I wish there was some other way."

"This is the best way," Miss Lillian declared. "I want my son to see her in action so he'll believe me."

Neil wanted to tell Lillian about the letter from Weezie and still wondered why she hadn't replied to his question about Sunny. In any case, he wanted to ask Lillian for the $5,000 for Weezie's block of marble, but now wasn't a good time. Maybe he'd tell her when this whole episode was over. She didn't need any distractions now. Had he invited Weezie to come to the picnic? He couldn't remember. He was pretty sure she wouldn't come out of the blue. She must be 70-something by now, about Lillian's age.

There would be plenty of time to help Weezie after they'd neutralized the threat to the island. After Kiki had been discredited and her alligator teeth pulled.

Exposure and the threat of calling in the police would put a stop to her attempts. Negative publicity would be worse than jail. But Neil wasn't so sure what Alex would do afterward. Would he stand by her, leave her, or just live apart from her, staying out of the divorce courts and away from a spread in the Atlanta media?

If this harebrained scheme didn't work, he didn't know what they were going to do for Plan B. But they had to try. Because if they didn't, Kiki would just get more and more devious. She'd eventually slip up and get caught, but it wasn't going to be at Lillian's expense.

If he hadn't seen Blackjack eat that fig, he might have thought Lillian was demented too.

They needed to stop Kiki now.

CHAPTER TWENTY-TWO

The day of the party dawned with a gentle heat, moist and breezy, with light clouds scudding across the sky. The perfect weather. When Sunny padded into the kitchen, yawning, she found Neil already there, mug in hand, pouring coffee from a steaming percolator. He'd solved the problem of Avery and Angus by spending the night in the dorm with them, despite their vigorous protests.

"Going for an early run?" Neil asked.

"You must have me confused with somebody else," Sunny said, scrunching her toes in her flip-flops. She remembered Kiki's gossip about Neil entertaining some woman on his sailboat. "I'm used to waking up early for work, and I run enough there."

"I'm glad of some company." Neil poured her a mug. "Let's have coffee out back. That way we can talk and be sure of not waking Miss Lil. I'll flip some pancakes when she's up. I promised the kids last night." He grabbed a banana for himself and tossed one to Sunny, then he took both mugs with one hand.

"You left the kids sleeping?" Sunny carefully peeled her banana on the way to the picnic table and began to eat it, trying to forget the symbolism.

"Nope. They took off in the Jeep to the beach to see the sun come up."

Sunny swallowed the last of the banana and pitched the peel into the 55-gallon drum Neil used as a trash barrel. "What? They saw that sun going down."

Neil looked at her, amused. "Did you expect it to stay down?"

Sunny shot him a murderous look. "This is so unlike her. On Saturdays I usually don't see the kid until noon." She lowered herself to the bench and swung her legs under the table.

"Don't worry." Neil set the mugs down on the table and took a seat on the other side. "It's an adventure. I had a talk with Angus last night. He'll look after Avery. I've brought him up to be a gentleman."

Gentlemen could be devious, Sunny remembered, especially teenage gentlemen, if that wasn't an oxymoron. As she reached for her coffee mug, Neil put a hand on her arm and nodded toward a tangle of greenery at the edge of the sandy yard. A small white deer nosed out, stared at them, and then began to browse the grass.

"I have to keep her out of the garden. But she's tame," Neil said. "Want me to see if she'll come to us?"

Sunny shook her head. "No, it's peaceful just watching her." And she might have ticks. She sipped her coffee in silence and then she just had to say it.

"I'm still worried about this . . . this trap we're going to pull off. What if something goes wrong?"

"Have a little faith, Sunny."

Rambo sauntered up, twined around their legs, and then settled into the Sphinx position, watching them through half-closed eyes. As if he knew the answer to the riddle.

"I worry about everything, Neil. Those kids."

"Why? Angus won't let anything happen to Avery."

Sunny shook her head. "Not that kind of safety. My daughter seems attracted to boys that will break her heart. I wanted her to come with me so she wouldn't be alone with a boy at home who's just using her for homework help."

"Angus knows better than to take advantage," Neil said gently.

Sunny avoided his eyes. "I know teenage boys."

"I know my own son," Neil said.

"Do we ever know our own children?" Sunny held out her hands, exasperated.

Neil smiled. "Hey, don't get philosophical on me. Come on. If it makes you feel better, we'll ride down and check on them. We'll get back before Lillian wakes up."

"But they've taken the Jeep."

"We'll ride the horses, sweetheart."

"But I don't know how to ride, *sweetheart*."

Neil grinned. "Come on, I'll teach you."

Sunny wanted to protest that she was afraid of the huge beasts, who might bite her or kick her or throw her off into the path of an alligator, but for some reason she got up from the bench and followed Neil down to the stable. She stepped as if molasses lined the path.

"Sunny," he said, slowing his amble to match hers, "you asked if we ever knew our own children. What I'm wondering is whether we know ourselves."

Sunny glanced at him. His eyes betrayed his casual expression. Her breath quickened, and numbness stole over her. "Now who's getting philosophical?"

They had reached the stable, and the horses whickered and chuffed in greeting. "It's not philosophy," he said. He took her hand, pulled her to him, and kissed her again, hard, cutting the last ropes that tied her to reason.

"We shouldn't." The tide was taking her farther from shore, but he was holding her close. She looked up at him, questioning, begging, but his eyes were soft. She could leave if she wanted. But she didn't want.

"Sunny. Don't think. Just *be*."

"But—" I'm going to North Carolina, Sunny thought, and then the thought flew away, and they were holding tight in the warm stable smelling of dung and dust, and she felt him hard against her, and her breath was coming fast, and there was no place no place no place they could go.

"Sunny," he murmured, and planted a kiss against the vein in her neck, and she tingled all over, pushing away the intruding thought that the kids might come roaring back in the Jeep.

Neil took her hand and led her down the path, past the nature center, to the old tool shed.

When he unlocked the padlock and opened the door, she gasped. It was a painter's studio, with two big windows hidden by outside shutters. On the walls he'd hung some wonderful framed watercolors, and other paintings were stacked in bins.

The shelves held brushes of various lengths and types in jars, and a couple of tool boxes probably held paints and more brushes.

"Don't tell," Neil said.

She was mute with surprise and joy, a lump rose in her throat, and she shook her head, not understanding why he didn't want to shout his talent to the world. She found that he kept a folding cot in the back, and he unfolded it and she knew she shouldn't be doing this. But what the heck, she was off to North Carolina and who knew when she might find somebody else again. Then again she might break her heart, but reason was out there, floating to the sky like a cloudy silver balloon.

On the cot in the studio with the shell-pink sunrise flooding through the windows, they rocked in sea-storm and current, roiling in the waves, and painted a new bright ring around the sun.

Sunny was lying in a delicious whisper of seafoam when the front porch bell began to clang.

"Oh my God, Miss Lillian's up!" She leaped up from the cot, shimmied into her shorts and t-shirt, found the sink, and splashed water on her face and hands. She took off running to the lodge, shaking her hands dry.

On the front porch, a stony-faced Miss Lillian, wearing her dressing gown, leaned forward on her crutches. "Sunny! Where on earth have you been!"

Sunny panted up to her, stitching together a story. "I went with Neil down to the stables. We were thinking of riding to find the kids, but then I heard your bell and came running."

Miss Lillian raised an eyebrow. "Is Neil on the way, or did he ride off? Oh, wait. I see him."

Sunny glanced around. Neil was striding up with untucked shirt. Sunny said quickly, "I explained to Miss Lillian about going to the stables."

He raised one eyebrow. "Right," he said. "Sorry, Lillian. We thought you'd sleep another hour."

The older woman drew herself up with an exasperated huff. "Who can sleep, with such excitement going on?"

My God, Sunny thought. She's really enjoying this.

Miss Lillian wanted to stay on the porch and drink coffee, so Sunny followed Neil inside, where a black-aproned Harris was already in the kitchen flipping pancakes. He greeted them, but gave Sunny that sinister look she was so afraid of. It was as though he knew everything that was passing through her mind.

"I'll run down to the Point later this morning and pick up the cakes and the fried chicken," Neil said casually. He filled two mugs with coffee, set them on the small kitchen table, and grabbed a plate from the stack on the hutch. "Harris, want to come?"

Harris shifted his eyes Neil's way but didn't move. "I think not, Mr. Neil," he said.

"Can't you just call me Neil?" Neil grinned.

"I think not, Mr. Neil." Harris piled Neil's plate with pancakes, as well as Sunny's. They sat down to eat while Harris finished the rest of the cakes and set them in the oven to keep warm.

Harris informed them that he planned to serve the leftover cold shrimp and slaw for lunch, accompanied by homemade potato salad and deviled eggs that could be taken to the late-afternoon supper picnic as well. A watermelon would chill in a tub of ice out back, along with the beer.

"I'll make some pineapple and ham sandwiches, too, for the picnic," Harris said. "We'll have a pick-up buffet for lunch."

"Did somebody say lunch?" asked Angus, coming in the back door. "How about breakfast?" Avery trailed after him, and Sunny was dismayed to see that she was positively glowing. Angus grinned back at Avery. "Pancakes! Great! Let's eat, and then I've got so much to show you."

Avery looked at Sunny curiously. "Mom, did you get sunburned already?"

After lunch, Sunny helped Miss Lillian inspect the Big House for any last-minute adjustments. The rambling old building's bedrooms had once been decorated in rustic elegance, but now, truth be told, they were downright shabby. Still, Miss Lillian liked to make sure they were comfortable. "I had them make up one for the senator, one for India, one for Alex and Kiki," she said. "I guess that's all."

Miss Lillian walked over and fingered a drooping ivory linen curtain in the last bedroom and gazed down at the courtyard in front of the house. Her eyes were distant, as if she was seeing something that wasn't there. "I remember a time when this house was full of family, friends, and full of laughter." She sighed. "Those were golden days, Sunny. It will never be the same again."

"But there will be more golden days, Miss Lillian," Sunny blurted. "There have to be! I mean we never know what's coming, do we?"

Miss Lillian turned from the window and looked at her curiously. "Well! Sunny, you surprise me. And of course, you're right. There's just so much of the past here."

The night before, Miss Lillian had taken her to visit the graves of Julie and the Doctor, so she could carry the potted orchids, brought over carefully in boxes. The purple one was for Duncan and the yellow for Julie, a merry yellow, a vibrant shade. Purple for wisdom, she'd said. She missed Duncan's wisdom.

Sunny had never seen Miss Lillian so vulnerable, and her heart went out to her. Suddenly she wished she could stay with Miss Lillian and not go to Pinehaven. Those paintings. Neil had a side he kept hidden from people, and he had trusted her. But not going was unthinkable. It was too risky, and she couldn't back out now.

"Come on," Miss Lillian said, dropping the curtain. "We're having a party."

Sunny helped to pack the picnic hampers. She loaded stainless steel utensils, red checkered cloths, paisley napkins, and bright blue plastic plates and cups. Harris gave her a large green insulated bag for containers of picnic goodies.

Neil and Angus loaded tables into the rusty island pickup truck. Miss Lillian had planned the picnic to be on the grand scale, but not as grand as those extravagances of Jekyll Island millionaires during the Gilded Age. Sunny marveled at the attention to detail, thinking of the beer and hot dogs and chips and store-bought brownies she'd packed for Kyle and their crowd in the days of the beach trips she'd dreaded.

Neil went down to the boat house to bring the inflatables and life jackets to the truck. Sunny's heart began to pound, and she took some deep breaths to quell her nerves. The plan, the plan. Get the picnic ready, put on her smiley face and be pleasant, look after Miss Lillian, and catch a murderess. All in a day's work.

Down at the beach, Angus and Avery were put to work pumping up the floats. There were going to be five of them, as well as his favorite, the inflatable sailboat. Neil checked the sky; a few wispy clouds and the light breeze promised a calm day, just perfect for a sunset picnic. Just perfect to catch a killer.

It had been just such a day when Julie had died. It had been just such a picnic, and now he recalled that he'd hosted no picnics since then, not even with Orrie. They'd carried beer and snacks when they went out in the big sailboat, the *Jolie*, but that wasn't the same thing.

Neil left them at the beach and drove back to the Lodge to get another load and greet his incoming guests.

At three-thirty they heard Harlan's boat puttering up the creek, and a few minutes later, Sunny, Lillian, and Neil were down at the dock greeting the senator and his daughter India.

But where were Alex and Kiki and the girls? "Harlan, you didn't go off and leave them?" asked Neil.

"I waited twenty minutes for them. They know my rules. When they didn't show yesterday, they waited till the last minute to call. Sounded a little tipsy, if you ask me. I told them to be on time today or else I was leaving." He spat in the water.

Sunny's heart dropped. All the planning they'd done, all the arrangements. Surely those idiots wouldn't stand them up! Surely they didn't get wind of the plan! Wait. She was being paranoid. There had to be some explanation.

"Just like them to be late," Miss Lillian said, unruffled. "Well, we'll just ignore their rudeness. Can you make another trip? They're sure to call with some cock-and-bull story. I'll pay extra, of course."

"Nope," Harlan said. "I've got another customer, and then I'm knocking off. Sharon and Nick are here, and Linda Faye's having a humongous cookout."

"They can find their own way here," Neil said tightly. "There are boats to hire at the marina."

Harlan and Neil took the bags up to the Big House, while Sunny pushed Miss Lillian in her wicker wheelchair up to the Lodge. Miss Lillian chattered with Wesley and India as if she didn't have a care in the world. Sunny wondered what she was thinking.

By the time Sunny had settled Miss Lillian and her guests on the porch with cool drinks, the disgruntled Harlan had left and Neil had rejoined them with a fresh beer.

Sunny had barely time to appraise the newcomer, India—a self-contained woman with a gentle manner and plain blondish bob—when a buzz reached her ears. A whiny buzz grew into a roar, louder and louder and louder. Neil sat up straight when he heard it slow to a growl and then stop.

"Excuse me a minute, folks," he said. "Sounds like somebody's here." He got up and headed for the path to the dock.

"I'll go, too," Sunny said, hurrying after him. She felt uncomfortable with the senator and his daughter, afraid they'd ask questions she couldn't answer. When they got near the water, she saw a speedboat drifting in with their four missing guests aboard. At the wheel was a boy, a young man really, with mercurochrome-red hair and a shiny black T-shirt and shorts. "I've seen that kid before," Neil said. He didn't tell Sunny, but it was the boy who had sped by and the pink-haired girl the time he and Oriana Welles had been out in the sailboat.

CHAPTER TWENTY-THREE

I t was just like Kiki to bring more clothes than she would need, even for a week in one of those Caribbean havens meant for James Bond and his ilk. Neil lugged his sister-in-law's two suitcases up to the master suite in the Big House, and left after syrupy thanks from the lady. Maybe she thought he didn't notice her wrinkled nose when she surveyed the comfortable, faded bedclothes and upholstery.

"Neil! Turn on the AC!" she demanded.

Neil cocked his head. The senator and India hadn't complained about their rooms. "We've never put it in. Really, this house stays pretty cool with the tall ceilings, the thick walls, and the overhead fans."

"I'm going to *die*," Kiki grumbled. "Why'd I ever come?"

"Now, honey." Alex gave her a warning glance. Maybe he'd told her to act nice on this trip or they'd never get anywhere with their plans for the resort.

Neil walked over to a window and shoved it wide. "I'll open both windows for cross-ventilation, turn the fan up to high, and bring you a window fan later. There are some extras over at the Lodge."

He was met with a resigned, baleful stare.

He'd just shut the big front door behind him, glad to be on his way, when he heard raised voices coming from the open window. He wasn't in the habit of eavesdropping, but there was too much at stake this weekend. He slipped back into the house by the French door of the library, inching it shut behind him, and stepped quietly to the door to the hall, opening it a few inches.

"For Chrissake!" Alex was yelling. "The girls are fourteen! Those guys are in college!"

"Oh, come on, Alex," Kiki said. "They're practically family. Trey Hedges is Eden Fairfield's boyfriend. Sydney thinks he's great."

"They're not *my* family," Alex said. "That punk Trey and his friend met the girls at that house party last month. I didn't want the girls to go, if you recall. Eden Fairfield is wild, older than they are, and her mother's too busy to care. Was Sydney even there, or did she outsource a chaperone?"

"Talking about Sydney. You seemed to be having a good time at her house. You wanted to stay."

He coughed. "I was in no condition to drive yesterday after you and Sydney kept the drinks coming and the hysteria going. I was so bored I overindulged."

"Really. Now it's *my* fault."

"That's beside the point," he said. "The point is that they had these boys' numbers on their phones. I could have just made arrangements to rent a boat from somebody at the Marina."

"But Trey came right over, and it would have taken a lot of paperwork and all that to get another boat, and I was tired. Don't be so stuffy."

Neil had heard enough. He closed the French doors and walked back to the Lodge. So the guy in the speedboat *was* one of the two that he and Oriana had seen when they were sailing.

Just then his phone buzzed, and he took the call. A voice on the line he didn't recognize said, "Neil McEvoy? I've been trying to get in touch with Senator Blackshear. His phone isn't answering, and he gave us your number in case of an emergency. I'm Corrie Stevens, helping Mrs. Blackshear, and she's been taken to the hospital. I'm sorry, but I think that he and India need to return."

My God.

He put in a call to Harlan, couldn't get him. Probably turned off his phone with his kids being home.

When he walked out to the front porch, Lillian was listening to India enthuse about her latest project for helping Haitian children and helping to build a school. The three of them looked so happy and relaxed in each other's company that he almost turned around and went back in so he wouldn't spoil their last few moments of contentment. No. He'd better tell them now.

After Neil had relayed the message, the senator slumped in his chair, all ease gone. "I knew I shouldn't have come."

"No you didn't, Daddy," India said. "We knew it would come sometime. We couldn't have known it would happen now." The young woman, calm and self-possessed, took charge of the situation. "How can we get back as soon as possible, Neil?" she asked." It won't take me long to pack our things again."

"I'll take you in my fishing boat," he said. "Outboard motor. Slow but sure."

Miss Lillian and Sunny stared at one another. They were losing their witnesses. They were losing Neil for the afternoon, probably. This was a bad omen.

Sunny watched the somber group depart, and turned to Lillian. "Maybe we should scrap this plan . . ." she began.

"Not a chance," Miss Lillian interrupted, and thumped her stick.

Neil returned in time to leave for the picnic. When the caravan started down the road to the beach, it was after five-thirty, the sun descending in the sky, hovering over the sea. Neil's Jeep, loaded with hampers and coolers, carried Miss Lillian and Sunny, while Angus followed in the pickup with folding chairs, soft drinks, and champagne, which now seemed out-of-place after the dismal news about Mary Lynn Blackshear.

Miss Lillian had ordered the champagne, along with silver-toned plastic cutlery, to give the picnic a feel of sumptuousness, and to put Kiki at her ease so she'd be off her guard. Now everything was upset. Everyone would be tense. But Sunny knew it would have to be hell or high water before Miss Lillian would abandon her plan.

The marshy wilderness around them gave off the smell of sweetish tidal mud. "Now remember, Neil," Miss Lillian said, "You're supposed to try to talk me out of going out in the boat or swimming. Tell me how dangerous it might be, and remind me of the rip tides. Remind me I'm not at a hundred per cent."

"Rip currents," Neil said automatically.

"Oh, bosh." Miss Lillian waved her hand. "It'll carry you out to sea no matter what you call it."

They had blamed Julie's death on the current. And the Red Cross book said a person could drown in sixty seconds. Sunny's pulse quickened. Surely Miss Lillian was demented to try this. Why couldn't they just forget it and go home?

"Anyhow, I'll argue with you," Miss Lillian was saying, "and say and do what I damn well please. That's the good part of being seventy-nine. Sunny?"

Sunny was checking to see if that bus Neil called a charabanc had caught up with them. The vehicle looked like a trolley car, with a frame for an awning on top, but no one had bothered to replace the old awning after it rotted away. Its slatted wooden seats didn't look very comfortable, and she was glad to be here with Neil in the evening light. She glanced at his glistening, tanned neck, and she yearned to touch the damp hair that needed cutting.

"Sunny? Your position?"

She coughed, realizing that Miss Lillian was talking strategy. "Sorry. Neil and I will be setting up some beach volleyball."

Neil chimed in. "Angus will be rigging the sailboat. Avery will be looking on."

"I don't know how he talked her into getting into a swimsuit and leaving her prosthesis behind." Sunny shook her head. If she's invited to a pool party, she usually wears a long sarong to cover everything up and doesn't go near the water. She thinks that residual limb will freak the other kids out."

"Angus has seen what nature can do to wild creatures, so he's unflappable. Also, he's very persuasive," Neil said.

"He must have gotten it from you." Sunny smiled, wanting to give him a gentle poke, but she couldn't with Miss Lillian looking on.

Neil shook his head. "Nope. He got it from his grandmother."

The horn behind them tootled. Startled, Sunny looked back to see Harris grinning as he drove the old charabanc up behind them. The kids and the others waved.

Harris was grinning! Well, that was a change from his usual expression.

At the beach, wearing her black swimsuit and an oversized white shirt, Sunny bit her lip while she helped Harris set up and arrange the tables, food, and serving ware. Knowing what she knew, that knot in her belly resisted all efforts to untie it. She was glad she wasn't sitting with the others, forced to be mute as a tangle of dried seaweed, while they talked all around the elephant on the beach—the future of the island. "Did Neil brief you on the plan?" Sunny whispered to Harris as she spread the red-checkered tablecloth across a folding table. She clipped weights to the four corners.

"I am informed," he said, and then murmured, "I have my own plan if anything goes wrong."

Sunny stared and whispered, "What do you mean?"

He didn't answer, because Alex came within earshot to get a beer from the cooler. "Where's the jug of gin-and-tonics I made?" he asked. "My wife and mother both want one."

Sunny dug around, found the Thermos, and handed it over along with two heavy, clear acrylic tumblers. Alex looked appropriate for the beach in a loose blue Hawaiian shirt and white canvas shorts. In contrast, Kiki accepted her drink in a black lace cover-up over a red bikini, accented with eye-catching gold and coral jewelry and black designer flip-flops, as if the island resort had already been built.

The girls moseyed up for cans of Diet Coke, and Angus walked over for two cans of ginger ale. "One's for Avery," he announced. Sunny didn't miss the glares that Blake and Ellery gave the interloper who dared to monopolize their handsome cousin.

The moment to hear about Harris's backup plan had passed. Sunny set out the fried chicken and the slaw and potato salad and chocolate cake, along with platters of sandwiches, tins of Charles Chips specially ordered, and jugs of water and home-brewed iced tea.

After Harris told Miss Lillian that supper was ready, she waved Sunny over and asked for a plate to be brought to her. Sunny prepared one as directed, and then went back for her own after the others had been served. She was too nervous to have much of an appetite, but she did love fried chicken. Miss Lillian suggested that Sunny sit on the low beach chair next to her.

The other adults lounged companionably with trays of food and drinks. Kiki occasionally threw in a comment, but kept checking her cell phone to see if it was picking up a signal. Just like her, Sunny concluded, to not join in the party. Or did Kiki have some plan in mind? Some plan of her own?

The kids camped on blankets. Blake and Ellery staked out one, Angus and Avery the other, like warring tribes eyeing each other across neutral territory.

Sunny kept a nervous watch on her daughter while Miss Lillian, using the kids as an excuse, began to tell stories most of the grownups already knew of old times on the island. She loved to recount the story about her great-grandfather Magnus T. Alexander winning the island and its house in a poker game. She said that the elder Alexander had found the old house in a state of suspended animation, as if people had left, meaning to come back.

Sunny sneaked a look at Neil and caught him looking back at her. His lips twitched into a half-smile, a conspiratorial smile. Her heart began to race, and warmth rose to her face. Damn that tell-all face! She could never be a spy. She'd never be able to play poker.

She longed to reach over and take Neil's hand. She ached to leave all these people behind and walk on the beach with him until they got far out of sight of everyone else, and then he would take her in his arms, and then they would lie on the soft sand . . . her face became even warmer, and then Neil raised his eyebrow to show her he'd noticed her blushing. Then he got a little color himself, as if he could read her thoughts. She forced herself to think that dry sand would really, really be a bad thing to have under you at a time like that. She hiccupped, trying to stifle a giggle.

She snapped out of her rainbow cloud when Angus said, "We want to go into the water now, Gran."

"Fine." Miss Lillian smiled contentedly and waved her hand. "Go have fun."

Angus helped Avery navigate her crutches to the beach. The girls ignored them, wading into the surf.

"Are they safe from sharks?" Sunny asked, thinking of the attacks in North Carolina and Florida not too long past.

"The kids are fine," Neil said. "There have been only twelve shark attacks in Georgia since 1837, none of them fatal. It's the geography of the coastline."

Miss Lillian turned to Sunny. "My dear, please ask Harris to pour us all another round of drinks."

But how many had she had already? "Miss Lillian, I don't think you really—"

"Hush, child," Miss Lillian said under her breath. "I know what I'm doing. You can have one if you like."

Sunny got up to do as she was asked. She badly wanted one of those cocktails, but she made do with a regular Coke. She needed every single one of her senses to be sharp for what they were about to do. She noticed that Alex took another drink, as well. She'd lost count of how many he'd had. Kiki? Sunny hadn't kept up with her drinks. In any case, the Dragon Lady still looked as alert as a bushy-tailed squirrel.

It was too soon when Angus loped back to where they were sitting. "Gran, you wanted the sailboat? We're ready."

"All right!" Miss Lillian said. She set down her glass, and Sunny noted she hadn't drunk very much. Alex's was almost empty. "Let's get going."

"I'm going with you," Neil demanded, as scripted.

Miss Lillian shook her head. "You stay here and watch the kids on those rafts." The girls had risen from their blanket and claimed a raft each, and were sauntering toward the waves.

Harris, wearing his black apron over a white guyabera shirt, packed up the rest of the picnic and began to carry it back towards the vehicles, refusing all offers of help.

"I still say you shouldn't go alone," Neil said loudly to Miss Lillian.

"Well, Sunny, you come with me," Miss Lillian entreated. "The children are already out on the rafts and I don't want to spoil their fun."

"Now, Miss Lillian," Sunny replied, following the script. "I'm really afraid of the water. Isn't there someone else who'll go?"

Neil looked pointedly over at Alex and Kiki. "What about one of you two?"

Kiki just stared down at her nails as if her manicurist had installed a mini-screen on her middle finger. "I don't want to get this suit wet," she finally said. "I do wish I'd worn the black one. It's back at the house."

"I'll go with you, Mother," Alex said, heaving himself out of the chair.

Sunny's stomach turned a flip. She hardly dared to look at Neil and Miss Lillian. She gritted her teeth and told her too-expressive face to stay still. Kiki had not taken their bait. Could they have been wrong? Had she seen through their ruse? How stupid they'd been to think it would work! They'd all be wearing life jackets, of course. Kiki had seen that, and they hadn't. Still. There were plenty of ways to drown, even in a life jacket.

There was nothing to do but to have Alex take Miss Lillian out in the sailboat.

"I'll go back and get my other suit and rejoin you. Maybe I can go out later," Kiki said sweetly. "Neil, will you drive me?" She languidly lifted her tote bag with one finger. Sunny looked on, dismayed. That would kill the plan for Neil to go back and get the fishing boat. Everything was going wrong.

Neil thought for a minute, glanced meaningfully at Sunny as if to say he'd retool the plan, and shrugged. "I'd better stay here and watch the kids. Kiki, why don't you ride with Harris in the Jeep? He needs to take the leftovers back to the lodge anyhow."

Kiki allowed the flicker of a frown cross her features. "That will be fine," she said, recovering a smile.

Harris had just come back for the last load and Neil briefed him that he'd have a passenger , tossing him the keys. Harris nodded slowly. Kiki checked her phone one more time before she got into the Jeep with Harris.

Alex waved and smiled at Sunny. "Come with Mother and me! There's always room in my boat for an attractive woman." Oh, good grief. Was he flirting with her? That was all she needed to make the day perfect.

"Yes, Sunny, come on," Miss Lillian insisted. Sunny knew that Miss Lillian was disappointed that the plan had fallen through, though she didn't show it. If Miss Lillian wanted her on the boat, then she'd go, because, to be honest, Alex looked a little drunk.

Neil helped them to cast off, and Sunny found that Alex actually knew how to sail the boat, despite all, and she told herself to relax. They glided along, a little farther out than Sunny would have liked, but still in view of the shore, though the children were looking tinier.

Miss Lillian pointed out landmarks and birds; she knew them all. She pointed out the beach area where the turtles often nested. Sunny reluctantly began to appreciate the salt spray, the shifting clouds, and the breeze. As long as she could shift her attention to the sky and the wind, she could hold back the fear of the water under her. She could endure this.

One more week, just one more week, and she'd be gone from these people, this island . . . and from Neil. She looked longingly toward the shore, and could barely make him out. Was he back standing on the sand, shading his eyes, looking out to sea—looking toward her?

Despite the plan's failure, Miss Lillian seemed to be taking advantage of the fine day and the company of her son. She asked him to tack in a bit so she could see what was happening along the coastline, since she couldn't get out there and walk it. "I don't see enough of you alone these days, Alex," she said. "I do wish you'd come to see me and let's have a heart-to heart, just ourselves."

Alex glanced back to shore as if he thought Kiki might be watching him, would need to give him permission to speak his mind. "I'd like to do that, Mother," he said. "I've been so busy lately. Maybe we can talk about something else besides this, uh, island."

He looked like a man who had suppressed a bad word, thought Sunny, watching him swing the sail to catch a fickle breeze.

"Now take this thing over toward Turtle Point," Miss Lillian said. Alex nodded and he headed northeast, the boat sliding smoothly through the gentle waves. Sunny's stomach was still tied up in knots, but they were loosening, and now she paid attention. She hadn't been to Turtle Point and wanted to visit there. When they got nearer, she saw fishing boats and some young people crabbing off a pier. She thought one of them might be Reggie.

"We'd better turn back now, Alex," Miss Lillian said. "I don't want to go too far. There might be a rip current near the sandbank."

The water was silky and clear, and Sunny thought it looked all right, but what did she know? Alex turned the sailboat back toward the picnic beach. Miss Lillian closed her eyes, and Sunny, loving the wind in her impossible hair, let her mind sail back to the day before, to Neil and the cot in painting shed. Only her fear of being out in the boat kept her from losing herself in the reverie, kept her from melting into a puddle. She forced herself to pay attention to her boss and the waves. Still, panic surfaced when she thought how deep the water might be under them.

She squeezed her eyes shut. "You're not a sinker, after all," she'd heard Flip say after the last lesson. She swallowed hard.

When they drew closer to the picnic beach, Sunny spotted the four bobbing rafts, a little farther out than she would have liked, Angus and Avery and Blake and Ellery aboard. Slathered with sunscreen, Sunny hoped. Then she noticed a strange pattern in the water ahead. Could that be the tricky current? The kids weren't near it, thank goodness.

Before she could tell Alex about it, she heard a whine and a growl, and then she saw it: a speedboat coming out of nowhere, heading in their direction. Her heart began to pound. That boat wasn't turning.

Alex squinted. "Hey, is that Sydney's boat? I hope it's not that wild daughter and her idiot boyfriend." As the boat hove into view, Sunny made out the driver and passenger, both wearing baseball caps pulled low, aviator sunglasses, black T-shirts. Looked as if Alex had called it. Sunny opened her mouth to scream as the boat came closer.

"Hey! That SOB's coming right at us!" shouted Alex. Reacting too late, he swung the rudder, trying to change direction. The speedboat roared by a few yards away, rocking them in the soaring wake. The small craft bucked and pitched, and Sunny felt herself tumbling through the air, smacking the water, sinking.

She bobbed to the surface, spewing salt water. Miss Lillian! Where was she? Alex surfaced, shaking his head. Miss Lillian, unable to move quickly in her cast, had apparently hit the water harder than Sunny, and the elderly woman floated limply, dazed and breathing hard. With horror, Sunny realized that the three of them had washed into the rip and were being dragged out to sea.

She gasped, swallowing more water, and then she spotted four empty rafts where the kids had been floating. That damn boat had pitched the rafts! The kids were in the water! Then she saw a raft heading out to the floating kids, powered by Neil.

Everything in her, her protective instinct for her child, tugged at her, called for her to go to Avery. But here was her charge. She could not abandon Miss Lillian. Neil. Could she trust Neil? A shiver went down her back. She *had* to trust Neil.

For a moment, the icy fear coursed through her, and she was back in the sinking trailer, panicking, trying to pull her mother through the window, knowing that if she failed, they both might die. She had prayed, she had cried, she had gulped the fetid water, but she had made it. She could do it again.

Miss Lillian, barely conscious, bobbed in her life vest, and her eyes flicked open, met Sunny's. Sunny saw trust there. A helpless person was depending on her, and she knew that feeling from the hospital. "I'm coming," Sunny shouted. "Hang on." She kicked out then, stroked over to Miss Lillian, grabbed under her chin, and pulled her head up. Sunny's stomach still felt cold, but she was kicking, treading water, keeping their heads above it.

She felt the rip tugging, pulling them out. She blinked salt water out of her eyes and saw Alex floundering, trying to get to them, but the alcohol had affected his coordination. What had that Red Cross book said? Go parallel to shore. Sunny right-angled and kicked for all she was worth, using everything that Flip had taught her. Alex made his way toward them. "Hold on!" he yelled. "I'm coming!"

Sunny kept kicking, pulling on reserves she didn't know she had, and finally she was free of the current. Before she could rejoice, a huge wave swamped her, and filled her nose with stinging brine. She choked, coughed, spat. And found she was a long way from shore.

Alex finally reached them, just when she thought she couldn't hang on. He took Miss Lillian from her, though she wanted to protest.

He held his mother in a perfect cross-chest carry, just like in the Red Cross lifesaving book, but he was thirty pounds overweight, and intoxicated. He wasn't getting anywhere, and his face was red. Now what? He wouldn't let her take Miss Lillian back. Could she grab the boat? Her legs were beginning to ache and fail, but she kept treading, looking for the inflatable craft.

The sailboat roiled on the current, heading way, way out to sea.

Oh, Jesus, thought Sunny. Oh, Jesus. Are you there, Jesus?

Her lungs were about to give out.

"Hey—o! Hold on!" she heard.

And then she heard the sound of a small motor, and there they were, two Geechees in a flat-bottom fishing boat, pulling alongside them. Alex shouted, "Hey! Nat! Robert! Thank God you're here! How did . . ."

Strong dark arms reached out for them. "Brother Harris watching out for trouble at the beach. When he see what happen, he come for us."

So that had been Harris's plan, to go for help if things went sour. Sunny could have cried with relief, if she wasn't already so wet and salty.

When they were finally all in the boat, Sunny, exhausted, bent over Miss Lillian, willing her to wake up, checking her pulse. "What happen, Mr. Alex?" the man called Nat was asking. Alex's teeth were chattering too hard for him to answer. "Take more than that to kill me," Miss Lillian murmured, and opened her eyes.

The adrenaline propelling Sunny was wearing off. Her teeth began to chatter, and her stomach rebelled again. She quenched the nausea by deep breathing. Shivering, Sunny checked the ankle cast, which looked okay, but would probably need replacing. Sunny wished she had the hospital nearby. She could use a stretcher herself.

"You'll be fine," she whispered, not sure at all.

Miss Lillian sneezed and choked once more. "She did it after all."

"It was an accident," Sunny croaked. But she knew Miss Lillian was right. Sunny's head felt woozy and her icy body couldn't seem to quit shivering. She couldn't pass out now. She had to see Avery, make sure she was all right.

She turned to one of their two rescuers. "The children? Are the children okay? Their rafts got swamped by that speedboat."

"They all safe," Nat said.

She could see somebody waving from the shore. Neil? She had just managed to lift her heavy hand to wave back when she heard a crash, a long way across the water.

CHAPTER TWENTY-FOUR

"That maniac that waked us," Neil muttered, when they were all back at the beach. "That idiot who brought the girls. I wouldn't be surprised if he crashed." Sunny reached out and touched him to get his attention. She wanted to tell him that Alex had said the speedboat looked like Sydney Fairfield's boat.

"What?" Neil asked, touching her hand.

She couldn't say it. The woman's name stuck in her mouth and wouldn't come out. "Miss Lillian said it wasn't an accident."

"She would say that," Neil reminded her. "Let's keep an open mind."

Harris arrived with the Jeep, and she lost her courage to say more. Sunny and Miss Lillian rode with Harris back to the Lodge, while Neil drove the charabanc with an exhausted Alex and the teens. As they drew up to the Lodge, Sunny blinked to make sure she wasn't seeing an illusion. On the porch, a woman wearing a flowing long gauzy skirt, with long, tangled gray hair, rose from a wicker chair and seemed to float down the steps. Sunny's heart plummeted, because she knew who was coming their way. She'd seen the woman's face, long ago and in a faded color photograph, looking much, much younger.

Weezie?

Sunny shut her eyes. What would happen now? Would Weezie unmask her, shame her before her daughter and everybody, saying that Sunny was a fraud?

"Lillian!" the woman cried. "Alex!" Sunny opened her eyes and saw Alex, limp as a jellyfish in the charabanc seat, straighten, hang over the side, and stare. Weezie skittered down the path, straight to Miss Lillian, and put both hands on her cousin's shoulders. "My God, look at you! What happened, Lil?"

Miss Lillian, never happy to be caught unawares, pushed herself upright into her dignified-matron pose, not easy since she was still wet. "Hand me my cane, Sunny. What's the matter with you, girl?" And then she stared at her cousin. "What are you doing here, Weezie?"

"You might have welcomed me after all these years," Weezie said gently. "But Neil invited me to the party. I wanted to surprise you."

Miss Lillian appeared to soften, but only a little. "You have certainly succeeded. But you missed the party."

Sunny looked from one to the other. Weezie, of course, had glanced her way, but her expression revealed nothing. Surely a mother would notice her daughter, even if they weren't speaking. But Neil was staring, giving them the fish eye. Damn it.

Weezie gave Miss Lillian an embarrassed smile. "I was running late. I was never well-organized, as you well know. But fate smiled on me—I managed to find a boatman that was bringing some kids over to Turtle Point, and he gave me a lift. When I got there, I saw Harris, much to my delight, and he brought me back here. Now tell me why you all look half-drowned."

"It's because we *were* half-drowned."

Miss Lillian and Weezie began talking a mile a minute to each other, as if they'd never lost touch. Miss Lillian explained their ordeal, Weezie asked questions.

Her supposed mother still didn't glance Sunny's way. Observing Neil's stony countenance, Sunny felt as though a hungry alligator had suddenly sidled up, ready to chow down. The Neil she saw now wasn't the Neil who wanted to rise to the moon with her on a carpet of clouds. The Neil standing before her had no use for poetry. Sunny swallowed, wishing she could push the Reset button and never walk in that door to Stonehaven. She could not say a word, her mouth was so dry. She felt frozen, unable to move.

And then Weezie turned her way. She glanced from Sunny to Neil and narrowed her eyes. "Is this . . ." she began. Sunny squeezed her eyes shut, waiting for the blow.

Miss Lillian rushed in. "Darling Weezie, yes, it is, it's Sunny! Don't you recognize your own daughter all wet? She's lost so much weight! I know you two have had your differences, but then, so have you and I."

Weezie regarded Miss Lillian for a long moment, and Sunny held her breath. Weight? She was supposed to have been heavy once? Weezie put her forefinger to her lips, considering. Sunny felt as if she'd turned into a chunk of marble about to be chiseled.

"Sunny," Weezie said slowly. "Come here. I want to look at you." The older woman studied her supposed daughter for what seemed like eons, and then she reached over for a hug. Sunny, a stone coming back to life, embraced her awkwardly. Weezie murmured in her ear, "We sure have a lot to talk about." And then, turning her face so only Sunny could see, gave her a slow, quick wink.

Neil, of course, didn't see the wink. He legged it out of the Jeep and hustled around to help Miss Lillian to the ground. He still hadn't said a word.

The kids had been piling out of the charabanc while all this was going on, uninterested in any grownups, even eccentric ones. Miss Lillian called them over, introduced the children to Weezie, and then ordered them to shower and change into dry clothes. "Wish I could stay and talk, Weezie," Alex said, looking both glad and mystified to see his older cousin. "I've got to go tell my wife what she missed. I wonder why she didn't come out when we got here."

"Yes," Miss Lillian murmured. "She missed it, all right."

And we missed our chance to catch her, Sunny thought. Kiki was probably lazing around with a drink and a copy of *Town and Country*, looking for opportunities to promote a new resort for the one per cent.

Miss Lillian closed her eyes. "Weezie, please forgive me. All I want is a bath and a nap right now. We have lots of catching up to do. Sunny, please entertain your mother until I'm in fit shape for company."

"Yes, Aunt Lillian." Sunny glanced back at Weezie before she helped Miss Lillian into the house. Weezie appeared to be enjoying herself immensely.

Sunny tried not to panic at the idea of "entertaining" Weezie. Just act. Just act all cool and calm, she told herself. Like an actress. After Miss Lillian's shower, Sunny helped her dress in a swirly pink and purple caftan, then settled her in bed and closed the door. She headed for her own shower.

Just as she peeled off her suit in her own tiny bathroom, she heard Alex, his voice hoarse and high-pitched, shouting for Neil. He was yelling so loud, she was sure he'd disturb Miss Lillian, and she needed to rest. She threw on her big shirt, which was long enough to cover her rear, and strode out, intending to tell him to pipe down and let Miss Lillian have her nap.

Neil's expression was perplexed and grim. "Sunny, have you seen Kiki anywhere?"

"No," Sunny said, taken aback at his sharp tone. "She's not in the Lodge." What a silly question.

"She's not at the Big House," Alex said. "I thought she might have come down here for something to eat."

"Nope. Did you check the dorm?" Neil scratched his head.

"The kids say she hasn't been there."

"The boat house?" asked Neil. "The nature center? The stables?"

Alex furrowed his brow. "She's not really a nature fan. And she hasn't ridden in years."

"Well, you check the stables and nature center now," Neil said. "I'll go to the boat house. Maybe she took my fishing boat. Or the canoe or kayak. Does she kayak?"

"Hardly," Alex spat. "Come on, man. She's missing!"

Neil's face reddened. "I'm trying to help you, brother."

"Wait," Sunny said. "Isn't there a footpath to the beach? One you can't drive on?" That was the way she'd taken to the beach, the path where she'd found the diamond.

"Oh yeah," Neil said. "It crosses the creek."

"Okay," Alex said, toning down a bit. "Maybe she went back that way and were surprised not to find us at the beach. But I honestly thought she'd be back here having a drink or studying the Big House trying to figure out—" he stopped, as if not to say too much.

A good reason for tearing it down, Sunny reckoned he was about to say.

Neil gave his brother-in-law a disgusted look. "After the boat house, I'll take a run along the trail to the beach and back. Then let's take the Jeep and search the island. We'll drive down to Turtle Point and see if anybody's seen her. Meet you back here."

Sunny thought about the alligators in the creek. Neil must have, too, because she saw him check his phone to be sure it was charged. Then Neil strode off toward the boat house, while Alex trudged down the path to the stables. She would have offered to help, but she felt very near to total collapse. And Neil was still being weird.

Why did stupid Kiki have to be missing? Maybe she was hiding on purpose, just to get attention.

Sunny trudged up the four wooden steps that led to the porch. She pulled open the screen door and walked inside, looking forward to bed. Weezie was sitting in the front room, under the watercolor of the Isle of Skye, as if she'd been waiting for her. She must have been listening to the conversation between Sunny and the men.

"Well, my darling daughter," the older woman said, with a mischievous smile, "Let's talk. Neil wrote and asked me about you. I didn't reply to his question, because I wanted to come and find out for myself what was up. It's a good thing I know Lil as well as I do. That look in her eyes meant she was up to something and didn't want me to spill the *haricots*. Out with it, Sunny. Who are you, and why are you pretending to be my daughter?"

Sunny sank to a chair and buried her face in her hands. "If I tell you, do you promise to believe me?"

Weezie's laugh tumbled out. "Where Lillian is concerned, I'll believe anything. Come on, let's sit outside so we can be there when the guys come back."

After they'd settled in the porch chairs under the slowly turning fan, Weezie gazed at her expectantly. Sunny took a deep breath. "It's like this. Miss Lillian didn't want Alex and Kiki to know I'm a hired hand. If I'm a long-lost relative, she figured they'd back off from pressuring her to move her into a retirement home."

"Makes sense," Weezie said, lifting the hair off her neck. "Boy, it's hot here. I miss Asheville. Go on."

"Not only that, she wanted me to be a party to all the conversations she was having with Alex and Kiki, especially about the island, and as a relative, they couldn't claim I was an outsider."

Weezie looked puzzled. "Why? What's happening with the island?"

Sunny filled her in on the ultra-luxurious resort plans. Weezie's mobile face became still. "I've seen what can happen. It's everywhere, and it's a shame. Pave Paradise and put up, you know. It's also a very big tangle. God, I loved this place when I was little . . ."

Weezie closed her eyes, leaned back, and sang a few bars of a tune about love letters in the sand. Sunny imagined two little girls on the beach with their tin shovels and pails, one in pink and one in blue. She'd seen such an illustration in one of those Dick and Jane books her mother used to buy at yard sales for a quarter. Mama would sell them to an antiques dealer for a few bucks, enough for another bottle.

Weezie suddenly broke into Sunny's bubble of reminiscence. "Why didn't Lil want Neil to know?"

Sunny clasped her hands. *Be calm.* "I thought that was a mistake, but I didn't dare say anything. It wasn't my place. Miss Lillian told me it would be easier if no one knew. Then no one could slip up. But Harris has always known."

Weezie looked around. "Where is Harris, by the way?"

Sunny remembered the earlier conversation about Harris and his sister. "Maybe he's at his sister's house. It's kind of a long story, but the accident made him go to his sister's place to get help, and I think they've made up their quarrel. He must have gone back for more visiting. And Neil and Alex have gone searching for Kiki. No one can find her."

"That's what I gathered," Weezie said. "I was just thinking, I might have heard her. It was very strange."

"Heard her? How? Where?" Sunny leaned forward, hands on knees.

Weezie surprised Sunny by rising from her chair. "Darling daughter, before we talk further, I could use a glass of wine and something to eat. I'm famished."

"Oh, please. I'll get it." Sunny gripped her chair to push herself up.

Weezie fluttered a hand, heading for the screen door. "Not a chance, sister. I'll get it. I haven't been in the water trying to save lives."

A few minutes later, Weezie returned with the half bottle of good California rosé Neil had stashed the refrigerator, two stemmed glasses, and a plate of leftover sandwiches and sliced cake. She sat down and tucked into a ham sandwich at once. "Ah," she said, munching happily, "I never had time to stop for food."

Sunny sipped her wine. It felt *gooood* going down, spreading warmth. "Now can you tell me where you saw Kiki, Miss Weezie?"

"Please, dear. Weezie. My soul's from California." She reached for a piece of cake. "And I didn't see Kiki, I heard her. This was after Harris dropped me off here. He'd asked me if I wanted to join you all at the beach picnic, but I was hot and tired from the trip down, and I needed a cool drink and a place to lounge for a bit before confronting Lillian. After all, it's been sixteen years."

"I decided I'd wait at the Lodge. Then here you all came, this raggle-taggle crew from the beach. *Surprise!*" She paused and sighed. "Not the way it turned out, but . . . back to the story. Here I was at the Lodge while the party was going on at the beach, and I'd just mixed myself a gin and tonic with a slice of lime when I heard a noise. It sounded like a speedboat had pulled up at the dock. When I heard a woman's voice, I picked up my glass and started to walk down there to say hello. I thought it might be one of you. Before I got very far, the boat pulled away. I walked on down to the dock, but no one was there. I think someone must have left. Do you think the boat picked up Kiki?"

"Oh, my God," Sunny said. "That was her. It had to be. And that could mean . . ."

Weezie's hand, reaching for another sandwich, stopped in mid-air. "Mean what?"

"That Miss Lillian was right. What if Kiki was driving that speedboat that came too close?"

"Tell me more about why Lillian was right."

Sunny gave Weezie a bare-bones sketch of their plan to catch Kiki in the act of attempted murder.

"I see," Weezie said, and took a long sip of her drink. "What do we do now?"

Sunny shook her head. "I guess we have to wait for Neil."

In the silence that followed, Weezie finished her sandwich, and Sunny drained her glass of wine. Then she saw Neil coming back up the path, his face looking even stonier than before. If possible.

She started to speak at the same time he did, but he was louder, so she closed her mouth. "I got a phone call about Kiki," he said stiffly. "The sheriff's on the way here."

"The sheriff?" Sunny's hand went to her throat.

"Where's Alex?" Neil asked.

Sunny saw him then, huffing his way up the path from the Nature Center. She nodded in his direction.

Neil walked down to meet him. Sunny saw him lay a hand gently on Alex's shoulder.

CHAPTER TWENTY-FIVE

Late that evening, all the adults, motionless as a sailboat in a glassy sea, gathered in the small front room of the Lodge. The kids began a Monopoly game out on the porch, within earshot of the adults. Harris, back from his sister's house, mixed everyone a strong drink and then hovered in the wings.

Alex had returned to the island. He'd gone with the sheriff and his deputy to formally identify the body. He was sunk in his chair, face blotchy, still in shock and denial.

The sheriff had told him and Neil that Mrs. Stirling and Mrs. Fairfield had crashed their speedboat into a boat full of beer-drinking, partying college students, injuring two. Mrs. Stirling and Mrs. Fairfield, the owner of the speedboat, were ejected into the water. Mrs. Fairfield suffered two broken legs. Mrs. Stirling had drowned.

Miss Lillian fidgeted, picking at loose wicker strands on the chair arm. She fixed Neil with an eagle stare. "Tell me what else that sheriff said. I was so shocked I didn't catch it all."

Neil leaned toward her and spoke gently, more for Alex's sake than hers. "He said that they'd taken a statement from Sydney before she was taken to the hospital. Apparently Kiki had been at the wheel; she'd told Sydney she wanted to show off for Alex, who didn't think she could drive a boat. Sydney claims it was an accident.

"The two of them had glanced back, Sydney said, to see if everyone was all right, after they'd come too close. They didn't notice the boat in their path. The college kids were a little drunk and they were taken by surprise. No time to get out of the way." Neil looked around the room. The sounds of game-playing had stopped from the porch.

"She wasn't trying to see if everyone was all right," Miss Lillian grumbled. "She wanted to see if I was dead."

"Mother," Alex said tiredly.

Miss Lillian didn't say anything more for a minute or so. Then she cleared her throat and spoke. "Listen, all of you. This has been a very trying day, and I've been very glad to have Sunny here. I hope she'll stay on. I can't let her go off and leave me now."

All eyes turned to Sunny. Neil's were still cold, but Weezie's gaze was encouraging. "What do you say, daughter? Not like Lil's putting you on the spot or anything."

Sunny knew she'd have to confess. It was her only chance to leave Miss Lillian and still keep Neil's friendship. A relationship with him had been doomed from the start, but a girl could dream, couldn't she? Only in fairy tales or romantic novels do the dreams come true. Everybody knew that.

"I need to tell you all something." Sunny took a long sip of her wine and blotted her mouth with a paper napkin.

"Please do," Weezie said, smiling.

Sunny sat up straight, hands folded. "My real name is Susannah Nadine Iles Magee. I've been nicknamed Sunny since I was in grade school, and Avery's father was not a doctor, but a country singer. He might even have made it one day, if he hadn't been so f—, that is, confused and mean."

"He wasn't mean!" Avery yelped from the porch.

Sunny didn't respond, and her gaze traveled from face to face. "I was hired by Miss Lillian to be her assistant, caregiver, second pair of ears, and, though I didn't want to admit it, bodyguard. This lovely lady," she reached out to Weezie, "is not my mother, although after meeting her, I wouldn't mind claiming her."

She stopped for a minute, blinked back tears, and continued. "My own mother was a hopeless alcoholic, and I made my own way through nursing school. I'm a registered nurse, and Miss Lillian's ankle is nearly healed. In another week I'll be moving to North Carolina where I'll have a good job with regular hours."

"I'll miss—" She couldn't stop the tears running down her cheeks. She gazed at Miss Lillian and especially at Neil, who didn't meet her eyes. "I'll miss all of you." She sank back into the chair and began to sob, the events of the day finally catching up with her.

"You have to stay!" Miss Lillian banged her stick on the floor so hard that everyone jumped.

Neil drifted over and offered Sunny a handkerchief, still not meeting her eyes. Well, she had lied to him, and she didn't blame him for being angry. She took the handkerchief, blew her nose, wiped her eyes, gulped, and straightened. "That's all," she said, and she felt oddly relieved, rid of a burden. "Except to say that I think we should all get some rest. If anyone doesn't feel well, come see me. I'll see what I can do."

The kids, understanding that the meeting was over, filed into the room. "Can we take some snacks to the dorm?" Angus said. His two cousins, though solemn, were dry-eyed. Angus slipped his arm around Avery, who leaned against him, daring any adult to say a word.

"Angus," Neil said, "Go ahead and get what you want from the kitchen. I'm depending on you to keep order tonight."

Angus looked straight at him. "Yes, sir," he said, two spots of color staining his bronze cheeks. The teens hurried back to the kitchen, ready to leave the adults to sort out their own mess.

"I want to go to bed, Sunny," Miss Lillian announced, and Sunny hurried over to help her out of the chair. Miss Lillian took the crutches Sunny held out. Then she made her way over to Alex, still slumped in his chair. "Son," she said. "I'm so sorry."

"Mother." He awkwardly pushed himself to his feet and hugged her, and the two of them clung together for a long time.

After Miss Lillian was settled in bed, Sunny made her way to her room and kicked off her shoes. She sank to the lower bunk and wiped her eyes once again.

She didn't know how long she'd been sitting on the edge of the bed staring into space when she heard a soft knock at the door. She pulled the last Kleenex out of the box and blew.

"Sunny?" A hoarse male whisper. "Are you decent?"

"Sure." She scuffed her toe on the rag rug. What did Neil want now?

"Come out on the porch for a minute. Everybody's gone." He didn't raise his voice, she guessed, so he wouldn't wake Miss Lillian.

"Why?"

"Just come. Please?"

"I'll meet you there in a minute." She got up and fumbled in her make-up kit for the pouch with the diamond earring in it. It would be her good-bye gift.

He indicated for her to sit on the loveseat next to him, under the yellow glow from the bug light. She hesitated, but tossed her head, sat down, and waited. The porch smelled of damp cushions and salt air and cedar. Drifting clouds blocked the stars, the moon was a fingernail sliver in the sky, and even the night sounds seemed muted. Sunny felt that a huge pit was opening up before her. She waited dully to be pushed in.

"That was a brave thing you did, Sunny, speaking up," Neil finally said.

She blinked. Right, say the good thing first, and then . . .

He continued, "You were brave out there today. But why didn't you level with me? At least, after—" He met her eyes, and his were accusing.

"I couldn't." That pit just got deeper when Sunny thought about the time they'd spent together, his touch, his kisses. "I felt miserable not telling you, but I had promised Miss Lillian. Who should I be loyal to? I figured you'd just forget all about me after I left, and why upset Miss Lillian when she was already so tense?"

She dropped her head. "Anyhow, now it'll be easier to let go. I have something I want to give you, though, before I leave."

"Give me?" he demanded.

She drew the pouch out of her pocket and shook the earring out into her palm. She held it out. "Miss Lillian acted all funny when I told her I'd found it. She told me to keep it. I thought you might sell it for the island."

He stared at it as if it were radioactive. "Damn!" He buried his face in his hands.

After a long silence, he met Sunny's eyes. He looked wrung-out and miserable. A lump rose in her throat. "What is it, Neil? Was that Julie's? I'm sorry."

He shook his head slowly. "She didn't wear diamonds. Kiki lost an earring the day of the . . . accident. I found it wedged in Julie's swimsuit, and I just threw it into the grass. I didn't want to give it back to Kiki."

Maybe Julie had been fighting for her life with Kiki, grabbed at her ear. Maybe she had plunged the earring into her suit as a message. Sunny didn't dare speak that thought. Maybe it had occurred to Neil, and that's why he'd cut himself off from everyone.

It hurt her to see him so torn, and she knew she loved him. She just had to make him see that love wasn't enough.

"Neil, listen. Suppose I did stay with Miss Lillian and see where this thing with us goes. I could move into her guest house and Avery could change schools, away from that boy who's using her for homework. Good for Miss Lillian and good for Avery. But not so good for me.

"You know, Neil, all my life I dreamed of being Cinderella. I wanted to find a handsome prince with a castle. Go to the ball. Get out of the sticks and live in splendor. And here I fall in love with somebody who wants to go all barefoot in the sand. It can't last."

Neil's eyes, the color of the sea and sky, were soft. "Is that all you want out of life, Sunny? That's what Kiki wanted. To be queen."

Sunny was quiet for a long minute. "I never told you where I came from, Neil. I never told you that I nearly drowned in a flood. I didn't grow up with Weezie guiding me, teaching me. I had to be the mother to my mother—and it was hell. I guess my dream was my way of wanting to be special, really special to someone, to be cared for, to be cherished. Princesses are always loved."

Neil smiled at her then. "I've known a lot of women who think they're princesses, Sunny, and they're loved only if they're good and kind. And you are good and kind. Do you think you could stand being special to just one person?"

"Well, there's Avery."

"She'll grow up and have her own life, won't she? Sure, she'll have challenges, but she's one tough kid. I'll make you queen of Issatee Island, and as for a castle, I can gussy up the Big House any way you please."

Sunny gave a little squeak. "Are you serious? I hardly know you!"

"I thought we knew each other quite well." He gave her a mischievous leer.

Warming from face to toes, she gazed back at him. "Let me understand this. If things work out, I'd have to live on this island. Surrounded by water. After Miss Lillian's scheme almost drowned me."

Neil leaned over and swallowed her up in a bear hug. "You acquitted yourself like a champ, my love. You kept Lillian's head above water while help was on the way." He lowered his voice. "And I've guessed the other secret you tried to hide from me. You're terrified of the water, aren't you? That's what courage is. You were there for her no matter what."

There was nothing she could say. Now he knew it all. Neil pulled back into a gentle embrace, and he was kissing her like the first time he had kissed her, deep and tender and tingly.

He knew it all, and he had called her *my love*. Lost, she was lost, she was way up in that moonbeam, all her senses aglow. The kiss broke off, and she gazed up at the tiny glowing sliver of the moon. Miraculously, the sky had cleared and the stars gleamed happily above. The dark shapes of the palms and the live oaks, the sea holly and the lacy ferns, all were silvered and shadowed, painted by a billion points of brightness in the sky. The sea chuckled and riffled in the distance, and the ocean breeze smelled of ancient ships.

She would really miss this place. She would.

"I don't do very well in love, Neil," she said, her voice breaking. "I had planned to go away and make a fresh start."

"A golf resort is no place to find a fairy-tale castle," Neil said. "No better than this island. How much do you know about this doctor you're going to work for?"

The question stung Sunny. "I liked him when he was at the hospital where I worked. He was nice to all the nurses . . ." She let the last sentence hang.

"I hear a 'but' in there, Sunny."

"Okay, so he had a nasty divorce and left town. So what? So have lots of people."

"But you don't know what caused the divorce, do you?"

"I heard some ugly rumors. I didn't want to believe them, because he was so nice to me." Sunny began to sob, then, great, heaving sobs.

"Hush," he said, and took her into his arms. He kissed her again, and the kiss went on and on, melting her resistance. Neil stroked her hair, and she laid her head on his chest. "How did you see Avery's dad as a prince? I thought you said he was a country singer."

"Oh, Neil. He took me up to Nashville and we drove around to Belmont and some of the other mansions. He promised me one of those if I'd stick by him while he made his way to the big time, support him through the lean years. And I did. And then it all fell apart."

"Did you love him, Sunny?"

Sunny looked out into the night then. "I thought I did. But maybe I was just in love with the myth. You dream up a prince, and when you meet somebody, you put your prince clothes on him. For a while, you see what you want to see. But one day, the prince clothes drift away into the air, and you see ripped jeans and a dirty T-shirt. And a nasty scowl."

The stars above wheeled past in their own milky stream, full of imaginary creatures, almost as if she could reach out and touch them, and she sank back into his arms. She took a deep breath. Troy Bentley had also been a prince of the imagination, hadn't he?

The weighty block of marble that had been sitting on her chest lifted, and she felt free. She didn't need to run any more. She didn't need rescuing. She had rescued somebody else today. And this place, this place she had feared so, had crept into her heart.

"No," she said.

"No, what?" Neil asked. "You're turning me down?"

"No, I won't cling to that old dream anymore. This place is growing on me, Neil."

He grinned at her then. "Come with me to the studio."

"That's not fair, Neil."

"Just to see my pictures."

She smiled at him, abashed. He took her hand and led her to the small, ramshackle former toolshed that held such magic.

He showed her all the paintings he had done, and told her the story of each one. She loved the picture he'd done of Blackjack high in a twisted tree. He moved a canvas aside and showed her the portrait he'd painted of Julie. "I never really captured her, so I just put it away. I'm much better with landscapes and animals."

Now she felt that she knew the island as he saw it, in his paintings, a dimension she never would have seen before. Her own world had been smaller, a bubble of work and home and the past, and she knew now she was ready to venture outside the bubble. She might just need to change the direction of her venture.

"If I stayed here, Neil," she said, "I'd have to live in a rundown lodge, wearing shorts and sandals and missing my favorite TV shows." She gulped. "With horses and crows and alligators and that big yellow cat. Helping you weed the garden, maybe even growing some flowers. All that stuff I've never done."

"You'd be great at it," Neil said. "And you could get to know the folks on the other end of the island, get to know Esther. She could teach you a few things about healing, and you could help her—if she'd let you. And I could teach you how to ride and to sail, when you're ready. And I'll even break down and buy a dish and a TV set if you really want one."

"And an occasional McDonald's hamburger?"

Neil laughed. "Why not? Maybe we can get off the island from time to time, go see Lillian." Neil put his finger under her chin and tilted her head up. "You'll miss her, I'll bet. Maybe one day she'll move down here with us, into the Big House."

Sunny's eyes lit up. "And maybe Weezie could come too, and start an art colony. Maybe you could let people know you paint. Sell more of your pictures."

Neil shook his head. "Maybe. I don't want the pressure. It would make me stop painting, love."

"Weezie can help you sell things. She knows the business."

"Maybe. And maybe one day, after she and Lillian are both gone, we'll let Alex convert the Big House into a B&B. Esther and her clan? They might help us run it, or have B&Bs of their own.

And I'll keep training Reggie so that one day he can take over my job, if he wants it."

She laid her head on his shoulder. "So many dreams. They can't all come true."

"The thing is to have them, Sunny. I thought I was through with dreaming, and that was a mistake. Now, the first thing is to get you some island shoes. Dirty white Keds, no laces."

No glass slippers, Sunny thought. But she had grown to love the roll of the sea and the smell of the marsh, the sunlight slanting through the ferny forest, the little white deer and the tracks of the turtles, and most of all, Neil. It wasn't a castle on a hill, but an adventure, right in front of her, stretching out like the pale rosy dawn shimmering over the long, long horizon.

And the sand, the sifting salt and pepper sand, was just another kind of glass. It would make a fine slipper.

BY THE SAME AUTHOR

Anne Lovett
Rubies from Burma
a story of love and war

*Can a young girl escape the shadow of her older sister and make a
choice that will change her life forever?*

From Kirkus Reviews

"Well-begun is half done, and debut novelist Lovett
captures us on the very first page of this story set in
rural Georgia in the middle of the last century.

What snares us so quickly is the narrator, Mae Lee Willis,
daughter of Gwen and Chap and long-suffering kid sister of the
insufferable Ava. Headstrong Ava is beautiful and sexy and damn
well knows it. She sets her cap for Duke Radford, scion of the well-
to-do Radfords. And she wins him just before he goes off to fight
in WWII. But true to form, she lets handsome Hardy Pritchett, a
married man, romance her while Duke is gone. . . .

Gawky Mae Lee is aware of everything and loves Duke from afar. The plot ignites with the appearance of Jack Austin, Duke's Army buddy, a thoroughgoing bastard who relishes chaos and seduction. Any conscientious reviewer needs to stop here, but it's no spoiler to note that Jack wreaks considerable havoc.

This book is wonderfully written. Every bit of dialogue rings true. . . .

Exceptionally satisfying; Lovett is the real deal."

—*Kirkus Reviews*

www.annelovett.com

NOTES AND ACKNOWLEDGMENTS

This book came out of my love for the Golden Isles of Georgia, which I first visited as a small child.

Of course, there is no real Issatee Island. That wild and lovely figment of the imagination has elements of Ossabaw Island, Sapelo Island, Cumberland Island, and Little St. Simons Island, all of which are wonderful places to visit. The most available island is Jekyll Island State Park, which the State of Georgia bought in 1947 from the Golden Age millionaires who had abandoned the island during World War II. The intent of the Governor and state legislature was to create a park where ordinary Georgians could afford a beach vacation. It's evolving and is now a charming place to visit restored "cottages" of a time gone by.

The other islands were in private hands until their upkeep became prohibitive. Most of Cumberland is now a national park, and is known for being the wedding site of John Kennedy Jr. and for beautiful and historic Greyfield Inn. The California owners of Little St. Simons are innkeepers of a lodge where lovers of bird-watching and rustic island life can visit. Ossabaw Island was inherited by Mrs. Eleanor (Sandy) West, who sold the island to the state in 1978 with the provision that she retain a homestead there for the rest of her life. Little did anyone realize that Mrs. West would reach the age of 104. She resides now in a personal care home in Savannah, having left the island only last year. I'm sorry I never met her, but she has my deep appreciation for preserving this wonderful place.

I'd especially like to thank the Georgia Trust for Historic Preservation for scheduling an excursion to Ossabaw, and to the Georgia Conservancy, whose working trip to Sapelo resulted in my cleaning windows in the Reynolds Mansion and meeting some wonderful stewards of our natural resources. And for also providing some Georgia-brewed beer, even though I normally don't drink beer.

Kudos to the Ossabaw Island Foundation, which sponsors trips to Ossabaw during the year and does wonderful work keeping the place tidy and raising funds. A stunning photography book came out just as I'd finished my manuscript of this book. I promise I have never met either of the authors, Evan Kutzler and Jill Stuckey. It's called *Ossabaw Island: A Sense of Place (Mercer University Press, 2016)*

I'd like to mention the Geechee community at Sapelo, who work very hard at keeping their culture alive, sponsoring a yearly festival to which all are invited. Special thanks to Cornelia Walker Bailey for her talk to the Trust visitors at Sapelo and for her book, *God, Dr. Buzzard, and the Bolito Man (Anchor, 2001)* which she wrote with Christena Bledsoe.

And, as always, thanks to Nanette and Peter and the Midtown Writer's Group, to the Holy Innocents' Short Story Group, to the Atlanta Chapter of Sisters in Crime and the Georgia Romance Writers, to the eternal inspiration of Zona Rosa, to my large and loving tribe, to my Dublin homies, and to my great first readers Anna and Louise, and also Joe, who tells me if anything is illogical.

CPSIA information can be obtained
at www.ICGtesting.com
Printed in the USA
LVHW111347140720
660679LV00002B/416

9 780996 070973